Revelation
By: Layla M. Gatlin

<u>Dedication</u>

This book is dedicated to my late Great Grandma, El Frita.

She always believed in and supported my writing from my very first hand written novella.

I think of you every time I start a new book and I hope you're looking down from heaven and seeing how far I've come.

Love you grandma.

Book One:
Change

-The Creature-

"Where issss she?"

The creature hissed as it circled the woman chained to a small metal chair. The woman, beaten and barely alive, ground her teeth together and looked up at the creature defiantly.

"Where is who?"

She muttered as blood dripped from her busted lip. The creature roared furiously.

"YOU KNOW WHO! Tell me where the child is or I'll kill you now!"

The woman laughed.
"Go ahead. I'll never tell you where she is. Besides, I'm sure you have the means of finding out. After all, you found me."

The creature growled and called for someone to take the woman to the dungeon.
"You will regret your arrogance. I shall find the girl and when I do you can watch me as I drag her to hell. Then I'll drag your people down as well."

Two men came in and unchained her from the chair. There was suddenly a bright light and an angel appeared. He shone with God's glory, blinding the two men just long enough to kill them and grab the woman.

"You!"
The creature spat with anger and disgust. The angel wrapped his wings around the woman and they were gone. Just like that.

-Aurora-

The sun beats through my window with such surprising heat that sleeping any longer would be impossible.

"Aurora! I know it's Saturday but are you really going to sleep until noon? I made pancakes!" Shawna yells from the kitchen and I smile.

Shawna is my adopted mother. She and her husband, Brent, adopted me from foster care when I was three. I don't remember anything from before then... I stand up and move to my dresser. My long brown hair is all knotted together and I reach for my comb. I stare into the mirror as I brush through the strands. My amber eyes shine with the light from the window. I've always thought my eyes were strange... I know other people have amber eyes but I've always been told that mine are unusual, well, most people say unique... Not that I don't like them, I enjoy the fact that my eyes are different. That could come from the sense that I've always felt a little different myself.

It doesn't take me long to get dressed and I make my way to the kitchen and take a seat at the table. It's already eleven in the morning but in our house it is never too late for breakfast.

"Morning sleepy head!" Shawna says as she sets a plate of pancakes down in front of me.

"Morning," I reply as I reach for a fork.

As usual Brent has already gone to work and Shawna will be leaving in an hour because it's the weekend. I scarf down my food and run to brush my teeth.

"Hey Shawna, can I go out today?" I plead as I re-enter the room. She frowns and I rethink the sentence.
"Sorry, mom, can I go out today?"

I'm seventeen now and have lived with her for fourteen years and I know she really wants me to think of her as my mom. And I do, think of her as my mom I mean, it's just hard to say it out loud sometimes… And I really have no idea why… It's just like somewhere inside me there's this feeling like I don't belong here. I don't know, it's weird.

"I guess so. Be careful!" She says and I thank her, grab my skateboard, and run out the door.

I don't bother putting on any knee or elbow pads because I don't really need them. Skateboarding is something I've been doing since kindergarten and I'm practically a pro now. I have really good balance and incredible reflexes. I've always assumed those are qualities I inherited from my biological parents, considering both of my adopted parents are equally clumsy. I kick the ground with my right foot to pick up speed and then I'm cruising down the sidewalk. Up ahead I see a turn on the other side of a building. I pick up speed and whip around it. I made it!

"Yes!" I cheer and fist pump the air... just before slamming into someone. Oops! I go sailing through the air and land on the person I hit.

"I am so sorry! I didn't see...."
I pause and stare down into a pair of gorgeous apple green eyes that belong to a cute dark haired boy I've never met before.

"It's cool," He says smiling up at me, "But could you maybe get off me now?"
I blush and jump up.

"Sorry..."
He laughs and stands up too. He quickly brushes himself off and offers his hand. I shake it awkwardly and inside I yell at myself for it.

"My name's Dayton. What's yours?"
I let go of his hand and try to get my mind back on track.

"Um..."

He laughs. "Well, nice to meet you Um."

I notice his eyes seem to almost shine in the sunlight and I'm entranced. The shine reminds me of the way mine look in the sun... So maybe I'm not the only one...

"Still there?" He asks and I pull out of it.

"Huh? Yea, Sorry. I didn't mean to stare, I just um..." I can feel the heat return to my face and I turn my head.

"It's cool. I get that a lot." His smile looks a little devilish as if he's trying to flirt but doesn't want it to seem obvious.

"I bet you do," I say hoping to sound like I'm teasing but it comes out more serious than I'd planned. His face lights up in a cocky grin and I can't help but laugh a little.

"Well, I guess I should get going." I say as I climb back onto my board.

"Oh okay. Well, I'll see you around then!" He says and then adds, "then you can stare at my gorgeous eyes some more!"

"Ha! Don't flatter yourself!" I shout over my shoulder as I speed off. Well, that was awkward. Was it really that obvious that I thought his eyes were gorgeous?

'Man, I stink with guys.' I think as I roll around another corner.

I can't stop thinking about Dayton, his short, spiky black hair and his amazing green eyes, and the fact that he smelled like smoke and vanilla. What a strange combination... But it smelled so good! It's so weird that I've never seen him before though. I mean, our city isn't exactly a very large town... By any means... It's weird that someone new would come around without everyone in town hearing about it. Especially considering that someone is a hot teenage guy.

-Michael-

He watched as the girl ran anxiously from her house and jumped on her skateboard. As usual she left behind any and all safety gear.

'Does she want to fall and bust her head open?' He wonders as he follows her, just out of sight.

Every once in a while she would do a trick or jump on the board that would make him rather nervous, but overall she was careful enough. There is a curve up ahead and he watches as she speeds up. He frowns and shakes his head disapprovingly. She whips around the corner and he moves after her but she's around and out of sight before he can catch up.

"Yes!" she shouts from around the corner. He slows down and sighs with relief.

'Thank goodness she made that turn okay.'
Suddenly a figure appears next to him and he turns. Standing beside him is Azieul.

"Why are you here Azieul?" He questions.
Azieul turns to him and there is a look of sorrow and fear in his eyes.

"I'm sorry to bother you but we really need your help, "Azieul frowns deeper and continues, "We've received word that something big is going down at the old warehouses tonight and I am afraid we cannot handle it alone."

He turns away from Azieul and back toward the corner the girl went around. She should be fine for a few hours while he's away helping Azieul and the others.

"Alright. Lead the way." He says and they leave together.

I grind down the rails in front of the post office and land safely on the ground. There aren't many people out today for some reason and the street is pretty clear. I come to the intersection at the only stoplight in town. There aren't any cars coming that I can see so I decide to cross. I'm rolling across the crosswalk when a black van just comes out of nowhere!

The van barely screeches to a stop in front of me and startles me so bad, I fall off my skateboard. Standing back up I rub my elbow. That's the second time I've fallen off today!

"Hey!" I start moving towards the driver's side window. "What on Earth do you think you're..."

I'm about to start chewing this guy out when the doors open and a group of about six guys in jumpsuits get out. One of the men, the driver, steps forward. He's tall, muscular, and artificially blond. He also doesn't look like someone who wants to apologize. I take a step back.

"Umm... you almost ran over me!" The men walk closer and I decide I should probably forget the 'tell them off' part and just beat it. "But it's okay. No harm done. I'll just get out of your way now. Bye!"

I turn to run but, unfortunately, I don't get far. Something hits me in my right arm and I look down. Upon seeing the small dart in my arm the situation dawns on me. My vision blurs and the world spins. I see the guys in the jumpsuits walking toward me and then I fall. My head smacks against the pavement but I'm out cold before I feel any pain. Strong arms lift me up and put me in the van. Then, the world is gone.

I awake what feels like ages later in a filthy, abandoned looking room, on a couch that has to have been here fifty years. A sharp pain slices through my temple where it had hit the ground. I instinctively reach for it and find it bandaged. The light suddenly flickers on and I jerk my head around to find the tall, blonde, muscular kidnapper from before.

"Good, you're up," He says, strolling toward me.

A few other men follow behind him. They are all still wearing the black jogging pants and matching hoodies. I sit up on the couch and pull my legs up against me.

"Who are you?" I ask, scowling. He grins,

"Not who, what."

My mind spins, trying to make sense of the statement. I gather myself and decide to be as 'smart alec' like as I can with this jerk.

"Oh, I know *what* you are. You're a psychopath! But I asked *who* you are!"

I briefly wonder why I'm not tied up but I decide I have other things to worry about. My captor laughs, not a normal laugh either. His laugh is a deep, evil, almost suffocating laugh that tells me I am not dealing with your regular milk carton kidnapping.

"Wh... Wha... What do you want with me anyway?" I gulp softly and try to compose myself. The last thing I can do is show fear. He turns toward me again and comes close. Too close in fact. He grabs my chin and lifts my face, only inches from his.

"How about letting me ask all the questions, okay?" He snarls in my face and I want to struggle, bite his nose, spit in his eyes, anything to

make him back up. But I don't. I hold firm and put on my most defiant
look. He smiles, "That-a-girl princess." He lets go of my chin and turns
to walk away and my lips curl into a frown.

"Don't call me that."
He stops and turns back, curiosity in his eyes.

"Don't call you what? Oh! Princess, you mean? Well, that is what
you are."

I laugh at that. "I'm sorry, but you have me mistaken for someone
else. I'm just an adopted teenage girl with a strong will and outgoing
personality. Sorry, but if you're looking for a princess try a palace in
England or something."

He seems amused by this. "It's so sad that you don't even know
what you really are."

I sit quietly, silently calling him all the mean names I can think of.
I'm almost sure he's some kind of raving lunatic.

"Maybe I am." He says.

I jump; Did I say that out loud by accident? No, I'm sure I only
thought it!
"Umm... maybe you are what?" I ask, trying to hide the quiver in
my voice.

"A lunatic? Isn't that what you were just thinking? That I'm a
raving lunatic?"
He smiles again and I feel the fear in my chest grow.

"How did you..."
I don't have a chance to finish because suddenly his voice is
inside my head.

"I read your mind princess."

I shriek and jump up, but he simply pushes me back down.

"Although I do enjoy watching you freak out, I suppose I should go ahead and explain. I'm what one might call, a demon, I suppose," He pauses and I stare at him, gawking.

Half of me believes it and is totally freaked out, and the other half is stuck on the 'he's a lunatic' idea.

"I see," he continues, "you don't believe me even after the little tricks I've shown you. Fine, you need proof? Here's proof."

He takes a step back and I watch as two silky black wings unfurl behind him. The feathers seem to almost glisten in the light and the wings take up a good ten feet in total left to right. I gape at him and his wings return to his back.

"You're a fallen," I say softly, still a little shocked.
But now it is his turn to be shocked.

"How did you know that?" He stares at me dumbfounded and I'm proud to have said something to make him that way.

"Books," I say as casually as possible, "I love books about angels. I always have."
At that he relaxes a little.

"No surprise. It's no wonder you'd be drawn to those types of books considering you're part angel yourself."

I stare at him as if he'd just told me I'd won the lottery. I mean, I've always dreamed about how awesome it would be to actually be part angel. Whenever I read a book about a girl who was a nephilim I'd always picture myself as her. I briefly wonder if I'm dreaming...

"You're kidding!" I can't help but smile as the possibilities dawn on me, " so you mean I'm a nephilim!?"

That earns another raise of his eyebrow. "You also know of the nephilim then?" He questions as I try to lower my excitement. I nod and try not to say anything else.

"I suppose these books you have read were either written by Nephilim or by someone who was being persuaded by them." He looks thoughtful for a moment before adding in a matter of fact tone, "They should be hunted down and killed for revealing our world to humans."

He suddenly seems very angry. Like the more he thinks about it the more he's sure that that's the proper decision for how to handle it. I have a quick mental image of my favorite author being killed by a band of demons and I swear my heart almost stops.

"No!" I shout suddenly, startling my captor, before adding, "I mean, people just think it's all make believe anyway, so why kill them?"

He seems to ponder the idea for just a moment and then says, "You're right. There are more important things at hand."

A thought suddenly occurs to me and I have to ask, "You still haven't told me, what is it you want me for anyways?"
He takes a seat in an old recliner chair in front of me and smiles.

"Oh yes, that," for a moment he's quiet and I wonder if he's even going to tell me, but then he continues, "Story time princess. Listen up. You already know of nephilim and how they are the offspring of humans and angels, correct?"

I nod and he continues. "Well, when the earth was flooded back in Noah's day the nephilim that were around were all wiped out. Angels never again came to the earth to be with a human. However, those of us, the fallen, who fell from heaven with Lucifer before the earth was finished, remained after the flood. Occasionally, a fallen one would find a female human and stir up trouble. Thus, the nephilim were once again on the Earth." He pauses to see if I'm keeping up and when I remain silent he continues. "Your Mother's father was one of the fallen. Your mother is one half angel… A nephilim." This time I jump in.

"So that means I'm a quarter angel?"
He seems frustrated by my interrupting him but nods before continuing on.

"Your mother also happens to be queen of Israel. So by blood, making you a princess." He seems to sense that I'm about to interrupt him again and stops. I start in,

"So I am an angel and a princess?"
He nods and I think of something else that troubles me.

"So if my grandfather is a demon, does that mean my mom is evil too?" I frown.

'And what does that make me?' I think to myself.

He frowns as well, and says,
"Unfortunately no. When someone with angel blood comes of age that's when their wings and powers appear. That is also when a messenger of the dark and light will appear to them. They then choose which side they will serve on. Heavens or hells. Your mother chose the straight and narrow."
He gives a look of disgust and I'm filled with relief.

"Good," I say beaming, "and I will too!"
I hope the statement will make him angry, but sadly all he does is shrug.

"Suit yourself. I really don't care what side you choose. You're only a quarterling and besides, that's not even the reason you're here." Now I'm the angry one.

"Then why am I here!? What do you want with me!? Just tell me already!"

He looks at me calmly and leans forward.

"You're here because I need your guardian angel dead."

"My what?" I ask, completely confused.

"Your guardian angel. All humans, and nephilim, have one. However, nephilim tend to get the more important angels as guardians. And your angel is very high up."

I try to think of all the angels I know of in the bible and mythology and wonder which one it could be. Suddenly my kidnapper's voice is in my head answering for me.

'Your angel… is Michael.'

-Gabriel-

The angel Gabriel scans the abandoned warehouse urgently. *'I'm too late; I didn't make it in time.'*

The thoughts run through his head endlessly as he searches the room for his friend. The floor is scattered with blood, weapons, and bodies. Both fallen and heavenly beings lie lifelessly around him.

'It could have been avoided. An unnecessary battle. If only I'd gotten here in time.' He steps over the bodies. None of which are his friend. *'Maybe that's good. Maybe there's hope...'*

A sobbing sound draws his attention to an old beat up vehicle at the back of the room. Gabriel moves swiftly around it and finds the kneeling form of his friend.

"Michael?"

Gabriel kneels next to him and Michael looks up. Apart from a few scratches and a bloody wing he seems okay. It doesn't take long for angels to heal so he should be good as new before long.

"Gabriel... so many were lost." Gabriel looks down and says nothing as Michael continues, "And for what? I was told it was an imperative mission... yet the whole time it felt so... wrong."

Tears form in Gabriel's eyes but he doesn't move to wipe them away.

"I'm so sorry my brother, but you are correct," Michael looks into Gabriel's eyes, searching, but he stays silent as Gabriel continues, "This mission was a set up..." A look of confusion passes through Michael's eyes as he tries to understand these words. "Michael, the fallen have taken the girl."

Realization floods across Michaels face and he shoots into the air without a sound. Gabriel remains seated on the concrete floor as he watches his friend soar out an open window. When Michael is gone from view Gabriel stands, a lone tear trailing down his face.

Already the bodies around the room have begun to diminish. They have begun to dissolve and the pieces will disappear. Angels and Demons do not have souls so they do not return to heaven or hell, they simply cease to exist. Gabriel watches as his fellow angels disappear, and then he closes his eyes.

"I'm so sorry."

He wraps his golden tipped wings around him and is transported back to heaven In the blink of an eye.

-Aurora-

Once again, I'm the only one in the room. The room smells like burning flesh and it is remarkably stuffy. I walk around looking for something to do to take my mind off of things.

'I have a guardian angel. And not just any angel, but the Archangel Michael himself.'

After he had told me I was completely amazed and disbelieving. Such a powerful angel coming down to Earth to watch over me? *'Wow.'*

The walls are gray cement blocks and the floor is concrete. I try the door, even though I know it won't open. It doesn't budge. There isn't a single window and there's basically nothing in the room but the couch, chair, and some empty boxes. I sit back down on the couch and sigh. Suddenly I feel bad that Michaels is my angel.

'He's such a well known angel and he's going to be killed because of me.' A flash of anger runs through me. *'But where was he when these freaks grabbed me anyways?'*

The moment I think it I'm ashamed.
'He's an angel. He has other things to do, heavenly things I probably can't understand.'

There's a crashing sound outside the room and I jump to my feet. Both fear and relief flood through me and I watch the door intently. Waiting and hoping this new development is a good one.

"Where's the girl Zantouron?" comes a deep, songlike voice from behind the door.
I listen as my captor, Zantouron, replies calmly.

"Hello, Michael. Come alone I presume?"

'Maybe he can save me. Maybe he won't be killed.' I think as I press my ear to the door. Then I do the only thing I can think of, I yell his name. "Michael! I'm in here!"

I hear swooshing sounds on the other side, and yelling. The words are another language and I can't understand them, but they make me shiver. They seem so familiar. Then I hear Michael's voice in my head.

'Stand Back!'

I do as he says and move away from the door. Then I stare as the door is splintered in two, down the middle, by a large glowing sword. In the books I'd read, angels always had swords of fire or flaming whips but this sword seemed normal except for a bright, white light illuminating from it. But the sword was nowhere near as glorious a sight as its wielder. Michael stood before me with golden hair and glimmering blue eyes. His entire body glowing with the same light as the sword and two beautiful white wings protruding from his back.

"Hello Aurora. We need to go."

He steps forward and extends his hand. I reach for it but hesitate. This seems too easy. *'Zantouron had seemed so confident he'd win. And he had Michael outnumbered.'* A look of shock registers on Michaels face and I quickly remember he can read my mind. He spins around so fast that for a second he is merely a blur. I look over his shoulder and watch as the six fallen surround Michael. All six are armed with swords of their own. Their swords aren't glowing like Michaels; instead they are black as night and smoke wavers from them as if they are on fire but without flames.

'Aurora...' Michael's voice is in my head again. He faces away from me and looks as if he's forgotten I am here at all. Had I imagined the voice? *'Aurora, Listen to me.'*

There it comes again and I know I hadn't imagined it. Zantouron steps into the circle to face Michael and he seems amused by the scene.

'Aurora, I don't know what all he's told you but he doesn't know everything.'

I frown, trying to concentrate on the words and not the scene before me.

Zantouron begins talking to Michael but I don't know what he's saying because Michael's talking to me again.

'He thinks you're a quarterling.'

The words surprise me and I think back, *'Aren't I?'*

Michael follows Zantouron with his eyes as if he is listening to him when in actuality he's talking to me.

'No, your mother was nephilim, your father was fallen.'

My mind puts two and two together and I gasp. Michael stiffens and Zantouron turns toward me. I suddenly realize my mistake.

'Think of something else! Now!'

Michael warns and I try to think of something else. Dayton. I think of the boy with the cute hair and green eyes. Zantouron studies me for a moment then turns back to Michael. Two of the fallen grab Michael and force him to his knees. He is no longer shining. Again he talks to me in my head.

'You're a triquarterling, the first in two millennia. You are more powerful than you can imagine.' I frown.

'That's cool and all but why tell me now? How does me knowing that help us?'
He is silent for a moment and I wonder if he heard me. But then he speaks again.

'It's time; you can manifest your powers if you try hard enough.' I swallowed hard.

'I thought they wouldn't appear until I'm eighteen... What if it doesn't work?'
Michael says nothing and fear bubbles up in me again.

'How do I do it?' I ask nervously.
He sighs aloud and then I hear him again.

'Believe. Then imagine your wings. Then you have to decide what you need.'

Believe? Check, I'm pretty sure I've had enough proof today, imagine my wings? Okay. I try to picture myself with lovely white wings. I see myself flying over a stream and up a waterfall. Check. Decide what I need? I need to defeat these guys and get home. I open my eyes to find everyone staring at me, mouths open. Michael smiles. I turn my head and find that I have large light gray wings attached to my shoulder blades. I'm not sure what to do now so I try to imagine the sword Michael has. After a moment a sword forms in my hand. It's not glowing like Michaels but it's a sword nonetheless.

Michael jumps at the opportunity and jerks free of the hands holding him down. His sword reforms and he swings it immediately. It hits the two nearest to him and they fall. One of the fallen recovers from his shock and dives towards me. I instinctively swing my sword and miss.

'Be one with your sword!' It's Michael again...

"Thanks Yoda..." I mutter under my breath as I twirl away from the fallen just before he can grab me.
Already I feel stronger and faster and my confidence builds as I swing again. This time I slice him in the arm.

"Yes!" I yell excitedly and turn, barely in time to see the other demon running up behind me.

"Whoa!" I scream out and drop to the floor.
The fallen trips over me and soars into the other demon that I have already injured.

Michael finishes off the two he'd been struggling with and flies over to me. The one I tripped starts to get back up but Michael stabs him in the chest and he falls lifeless. I cringe as he does the same to the other that I hurt and turns to me again.

"You okay?"

I nod and look around.
"What happened to Zantouron?" I ask, noticing he's not among the bodies.

"I assume he transported back to Hell. He'll be back though," he says and
then takes my hand, "Hold onto my hand, flap when I say." My eyes widen but before I can protest we're in the air.

I'm surprised that I got the hang of flying so quickly. In all of the books I've read flying is usually a hard process, and the nephilim have to practice a lot before they can do it well. Michael is flying next to me and I no longer need his help.

He nods and says, "Yes, but you are more powerful than the nephilim in your books. You have more Angel blood in you and so it comes more naturally for you."

I sigh, "That's really invasive you know? The whole mind reading thing?" He doesn't respond.

"I have a question." I announce.

"I'm sure you do." He sounds a bit irritated but I go on anyway.

"Am I going to have to move?"

Michael frowns, "No, it will not do any good."

I stay quiet for just a moment before arguing, "It took them 17 years to find me this time."

I thought it was a good point but then he said, "Last time you didn't have your powers. Now that you do they could track you in a heartbeat. You give off spiritual energy that other angelic beings can track effortlessly."

Okay, so I'm basically a sitting duck anywhere I go? Lovely.

"I have another question." He groans but doesn't stop me. "My dad, umm... Did he... Was I..."
For a brief second I think I see him blush but it's gone in a flash.

"No, they were..." He pauses to consider his wording and then finishes,
"in love."
I breathe a sigh of relief.

"Then did he leave her or... what happened?" I watch him as I wait for him to respond.

"He had to leave in order to protect you. When you were born he knew if he stayed the other fallen would know what you are and would come after you."

When he finishes the explanation I feel sick. I want to cry. It's hard knowing my dad left my mom to protect me, even though I've never met either of them. I suddenly have a headache from trying to hold back tears. Michael glances over at me a moment then points downward. My gaze drifts down in the direction he's pointing and I see my house. There is a strange humming sound inside my head for a split second and when it's gone, so is my headache.

'No tears please.' Michael says in my head, *'there have been enough of those today.'*

I have no idea what he means by this or what he did to stop my headache, but I don't ask. Michael tilts his left-wing down slightly and begins to descend. I imitate his movements and soon we are landing in my backyard. My wings dematerialize and I'm about to walk in the back door but then I turn back to him.

"Last question." I say and he narrows his eyes, "if you're always watching, where were you today?"
I don't say it harshly, I'm just curious, but his face looks pained and I'm sorry I asked.

"I was," he closes his eyes, "tricked. I wasn't thinking and so many..." He stops suddenly and opens his eyes. "You need to get some sleep. I'll see you in the morning."

Then he flies off without finishing his explanation.

- Aurora-

"Aurora, get up. It is time for church."
A voice in my room tells me. I moan into my pillow.

"Oh, come on Brent! I had a rough day yesterday. Let me sleep!" I wrap my pillow around my head and try to drown him out.

"I am not Brent. Now get up please."

The voice announces. The words run through my half-asleep mind until I finally understand them. The voice is definitely male and once the part where it said, '*I'm not Brent,*' finally becomes clear I bolt upright and whip my head around. Michael stands in my doorway leaning against the wooden frame. I groan and let my face fall back into the covers.

"How did you get in?" I mumble it through my sheets.
It's a stupid question, I know. He doesn't even bother to answer. He's an Angel. He can get into a human's house easily. Before I know it I'm up, dressed, and sitting on a pew at church. I've always gone to church and believed in God. However lately I have been slacking off a bit I suppose. But I get a feeling I won't be anymore. After church we start walking back to my house. Yes, walking. Sadly, Michael says we can't just go busting out the wings anytime we want.

We're about halfway there when Michael turns and says, "There is someone you need to meet."

Before I can reply there's a blinding light in between us. I try to shield my eyes but as soon as I do the light goes out and in its place is another Angel. This Angel has Golden hair like Michaels only it also has white streaks throughout it. His hair is long and wavy and goes just past his shoulders. He has on a white shirt and white pants with a golden belt around his waist and golden sandals. On his back is a leather tube shaped carrier. It is held on by a single shoulder strap that goes over his left shoulder and under his right arm. I notice that his eyes are sad but at the same time he's smiling.

Michael steps forward a bit, "This is the Angel Gabriel."

No way...
"The Gabriel?" I ask excitedly, "like the Gabriel that appears to Mary in the Bible?"

Gabriel nods, "It is nice to finally meet you in person Aurora."

Michael starts up again, "Aurora, there is something you need to know how to do. In case anything like yesterday happens again, you have to know how to get a message to Gabriel." After I confirm that I'm listening he goes on. "When you need to contact Gabriel you pull a feather from your wings. It will sting but another will grow back. Then hold onto the feather and think of the message in your head. Then release the feather. It will dissolve and go straight to Gabriel."

"Wow! That's so cool!" I shout and Michael shushes me.

He nods, "Yes, It is. Now I need to have a private conversation with
Gabriel. We will be right over there."
He points off to the side of the street at a gas station, and then they walk over to it and begin whispering. I'm just starting to get bored when I see a familiar face out of the corner of my eye.

"Dayton!" I holler his name as I run over towards him. At first he stiffens upon hearing his name, but once he sees me his shoulders relax some.

"Hey." He says as I stop in front of him.

I smile, "Hey! Sorry to bother you but I don't think I ever actually gave you my name yesterday."

He shakes his head and grins, "No, I don't think you did. You didn't give me your number either."

I laugh, "Ha ha. Smooth."

He shrugs, "I try."

Oh my goodness! I think he likes me!

"Well, my name is Aurora."

"Well, that is a beautiful name for a beautiful girl." He says, smiling flirtatiously.

I feel my cheeks burning the second the words leave his mouth. I'm trying to think of a witty response, when my eyes happen to glance over his shoulder towards the gas station. Gabriel is gone and Michael is staring at me. He looks stricken and I panic.

'Something's *wrong! Did the fallen find me? Is Zantouron here? Does he know what I am? So soon?'*
Thoughts run through my mind in a rush.

"I'm sorry. I just remembered I have to be somewhere." I say turning back to Dayton.
His face looks a little pale and I wonder if I did something angelic without realizing it.

"It's cool," he assures me, "I have to go too. I'll uh... catch you later!" He turns to leave and I turn toward the gas station. Michael is already on his way over.

"What's wrong?" I ask but he doesn't answer.
He simply grabs my arm and says,
"Let's go."

- **Dayton** -

Dayton walks away from Aurora and around the corner. Yesterday he had been run over by the beautiful girl on a skateboard and had thought she seemed different than others. Somewhat unique. But today his suspicions were confirmed. When he was certain he was out of sight he broke into a run. A set of midnight black wings burst from his back and he was in the air in seconds. When he walked past her just moments ago he'd heard her call his name and could hear the energy in her voice. For a moment he'd frozen. Why would a nephilim know his name? But then he'd seen the face and had understood. He was right; the girl does have Angel blood in her. She was flirting with him and he was flirting back. Being a fallen doesn't mean you can't have some fun…

The whole time they had talked he was reading her mind, searching for any hint that she suspected him of being fallen. None. She must not know much yet. No surprise though, considering she had obviously changed just since the last time they'd talked. Everything was looking good until up to the last minute. She had suddenly gotten scared and jumpy. He'd read her thoughts and paled.

'Michael *looks stricken. Something's wrong! Did the fallen find me? Is Zantouron here? Does he know what I am? So soon*?'

He had almost panicked himself at that point. And then her thoughts repeated something that shocked him even more.

'*3/4ths. I'm 3/4ths. 3/4ths.*'
That's when she'd said she had to leave. Dayton's stomach had turned a flip but he had tried to act as normal as possible. Then he'd left.

'She's *a triquarterling*!' Dayton frowns as he flies and thinks things over.

'That would mean she is almost as powerful as a full blood. And if Zantouron is after her she is in serious danger. Zantouron is almost as evil as the devil himself!'

Every demon under Satan's rule will be after the girl in no time. But Dayton isn't under Satan's rule any longer. No, he had rebelled against the devil a long time ago. A rebel. That's what he is, it's what he's always been, and it's the reason for everything that has happened in Dayton's life. Both good and bad. But this girl, this girl is one of the good things. He doesn't know why but he's drawn to her. She's the most beautiful creature he's ever seen in heaven or on earth. (Excluding the Almighty only.) No, he's not your typical demon, and Aurora is no typical nephilim either.

They belong together. It's destiny. It has to be...

"No! That's impossible... " I shake my head and Michael repeats what he has just told me.

"He is a fallen one."

My eyes fog up, "Are you sure? How do you know?"

He suddenly looks disgusted, "Could you not smell him?"

I'm appalled!
"What do you mean couldn't I smell him? He smelled amazing! Like smoke and vanilla!"

I'm furious and I'm trying to blink back tears. There I went thinking that there was still something normal in my life. Thinking I was still just a teenage girl with a crush on a cute guy, only to find out I'm a nephilim with a crush on a demon! I assume Michael read my mind because after I think it his face goes soft again and he looks sympathetic.

"I'm sorry Aurora but the smoky smell was the sulfur of Hells fire." I believe him but I refuse to look him in the eye. He goes on, "All fallen smell like sulfur."

I wipe the tears from my eyes and mutter, "But he also smelled like vanilla."

Michael nods, "Yes, they usually do have a second smell to cover up as much of the sulfur smell as possible. Which is why, if you noticed, Dayton's sulfur smell was like smoke, while Zantouron's was purely the smell of sulfur and flesh."

I had noticed, but I don't say anything. Then I think of something and I have to ask him about it.

"Well you smell like cotton candy. Do all Angels smell like cotton candy?"

He raises an eyebrow at me and then laughs. "It is actually the aroma of incense but I suppose it does smell a lot like cotton candy. Yes, all Angels smell this way. It is the smell of heaven. This is how you can tell if an

Angel or a demon is close by, usually."

He smiles. I'm starting to cheer up again but Dayton's face keeps popping into my head. It's just so hard to believe that he could be a demon, or even dangerous at all.

"How do you know Dayton's dangerous?"
I ask it without hesitation. Michael's smile disappears again.

"All fallen are dangerous."

"Yeah, well, maybe he isn't a danger to me!"
I feel the anger building back up. Michael looks as if he might get angry himself.

"Fallen are not to be trusted under any circumstance. I'm sure he read your mind back there and now he knows you're a triquarterling and he will probably be back. Stay away from him. Do you understand?"

Stay away from him? I don't think I can. I feel drawn to him, connected somehow. And that feeling only got stronger after Michael told me he's fallen. My mother fell in love with a fallen didn't she? Maybe I will too. Michael reads my mind and begins to protest. I respond by drawing out my wings and shooting into the air.

'I *make my own decisions thank you.*'
I think back at him as I fly towards my house. Besides, I just know Dayton wasn't pulling one over on me. He was sincere. I'm sure of it!

What if we're meant to be together? What if it's destiny?

- **The Creature** -

"You're certain?"
The smooth, dark voice questions.

Zantouron nods, "Yes, I'm sure. She has yet to come of age but her powers have already manifested. Her mother, as you know, is a half blood but her father is a mystery. The girl is incredibly powerful and there's only one other case, I've heard of, matching this."

The figure in front of Zantouron considers this only a moment before saying, "Very well. Forget the Angel. I want the girl."

Zantouron smiles maliciously at the order and bows slightly.
'This *is going to be loads of fun.*' He thinks as he stands back up again.
"As you wish, master."

Then he turns on his heel and allows his wings to unfurl behind him. He holds up his hands and a fire forms around him. The flames spin around him faster and faster. Then in a puff of smoke he's transported back to earth. Once he's gone, the creature he had left behind steps out from the shadows and transforms into the shape of a man.

'*Finally,*' he thinks as he watches the flame die,' *another three quarters Angel has appeared. I've waited 2000 years for this. She must be won to my side. Then I can finally have my revenge.*'

The creature knew of the girl's existence the moment she was born. He had at the time kidnapped her mother trying to find the girl, however, when that pesky Angel had appeared and saved her he had not bothered to look any further. After all, at the time, he had thought the girl was only a quarterling and therefore, not worth the trouble. The flame that had been dancing across the floor is little more than a pile of ash now. The man/creature returns to his shadowed throne and listens to the screams of those he has already won.

The footsteps chasing me are getting closer and I try to speed up. I'm breathing hard as I race down the dark alleyway in a panic. Zantouron's after me... He is so close now I can almost feel his breath on my neck. I trip and fall flat on the concrete, skinning my knee. A hooded figure steps in front of me. I crawl back as far as I can until I'm against the cold brick building behind me and let out a blood curdling scream. Suddenly, Michael drops down from above and lands between us. His sudden appearance startles my pursuer who falls backwards. Michael's sword comes down slowly and flips the hood from atop the man's head.

"I don't want to hurt her!"
The face below shouts. And that face belongs to Dayton. I gasp and the image fades from my mind. I groan as I awake from the dream and my eyes slowly flutter open. I look out the window and see it's still night time. I start to close my eyes again when I hear,

"I swear! I don't want to hurt her!"
I bolt out of bed and dive to the window. Below, I see Michael with his sword drawn and pointed at someone's neck. Dayton's neck!

"No!" I yell, forgetting Shawna and Brent are sleeping.
My wings explode from my back and I leap from the window. I land to the right of them and retract my wings. Michael has a scowl on his face and doesn't turn his attention away from Dayton for even a second. Dayton on the other hand is watching me. He has a sword to his throat but he acts like he doesn't notice anything but me. I suddenly feel self-conscious about being seen by him while I'm in my white tank top and purple pajama pants.

'I *won't hurt you*.' He says in my head.
It's strange, but somehow I know he's telling the truth. I can feel it.

"I know." I say out loud
Michael glances at me a brief second but then turns back to Dayton.

"Michael, stop!"

I glare at him and his jaw tightens but he makes no move to pull away. I sigh and form my own sword in my hand.

"What do you think you're doing?" Michael demands.

Dayton's eyes lower to the ground and I shake my head.

"I said, stop. He isn't here to hurt me. Put away the sword."
Michael laughs, amused by my threat. I'm getting angry and I stand up straighter.

"Michael, I'm serious. I may not beat you but I will sure try." He growls but lowers his sword.

"If you even think about harming her, I'll kill you." He says to Dayton.
Then he turns to me,

"And I hope you know what you're doing."

He steps back but doesn't let us out of sight. My sword disappears and I turn my gaze away from Michael and back to Dayton. I'm suddenly nervous. I know he isn't here to hurt me, how I know I haven't a clue, but he's still a demon...

"Why are you here?" I ask.

He puts on that cocky smile of his and replies, "I wanted to see you again."

My heart seems to skip a beat. Normally I'm not one of those girls that gets all lovey-dovey and stuff but what really got to me just now is that I know he means it. Michael, off to the side, lets out a small laugh like snort that helps me snap out of my trance.

"Michael could've killed you." I point out.
Michael mumbles something that sounded like, "could have, would have, probably will."
I ignore him. Dayton shrugs,

"A risk worth taking. A prince must first face the Dragon before finding the Princess you know."
I can't help but smile at the comparison of Michael and a Dragon. Michael growls and I try to stifle a laugh.

"Well, you found me. Now what do you need to tell me?"
I can smell the smoky vanilla on him and briefly wonder what I smell like to him.

"Honey." He says and I jump.
I keep forgetting they read minds.

"Oh... Okay." I shift my weight back-and-forth and he continues,

"I came to warn you. As of an hour ago, Satan has a price on your head. You're officially wanted by the devil." His smile has faded and he stops making eye contact. He runs a hand through his hair absently and goes on, "you're going to need protection."
Michaels' eyes light up with anger,

"I'm protecting her! I don't think....."

Dayton interrupts him by adding, "I know Michael's your Guardian and he's doing a great job but not even the Archangel Michael can take on every demon under Satan alone. He will need help and I promise I'm going to be part of it whether he likes it or not."

Dayton steals a quick glance at Michael who looks about ready to explode. Then Dayton looks back at me and when our eyes meet it's like I can see straight into his soul. (If angels and demons even have souls).

"I feel," he begins slowly, "connected to you somehow. I really want to keep you safe."

He looks away but not before his cheeks turn pink in a blush that is both cute and awkward at the same time. Again it's as if I'm a human lie detector and I can feel he's telling the truth. Michael starts talking in my head telling me not to trust him and reminding me he's fallen, but I don't care.

"Thank you." I say and Dayton turns back to face me.
He seems to search my face for any sign that I'm being sarcastic and when he finds none he smiles again.

"I won't let anything happen to you. You can trust me. I promise." I nod and turn to face my house. Michael turns the other way and stomps off angrily. I stop and turn back to Dayton,

"About what you said, about feeling connected to me," I pause and he looks like he might blush again, "I feel the same way towards you."
Then I let out my wings and flew back to my room without another word.

-Gabriel-

This is the angriest Gabriel has seen Michael since his dispute with Satan over the body of Moses.

"How can she be so stupid? Trusting a demon! Of all the reckless things..."

Michael paces back and forth while he vents. Gabriel watches his friend a moment and then says,

"Now Michael, you know her mother was in love with a demon and that didn't turn out to be so bad."

Michael scowls,

"Yes, but that too was reckless. Just because one relationship between nephilim and fallen didn't end in disaster doesn't mean another won't."

Gabriel thinks for a moment then says,

"Aurora is a smart girl and more Angel than human. So it is strange that she is not being more cautious. She did not say or think anything that might help us understand why she is so trusting of this fallen did she?" Michael stops pacing and thinks back.

"I don't know. She just kept thinking that he's telling the truth. She thinks she knows he is. She's a teenage girl and she's hormonal and thinks he's good-looking, so of course she's going to believe..."

He suddenly stops and looks as if he's thought of something. Gabriel waits for him to share his sudden realization.

"Gabriel, you don't think she has the power to distinguish between truth and lie do you?" Michael asks.

That would be interesting. Very few Angels have that particular gift, nonetheless a mere nephilim...

Gabriel shakes his head, "I don't know brother. But these are strange times and anything is possible."

-Dayton-

'She's kind of cute when she sleeps,'

Dayton thinks to himself as he watches Aurora sleep. It's almost dawn and the sun will be rising soon. He hates that he has to wake her, well he doesn't really have to but...

"Psst... psst... Aurora!"
Finally she stirs awake and rolls over to face him. She registers his face and bolts straight up in bed.

"What are you doing here?" She demands worrisomely.
He smiles and holds out the caramel frappe he'd gotten for her at Starbucks.

"Thanks..." she mutters, "but you probably shouldn't be here. If Michael sees you he'll…" She trails off and Dayton laughs.

"Your Angel friend is at a meeting right now. Besides, there's something I want to show you. Get dressed to meet me outside, okay? Try to hurry." Then he jumps out the window. He waits for her down there and before too long she is at the window, spreading her wings, and swooping down to meet him.

"Where are we going?" She asks him suspiciously and he smiles,

"You'll see. Just trust me."
She hesitates only a second before nodding. Dayton leaps into the air and his wings burst from his back.

"Follow me." He flies off and she follows behind him. He reads her thoughts as they fly.

'He *is so cute*.' And ' *I wonder if he likes me*.' Were only two of the many thoughts that had him smiling the whole way. She just found out she's part Angel and yet she's thinking more about him. How cute.

I have absolutely no idea where he's taking me. Maybe I didn't think this all the way through. My Guardian Angel goes off to a heavenly meeting and I follow a demon to some unknown location, willingly. But man is he a hot demon. I get the feeling all Angels, fallen and heavenly, are supposed to be attractive. However, attractive or not, a demon is a demon. Am I making a huge mistake by trusting him?

We've been flying about 10 minutes when we come upon a mountain.

"You're not going to move mountains are you?" I tease him as he lands on the edge of the small ledge near the peak. He laughs and I land next to him.

"No, that's more of a heavenly Angel thing." He assures me.
We sit on the edge and he points ahead.

"Watch right there."
I follow his finger and watch the sky. It suddenly fills with colors: pinks, purples, oranges, and yellows streak across the horizon. The sun rises and I stare in amazement.

"Wow." I inhale then exhale slowly, "it's beautiful."
It's the most beautiful thing I've ever seen. I'm breath taken. Next to me, Dayton nods in agreement.

'You're *the most beautiful thing I've ever seen.*'

His voice fills my head and I turn to look at him in surprise. It was just so unexpected. He is staring at me intensely and I stare back, into his gorgeous green eyes. For a moment I think he might lean forward and kiss me. Then I instantly regret it, remembering he can read minds.

He gives a thin smile and announces that it's time to go back. Then he stands to his feet and leaps from the cliff. I inwardly yell at myself for ruining the moment and then follow behind. On the way back I try not to think about what just happened on the mountain. I know he would just read my thoughts and see how embarrassed I am. I decide to start a conversation to keep my mind off of it.

"Last night you said every fallen under Satan's rule would be after me." I begin and he glances at me curiously, "but aren't you under his rule too?

Or have you gone rogue or something?" I ask, smiling but totally serious. He sighs.

"No, I'm not under his rule. Never really have been." He looks away but now I'm really curious.

"But I thought since you fell…" I begin but trail off.
He understands though and explains.

"No, I didn't choose Satan over God. When we were asked to choose sides I got a little rebellious." There was a pause as if he were trying to think of an easier way to explain it, "okay, so you know how when a kid's parents get divorced and they ask the kid to choose which one they want to live with? And then the kid yells and complains and says both or
neither? Yeah, well, that's pretty much what I did."
I nod and he's silent for a moment before continuing,
"I basically said the whole thing was ridiculous and they should just stop the fight instead of forcing us to choose. Then I said if they didn't stop, and we had to choose, then I choose neither. And for that God sent me down with Satan, but I still didn't choose him. So I went solo."
I watch him and listen silently. When he's finished I ask,

"Do you ever regret it? Not choosing, and getting kicked out anyways?" He turns to me and looks deep into my eyes.

"I did. But then I met you."

- Michael -

When he gets back from his meeting with Gabriel, Michael finds the girl gone. He can feel her powers dimly, coming from the west. They seem to be getting closer so she is probably coming home. Michael leans against a tree to wait for her arrival. Why does she insist on putting herself in dangerous situations? She should not have left the house without him! She lands in the yard, along with her demon friend. Michael steps out from behind the tree angrily.

"Where were you?"
His sudden appearance must've startled the girl because she jumps.

"Michael, chill, Dayton just took me to see the sunrise. It was beautiful." She explains but blushes on the last sentence, as if hiding something.
Michael tries to read her mind but she just keeps thinking about Dayton.
Michael narrows his eyes,

"And why, pray tell, did you decide to take her to see the sunrise?" He questions the demon, looking for any sign of hidden intentions in his eyes. Dayton shrugs,

"Her name means dawn. I thought she might like to watch one with me." He shoots a sideways smile at Aurora and she smiles and blushes again.
Michael sighs,

"Whatever. You're back now and we have things to discuss."
The demon waves and begins to slink away. Michael frowns,

"You too fallen. Come on."

I can tell Michael is mad that I went off with Dayton this morning. He's trying hard not to show it but I can still see it in his eyes. He hates Dayton and I'm surprised he's letting him sit in on this discussion he has called. We are all in my bedroom sitting in a triangle on the carpet. Luckily, Brent and Shawna are already at work because I doubt they would be happy to find two guys in my room.

"There is something I need to know about you, Aurora."

Michael says it and then looks curiously at me. I'm suddenly a bit nervous as if he's about to give me a pop quiz or something. Michael turns his head toward Dayton and says,

"I've decided to completely trust you."
Dayton looks completely taken aback and Michael turns back to me as if he expects me to say something.

"No you don't, that's a lie." I say defiantly.
Michael smiles knowingly but still he asks,

"How do you know?" Now both Michael and Dayton are staring at me intently.

"I don't really know how to explain it," I say unsure, "it started last night and I can just tell when people are telling the truth and when they aren't."

Michael smiles proudly. Dayton looks shocked for a moment but he recovers quickly and says, "Oh come on Michael. You still don't trust me?"

Michael stops smiling and shoots him a look. Dayton laughs and sends a smile in my direction.

"Aurora," Michael begins, "I believe you have what's called the power to distinguish between truth and lie. It's an extremely rare gift that only a few angels possess."

He continues and goes into the history of the power, but I'm no longer listening. Dayton's voice appears in my head.

'Congrats *on the power. Super cool.*'

I try to act like I'm still listening to Michael so he won't try to read my thoughts.

'Thanks, *I guess*.' I think back to him.

'So what do you say, maybe ditching the Angel later and getting some lunch?'

I consider the offer for a moment. I get a mental image of Dayton and I sneaking off together and I smile. I've never been the rebellious type but the thought of him and I together gives me chills and I decide that for once, I'm going to be. Dayton's smile falters for half a second and I'm not sure why but I figure it's nothing to worry about.

'Sure,' I reply, '*Why not? I'd love to! But you know he'll just track my powers if he has to.*'

'Let *him*.'

He says before speaking out loud and addressing Michael, "Dude, what does this have to do with me? Why do you want me here?"

Michael stops his droning and sighs. "Because of last night. Aurora has the power to tell if you're lying and you said last night that she can trust you. She obviously thinks you're telling the truth. I refuse to trust you myself as of yet, however, I'm willing to let you have a chance to prove yourself to me."

Dayton narrows his eyes suspiciously and turns to look at me. I nod to let him know Michaels telling the truth.

"Umm...thanks." Dayton mutters and looks down. Michael turns to me again.

"There are a few things you should know. The first of which is why Satan wanted me dead." I admit I had been wondering that since Zantouron first told me but I hadn't wanted to ask. Michael goes on, "He wants me dead because just before the tribulation takes place on earth, Satan and his demons will return to heaven for one last fight. I'm supposed to lead the angels of heaven against Satan. We will win and I will bind Satan and
toss them into the abyss for 1000 years." He pauses and glances at Dayton who remains silent, "this is described in Revelation chapter 12 in the Bible. Although some interpret it as the original fall from heaven, it is actually describing a future event. One I fear, may be closer than we think."

I consider this and do a brief recap to make sure I understand.
"So Satan wants you dead because you're going to defeat him, bind him, and throw him into the abyss?"
Michael nods, telling me I have the right idea.

"Okay," I begin again, "so why does he want me so badly?"

"That is the other thing you should know," he starts, "you see, good and evil are on a scale of sorts. When an Angel chooses a side it tips the scale one way or the other depending on what side the Angel chose. But because all full-blooded angels are male, then there can't be any more angels in the future to choose. Half bloods don't count for much and quarterlings don't really count at all, as far as the scale goes anyway." I can already see where he's going but I let him continue anyway.

"Triquarterling's, like you however, being more Angel than human, do count. Right now the scale is tipped in the favor of good. During the tribulation the antichrist will rise and the scale will be balanced out for a while but good will still prevail in the end. But if you were to choose evil it would balance the scale out now. Then when the antichrist rises it would tip in favor of evil and, although Satan will still be defeated eventually, he will deceive millions more than predicted in the Bible. If you choose good however, the scale will always favor good and never even out. Less people would be deceived and therefore more will be

saved and taken to heaven than predicted."

He finishes his explanation and I frown,

"So basically I have the fate of millions of souls resting on my shoulders?"

Michael nods solemnly and Dayton turns away, avoiding my eyes. I continue,

"But I'll always choose good! Satan is stupid if he believes I'd ever even consider choosing his side!"

Michael looks uneasy,

"Satan is wrong in his ways but he is far from stupid. If he gets a hold of you he will give you the choice between either choosing him or being killed. And he wouldn't just kill you either. I'm afraid he'd try to torture you into joining him. I'm sorry, I know it's a scary thought but you need to know the truth."

I swallow hard and try to push the images of torture from my mind.

'I *won't let that happen*.' Dayton assures me in my head, and I relax just a bit, knowing that he means it.

"In order to ensure your safety, you will need to learn how to use your angelic weapons more skillfully."

Michael says it as he moves to the window and waves for us to follow. Then he leaps from the window and I glance at Dayton, who shrugs and does the same. I follow them down to the backyard and watch as Michael draws his sword.

"You will need to train." Michael says and I draw my own sword in imitation. Dayton takes a seat by a nearby tree and announces that he will be watching from there.

"Umm… What exactly did you have in mind?" I ask Michael, although I have the feeling I'm probably not going to enjoy whatever it is.

- Dayton -

Michael's the kind of guy that believes in learning by experience. Therefore, his idea of training for a fight is by fighting. However, Dayton had guessed this was the case from the start, which is exactly why he wanted no part in it. He can't stand the thought of possibly accidentally hurting her in a fight. How would he live with himself if he did? After a few hours of training Michael finally decided they were through for the day.

Aurora looks as if she might pass out and Dayton doesn't blame her. Michael definitely kept her on her toes during their battle. In fact, a few times it got so intense, Dayton almost jumped in to help her.

"You've done well." Michael states, "That's enough training for today." Dayton springs to his feet and trots over to them.

"Finally! I was starting to think you were going to keep fighting until she passed out." He says to Michael.
Michael looks irritated and Dayton smiles, he loves that he has that effect on the Archangel.

"Perhaps if you had helped it would have gone quicker." Michael says it heatedly and Dayton shakes his head.

"Right. So you could 'accidentally' stab me? No thanks."

He says it as he loops his arms through Aurora's. She blushes but doesn't pull away. Michael looks at their arms and his face floods with disapproving anger, but before he can say anything Dayton unfurls his wings and says,

"Now, if you're done waving your sword in her face, I believe she and I have a lunch date to get to."

The Archangel looks at Aurora, who is about as shocked as he is. Dayton realizes Michaels talking to her thoughts and he tries to read her mind. She's getting better at blocking him out, which is both annoying and impressive. After a second he is in, just in time to hear her tell Michael it's her life, her choice, that she trusts Dayton, and not to follow them.

Dayton smiles at that and waits as she unfurls her wings. She has to be the most amazing girl he's ever met, human and nephilim alike.

"McDonald's? How romantic."
I tease him as we land behind Mickey D's and he smiles,

"Only the best for you Princess."
I laugh and follow him around to the front of the building and in through the front door. Dayton asks what I want and because I don't want him to have to pay a lot for mine I just say a hamburger and fries. So I'm a little shocked when he orders...

"Two cheeseburgers, two medium fries, two large soft drinks, two Apple strudels, two bags of chocolate chip cookies, and two Oreo blasts. And I need it all to go."
The lady behind the counter is staring at him like he's crazy and turns to me for an explanation. I shrug, I don't understand him sometimes but I know I trust him and that's all that matters. The lady finishes ringing it up and Dayton pays in cash. Then we move to get our drinks from the fountain while we wait.

"I doubt very seriously we can carry all of that let alone eat it all!"
I tell him and he grins again,

"Don't worry. I think you'll be surprised how much you can eat. You see, Angels and demons don't have to eat, so we can eat as much or as little as we want and it won't affect us."
I consider this a moment and correct him,

"But I'm not full Angel. I'm still human too."
He nods in agreement, "Exactly. So you have to eat to survive, however, the angel part of you will burn food off almost as fast as you can eat it.
So you can eat all you want, no problem."

Wow, that is so cool! Our order is ready and Dayton grabs it then heads to the door and I follow him. We walk around the restaurant again and take off into the sky.

"Where are we going this time?" I ask it, hoping he'll give me more of an answer then he did this morning.

"A mountain."

"The same one we went to this morning?"

"No," he explains, "this morning we went to the San Gabriel Mountains. Now we are going to Mount Baden Powell."

"Okay, so why are we going?" Since I'm getting straight answers from him right now I figured I may as well ask that too.

"Now that one you're just going to have to trust me on." He says it in a playful, taunting tone and I laugh,

"Of course."

When we get there instead of heading to the top like this morning, he leads me to a large open field at the bottom of the mountain. In the clearing is a small checkered blanket with a bouquet of roses in the center.

"When did you have time to set this up?" I ask, awestruck. I sit down on the blanket and reach to feel the pedals of a rose; it's incredibly soft.

"This morning, before we went to see the sunrise." He says, as he sits on the blanket a few feet away from me. I smell of a rose and smile,
"How did you know I'd say yes to going to lunch with you?"

His smile fades and he looks at me seriously this time. "I didn't. But I hoped you would..."

I feel my cheeks fill with heat and I decide to distract myself by eating. We managed to eat all the food after all and I'm amazed that I'm not sick to my stomach. Dayton points toward the mountain and I look up. The sunlight shines down over the fall trees and all the brilliant colors are exposed. It's an amazing sight and just as beautiful as the sunrise this morning. A thought suddenly occurs to me and I turn to Dayton.

"Dayton, why do you keep showing me such beautiful things that have to do with light?"

He turns away from me and looks back up the mountain with a sad look in his eyes. "You should always choose light. Choose good over evil when the time comes… Because believe me you'll regret it if you don't. In all your decisions you should always choose light instead of darkness." He still doesn't look at me and I get the feeling he's not just talking about what side I'll choose when I turn eighteen. I get the feeling he's talking about himself.

"Dayton," I start to tell him he's not evil. I want to tell him how I feel about him. That I think I love him, despite the fact that I just met him,
"you're not… I mean I…"

All of a sudden he leaps to his feet and looks totally freaked out. He puts a finger to his lips to let me know to be quiet. Then he draws his sword and looks around us nervously. I'm suddenly aware that the air is filling with a heavy smell of smoke and fear streaks through me. I stand up beside him and my own sword forms in my hand. Out of the woods around us steps fallen after fallen. About 20 of them surround us now and Dayton puts his hand behind him to tell me to stay back. I don't. In fact, I step up next to him.

'What *are you doing*?' He thinks at me.

'I've *been training all morning. I'm ready to put it to the test.*' I think back at him and he smiles.
My wings unfurl and I quickly pluck a feather from them.

'20 fallen surrounding us at the bottom of Baden Powell.' I think and release the feather.

It disappears and I hope it gets to Gabriel in time. The fallen begin to charge and Dayton squeezes my hand really fast then let's go and darts toward them. I take a deep breath and before I know it I'm doing the same.

- Michael -

Michael had known that letting the girl and the demon go off without him would be a bad idea. That is why he had tried to talk Aurora out of it but she is the most stubborn, independent, child he has ever encountered.

He'd considered following them but he knew they would sense him. Besides, he had thought, he had said he'd give the demon a chance and how is Dayton to win his trust if he never gives him the opportunity to do so. So he had let them go off together. And now he's flying through the air as fast as his wings can carry him to go save their stubborn, uncareful, love struck rear ends.

Just a moment earlier, Gabriel had appeared in front of him in the girls' backyard and relayed the message. When Gabriel had first appeared with a look of intense worry in his eyes, Michael immediately knew something had happened to the girl. His first thought was that the demon had let her into a trap but then Gabriel had said that they were both surrounded. Then Michael had taken off and now he's headed straight for mount Baden Powell, angry at himself for letting them go off without him in the first place.

He gets close to the mountain and searches it with his eyes. Below he easily locates them, Aurora and Dayton, barely managing to hold off the fallen that are closing in around them. *'At least I managed to get here before it was too late...'* He thinks to himself as he nose dives down towards them at top speed.

Of course, because all of the fallen are after me and not him, they ignore Dayton and come straight for me. All 20 of them dive towards me at once. Dayton leaps between me and the closest two and tries to hold them off. Four of the fallen charge at me from different directions. You know how in movies when that kind of thing happens the hero just ducks and the bad guys end up stabbing each other instead? Yeah, well, that doesn't typically work in real life, and I should know.

I duck down hoping for the movie effect but instead they simply stop and point their swords down at me. Uh oh. Between them I spot Dayton battling it out with three fallen at once. The two he had blocked earlier lay in the grass nearby bleeding, most likely dead. This is all happening very quickly, in fact, the other fallen are still running from the trees. Dayton, I notice, is extremely skillful with a sword. He stabs one fallen in the chest and spins around quickly to the other. Their swords meet with a clang and he ground his teeth from the effort.

One of them that is surrounding me grabs my arm roughly and yanks me to my feet. Michael chooses this moment to swoop down from overhead, out of nowhere, and land on the guy that's holding me. He releases me as he falls to the ground unconscious. I don't waste any time. Before Michael can even draw his sword, I'm whirling around to face the other three that are behind me and swinging my sword violently. It catches them off guard and they don't even have time to move before my sword collides with the first one's gut. It continues on and hits the second one but by then the third fallen has pulled himself together and sidestepped my attack.

The momentum from the strike has my sword still sailing through the air and I struggle to stop it. While I'm trying to stop my sword the fallen lunges at me but Michael steps in with his own sword and thrusts it into the fallen's chest. I get control of my sword just as another fallen plows toward me. I dive sideways and roll across the grass. I had envisioned hopping right back up into a catlike pose and preparing to strike. But I guess that's just another thing that only happens in the movies, because I only end up face down in the grass with a scratch on my face and holes in the knees of my jeans.

I look up and watch as Michael kills off that fallen along with two more. Dayton has already killed the three he was fighting and is now facing only one. But that one, is Zantouron himself. The remaining fallen retreat back into the trees or wrap their wings around them and disappear, back to hell I assume. I stand back up and dust myself off swiftly. Dayton suddenly cries out in pain and my eyes dart toward him. Zantouron grins as he pulls his sword from Dayton's shoulder and lets him fall to the ground.

I shriek in horror and then fury as I run toward him, sword posed to strike. Zantouron laughs and pulls his wings around himself; he's gone before I can reach him. I race to Dayton and fall to my knees at his side. His shoulder is bleeding badly and I can feel the warm tears starting to run down my cheeks. He smiles up at me and says,

"Don't worry too much. We heal fast, you know. I'm not saying it doesn't hurt like…"

That's when I lean down and kiss him, wrapping my arms around his neck tightly. At first his eyes go wide with surprise but then he wraps his arms around my waist and kisses me back. Michael, standing off to the side, growls in disgust but I don't care. We kiss tenderly and I run my fingers through his hair. He loosens his grip on my waist a bit and I pull away just an inch and look at him. He searches my eyes and I know he's trying to read my mind so I decide to make it easier for him.

'I think I love you...' I tell him in mind speak.
He smiles and pulls me back in to kiss again. This time he kisses me more passionately and says in my head,

'You *know what? I think I love you too.'*
I can feel my heart beat quicker at the words. Just then a hand grabs my shoulder and pulls me away from him.

"That's enough. We have to go before they return." Michael says it with a hint of anger in his voice. I know he's right but I'm still frustrated at him for interrupting the moment.

I look back down at Dayton and already his wounds are almost completely healed. He smiles and pushes himself off the ground, then he offers his hand to me. I take it and he helps me to my feet. Michael grinds his teeth together and crosses his arms but he doesn't say anything.

"Michael's right," Dayton starts, "you should be going." I frown as I consider this.

"What about you? Aren't you coming with us?" He smiles, his wounds are completely gone now but his clothes are shredded.

"I've got to go find some new clothes. I'll catch up with you later." He gives me a quick kiss before flying off.

-Aurora-

We fly in silence for a few moments before Michael finally looks over at me and says,

"You're getting too involved with that demon."

My face goes red with anger and embarrassment. Why does he always have to be against me? Against us?

"Don't tell me, it could tip the scales or something right?

Michael shakes his head. "No, but it isn't fair to either of you."

This response confuses me and I frown again. "What is that supposed to mean?"

That loving each other isn't fair to us? Michael sighs and looks away from my eyes. It appears he is reluctant to answer but he does after a moment.

"Aurora, you know about the tribulation and the antichrist, correct?"

I nod, "Yes, but what does that have to do with me loving Dayton?" I demand an answer, now thoroughly annoyed. He still doesn't meet my gaze as he replies.

"After the antichrist's reign comes to an end all of the remaining people that turned to God will be called into heaven. Then the earth shall be destroyed and Satan and his followers will be cast into the lake of fire to suffer for all eternity."

Understanding hits me like a sledgehammer and I fear I might fall from the sky.

"Dayton…" I mutter aloud and Michael nods.

"Yes, your friend may not choose Satan but he is still a demon and will ultimately suffer the same fate. If you get too attached to him it will only make his fate harder on the both of you. He knows where he will end up and it will be easier for him to accept it if he isn't leaving the ones he loves. So it isn't fair to either of you to remain involved with each other." Michael finishes the statement matter-of-factly.

I'm crying, again. This whole system is just so messed up! Why did this have to happen to me? It all makes sense now though; Dayton showing me how great the light is, trying to convince me to always choose good, not kissing me during the sunrise, and feeling unworthy of me on the picnic. He wants me to choose good so that I won't perish with him. He's trying to protect me!

"No!" I shout and Michael looks at me shocked.

"No what?" He asks, concerned. I clench my fists together.

"No, I won't let that happen to him! I'll find a way. I'll do anything! There has to be a way…"

We touch down in my backyard and tears flow down my cheeks steadily but I don't move to brush them away. Michael shakes his head and gives me a look that's halfway between pity and annoyance.

"There is no way. The Almighty has decided it and so it shall be. No one other than he can give or take away such a thing."

I look directly into Michael's eyes, "Well, then I guess I'll just have to take it up with him."

I curl my wings around me the way I had seen the fallen do it and think of heaven. Michael's face looks bewildered and frightened. He leaps toward me but it's already too late. The earth around me begins to blur until in its place is a new place entirely. The streets are made of gold and a huge wall surrounds it made of smooth Jasper. I stare around me in amazement at the beauty of it all. There aren't even words to describe the splendor of it. But I'm not here to admire the surroundings, I'm here to find God, literally.

-Dayton-

Dayton pushes through the door of his small, rented apartment and shuts it behind him. On the floor is a yellow slip of paper stating that his rent is due. The apartment only has one bedroom and one bathroom and the kitchen and the living room are together as you enter. Dayton magnets the paper to the refrigerator as a reminder, although he's not entirely sure he plans on coming back after today. He has one couch and a small coffee table with the 19" TV sitting on it in the center of the room (although he's not sure how he came across either of them). At the back is a stove, refrigerator, and the sink that all came with the apartment. There are two cupboards under the sink where he keeps paper plates, cups, silverware, and any canned or boxed foods. Of course, he doesn't need the food to survive but sometimes it can be a comfort.

Everything in his apartment is neat and well organized. Dayton moves to the bedroom and pulls his shredded shirt over his head before tossing it into the trashcan next to the four drawer dresser. His bed on the other side of the room is neatly made with midnight blue sheets, blanket, and a body length pillow, all of which are merely there for looks considering he doesn't need to sleep and typically doesn't have time for sleep. After showering Dayton changes into a clean pair of jeans and puts on a dark gray crewneck T-shirt. He stands in front of the mirror, looks at his reflection, and sighs.

'What now,' he thinks as he stares at the image before him, *'why is it that for me fate is crueler than death?'*

Dayton had long ago accepted his fate and had decided that by that point in time there wouldn't be anything left to live for anyway. But now…? Now he had a reason to fight fate. She's fallen in love with him. What will she feel when she realizes he has to suffer for eternity and she has no way to stop it? And how could he go on if she chooses to stay with him even though it would mean suffering the same fate? But what can he do? The judgment at the original fall was final… Right? There can be no forgiveness to the traitors of the throne…

"What can I do," he thinks aloud as he moves towards the door, "except try to prove myself to God and beg for his mercy. And hope the God who is the very essence of love will understand my situation and offer me his grace." Then he flips off the light and walks out the door.

-Michael-

When the girl had wrapped her wings around her Michael had been dumbfounded. He had not even known that it was possible for a nephilim of any degree to transport dimensions before coming-of-age. Even the last triquarterling had not been able to transport before then and even after that he had to have help the first time. So in his transfixed state Michael was not able to react quick enough to stop her.

Now he folds his wings around himself and transports to heaven after her.

'She *doesn't know what she's getting herself into*.' He thinks as the Earth disappears in the heavens come and view. '*Hopefully I can find her before she finds the creator*.'

The moment everything is steady again Michael spins in search of her and he catches a glimpse of her black sneakers as she rounds a corner nearby.

'Stupid, *foolish, arrogant girl*!' Michael grumbles in his head as he speeds after her. *'Doesn't she realize that there is a lot more at stake than her impractical romance with this demon? There are a lot more lives, innocent lives, at risk than that fallen Angel's. What does she expect to do anyway? Walk up before the King of Kings and demand he, her creator, forgive the demon who betrayed him? Doesn't she know there is no grace for those who fell? She's going to get herself in even more trouble than she's already in...'*

"Let me go!" I scream at Michael as I struggle against his grip, "Let go! I have to save him!"

Tears are streaming from my eyes again and I'm getting seriously sick of crying so much.

'How *did Michael find me so fast anyway?*'

Around us several Angels have stopped singing or praising or whatever they're doing to stare at us. I remember when I was younger how the Sunday school teachers would always tell us that there are no tears in heaven. Well, I'm in heaven and I'm bawling my eyes out. So I suppose I understand the shock and confusion on all of the faces around me. They probably don't even know what tears are…

Or perhaps they are staring because the Archangel Michael is standing in the middle of heaven's streets wrestling a nephilim teenage girl who also happens to be screaming and crying. Yeah, that's probably it.

"Aurora, for goodness sake! Settle down before all of heaven starts to panic!"

Michael restrains me further and I finally stop struggling and sigh. He releases me and I grit my teeth.

"I have to talk to God, Michael. I have to save Dayton. He doesn't deserve…" I choke on the thought and shove it aside. Michael nods,

"I understand your intentions and it's very noble of you but it's also no use. There is no forgiveness for a fallen."

I can feel he's telling the truth but there is something else there too. He believes he's telling the truth but it appears Michael is not 100% sure. And that means there could be hope!

"I don't believe it! I'm going to talk to him and you can't stop me!" I spin on my heel and he grabs my arm again.

"You cannot go before the creator." He says it softly.

"Yes, I can and I will. Now please let me go." I say it roughly to convey my seriousness.

"Aurora, like it or not you're still part human and human eyes cannot behold the maker. You could go blind or worse. If you insist on doing this you will have to take it up with the Son." Michael finishes with a sigh and I turn to look at him.

"You mean, Jesus?" I ask him in amazement and he nods.

"Yes, humans have to go through Christ in order to get the creator. That's why some say 'in Jesus name' at the end of their prayers. Jesus is like your lawyer when it comes down to it. He goes before God and pleads your case for you."
I smile at Michael's comparison.

"Perfect, then let's go see Jesus." I start to walk away and Michael frowns before moving ahead of me to lead the way.
After a few minutes of walking Michael stops and I almost plow right into him.

"Wait here." He commands before flying upward.

I follow him with my eyes until he has completely vanished into the clouds above. Moments later he lands again, grinning from ear to ear. A figure lands next to him and my mouth falls open. You know those pictures of Jesus you see in a church of him looking like a normal guy with long brown hair and soft eyes? Yeah, well, he may have looked like that while he was on earth but here, not so much. In fact, John described him pretty accurately in Revelations. His hair is as white as snow and his eyes are a fiery orange that seem to flicker like flames. He's wearing a long robe that's almost the same color as blood and has a Golden belt around his waist and a sash across his chest. His whole body glows brighter than Michael's sword and when he smiles I fall to my knees. I can see why Michael is smiling so brightly. Just being around the Son of God has filled me with so much joy I almost forget why I've come. Jesus offers his hand and I take it shakily. He helps me to my feet and embraces me before questioning me about my quest.

"Hello friend, why have you come to me?" When he speaks his voice is so smooth and calming like the sound of rushing water.

"Umm…" I'm suddenly nervous and I take a deep breath and explain everything to him. He listens intently, nodding occasionally to show he understands. When I finish explaining everything he smiles again,

"You are a sweet girl and have a very big heart. I will take it to my father and let him decide what should be done. Please remain here; it should not take me long."
Then he rises into the air, without wings. Moments later he returns and my stomach turns flips.

"My father has a proposal for you," he begins, "Michael has told you of the war to come and it is all too soon arriving. You will not be of age by then, but if you choose to fight on heaven's side in the battle and remain loyal to him then my father will forgive the fallen one. Then he will be allowed to return to heaven. You and he may remain together also; however, he too must fight on heaven's side in the war. Only then, will I grant the desire of your heart." I smile and let out a cry of joy.

"Yes! I accept! Thank you!"

When we re-appeared in my backyard Dayton was there waiting.

"Take a little trip to heaven did ya? A little early for that, don't you think?" He says it and looks to Michael for an answer. "Did you at least bring me back a souvenir? Because you know if you're…"
I interrupt him by leaping into his arms and knocking him backwards. I plant my lips on his and kiss him deeply.

"Whoa!" He starts and gently pushes me up, "not that I don't like it but what's the occasion? I've only been gone an hour, did you really miss me that much?"

I laugh. He tries to read my mind but I block him out. I want to tell him this from my mouth. I'm trying to think of a mysterious way to put it but I end up just blurting it out.

"I met with Jesus and he agreed to forgive you and let you back into heaven if we both fight on heavens side during the upcoming war!" I suck in a deep breath and I watch his face as the words set in. He looks disbelieving at the possibility.

"But how could… Why would… I don't… Is this for real?"

I smile and try to keep from jumping up and down. Michael nods at Dayton, who then fist pumps the air and yells various cries of joy and thanks. Then he grabs me and pulls me close. Our foreheads touch but he doesn't kiss me right away.

"Thank you so much. I owe you my life. If it were mine to give I'd give you the world." He whispers it to me and I smile.

"You're the only thing I need." I whisper
back. He leans forward and I lose myself in his
kiss.

-Zantouron -

"The girl has fallen in love with the demon that has chosen no side. She's made a deal with heaven to 'save his soul' from the lake of fire." Zantouron relays the news to his master and the creature frowns.

"Love is powerful; even more powerful than hate. She can no longer be won to our side. However, love may work to our advantage this time. The fallen loves her back and I'd be willing to bet he would gladly give his life, and service, for her safety."

Zantouron nods understandingly and awaits his instructions which the creature doesn't hesitate to give.

"Bring me the girl. Make sure that nuisance Michael isn't around and be sure the love struck demon follows."

The creature says it thoughtfully as he paces. Zantouron takes a small bow then gathers up a few others to help him. The Great War will be in only a matter of days and Michael will be preparing. The Archangel most likely transports off to heaven each night to prepare while the girl sleeps. It's likely the demon will be watching after her while Michael is away.

'So some of us will distract the boyfriend while the rest of us grab the girl.'
He plots as they transport back to earth. He doesn't completely agree with the beasts' plan of capture.

'If she can't be won then why not just kill her and be done with it?'

The group of fallen flicker back to earth and the sun is just setting overhead.

'Love may be powerful, but when it ends, it ends in pain. Perhaps an even greater pain than hate itself can cause...'

-Dayton -

It's hard for him to believe any of this is actually happening. In just a few days Dayton will fight alongside heaven again. He watches the beautiful girl sleep. She has not only taught him to love again but has also saved his life. He gently kisses her forehead, careful not to disturb her slumber. He can no longer imagine living without her. A noise outside catches his attention. Dayton moves to the window and a very familiar smell wavers up to him, sulfur. Down below there are three fallen stalking across the backyard toward the house.

"Crap!" Dayton mutters under his breath. He takes another glance back at Aurora before spreading his wings, drawing his sword, and leaping from the window. He lands directly in front of them.

"Leave this house immediately." He warns them with a low growl. The three intruders laugh and form their own swords. "Fine, have it your way. But I won't let you hurt her."

With one swift launch he's upon them. This battle hardly requires any effort from him. He has battled many more than three at a time before. The fight only lasts about 10 minutes tops. Dayton was meant to be a warrior Angel before the fall and had received extensive training.

'Did Zantouron really think that a mere three demons could...? No Zantouron would know better, so why did he...?'
Suddenly it dawns on him and he shoots up the side of the house and through the window.

"No!" He growls, outraged upon finding the bed empty. There's a small note on the pillow that reads,

"Meet you in hell lover boy." And, unsurprisingly, it's signed by Zantouron.

I had tried to yell for Dayton as the hands grabbed me but they were too quick. They gagged me and bound my wings and hands behind my back. Zantouron had placed something on my bed, but I couldn't see what. I hope with all my heart it wasn't a bomb, for fear of Shawna and Brent getting hurt, or worse. Then Zantouron had grabbed me and transported us both to the underworld where I am now. I'm sitting on the floor next to a throne made up of bones. On the throne is the one and only devil himself.

So you know how Satan is usually imagined as a red creature with horns, a tail, and a pitchfork? Well, I suppose he could probably look that way if he wants but for right now he just looks like a man. Granted, he looks like a man who's killed thousands of people, but still human looking overall. He doesn't talk to me; in fact, he hardly seems interested in me at all. I wonder if perhaps he's after Michael again. The silence is becoming extremely awkward and creepy.

I'm considering trying to talk through the gag when a fire suddenly appears about 5 feet before Satan's throne. The flames swirl around a moment creating a cylinder of shadowy black smoke too thick to see through. When the flame dies and the smoke clears Dayton stands in its place with a furious expression. He spots me and his eyes soften but then he turns back towards the devil looking angrier than I'd ever seen him before.

"Lucifer let her go! She won't side with you. Give it up." His voice is strong but I can see in his eyes that he knows that Satan isn't going to just give up.
Lucifer laughs,

"Oh, I know. She's made a deal with heaven. She's in 'love' with you. I know she can no longer be won."
Dayton narrows his eyes,

"Then let her go. She's of no use to you."

The devil stands and moves toward me. He stands behind me in a way so that I cannot see him but I can feel he's there. Dayton goes stiff as he watches Satan over my shoulder.

"I could just kill her…" Satan says from behind me.

"Don't you dare lay a finger on her!" Dayton hisses.
Lucifer appears from behind me and returns to his throne of death.

"I suppose I could be willing to spare her life and set her free, if you're willing to make a little deal."
I shake my head violently, '*Don't do it*!' I think at Dayton. He frowns,

"What kind of deal?"

Lucifer grins, "Fight on my side in the war and I'll let her go safe and sound."

Dayton clenches his fists and looks away. Satan is supposed to be a liar and if so, why would Dayton even consider believing him? Because this time he's telling the truth… My "gift" is telling me he means what he says. But if Dayton does what he's asking then he will perish in the lake of fire and I'd lose him forever.

"Fine." Dayton refuses to look at me as he says the word.

'No*! Dayton please! No*!' I scream it at him in my mind but he ignores me.
Satan smiles again,

"Good, but I don't take word-of-mouth."

His smile gives me chills as he hands Dayton and old, wrinkled, yellow colored paper. Dayton looks completely defeated. He reaches behind him and plucks a raven black feather from his back. There's blood on the end and he uses it to sign the paper. I suddenly realize that my hands are tied close enough to my wings that if I twist them just right… I manage to pluck a feather from my back and send a message to Michael. As I release the feather I pray he can get here in time to stop this before it's too late.

"There, happy now?" Dayton snarls as he hands the paper back and lets his feather disappear. Satan takes the paper and it vanishes with a puff of smoke in his hand. Dayton shoots me an apologetic look and I tear up again. Then without warning Michael appears with a burst of light in the room.

"Lucifer!" He bellows fiercely, "you have no right to…" He notices Dayton's helpless look and stops abruptly. Satan leans back against his throne and smiles victoriously. "I'm taking the girl." Michael finally says and moves to untie me.

I look to Dayton begging him for an explanation but all he says is,

"I'm so sorry…"

I start to go to him but Michael grabs me. I try to push past him but he wraps his wings around us and transports so fast I barely have time to register what's happening. When I try to yell to Dayton my voice is lost in the wind and the last thing I see is a look of devastation on his face.

"What's going on?" I demand as Michael releases me in my backyard. He looks distracted, like he's in deep thought. "I mean it! I want answers! Where were you this time? Why didn't Satan kill me? Why did he want Dayton? What was that paper Dayton signed with his feather? And he isn't seriously going to fight for Satan is he? I'm safe now can't he just refuse Satan?" I'm out of breath by the time I finish and Michael looks me over nervously.

"I'm so sorry Aurora. I'll answer your questions but you won't like it. I was in heaven preparing for the war. Satan didn't kill you because he wanted Dayton. Had he killed you Dayton wouldn't have cooperated. Satan still wants to tip the scale but he knew that after your deal with heaven you would never choose his side. And I hadn't thought about it before but because Dayton technically never chose a side, he could tip the scales. Satan knew Dayton would do anything to save you and so he made the deal to spare your life in return for Dayton's service. The paper Dayton signed was called a blood bond. It's signed in blood thereby binding you to it through your blood. I'm afraid he can't refuse Satan because if he breaks the blood bond both you and he will die."

He finishes and I gasp,

"No! There has to be a way to break it without it killing us! Michael
please! There has to be a way, there always is…"
He is suddenly fidgety,

"There is no way."

I frown, "You're lying."
Why does he even bother trying to lie to me? He knows I can tell.

"Aurora, it's too dangerous. I can't allow you to…"
He stopped short and his eyes lower to the sword that is suddenly at his neck. I'm angry, Michael of course knows that I would never go through with it but he sighs and agrees to help me nevertheless.

"The only way to break a blood bond is for the signer to eat from the tree of life."

I lower my sword and look at him.

"You mean the tree of life that was in the Garden of Eden?" I ask curiously and Michael smiles softly,

"No, the tree of life that *is still* in the Garden of Eden."

"Iraq? We're going to Iraq? Isn't there a war going on there right now?" I asked Michael, a little surprised that the Garden of Eden is supposedly located in such a poor, evil filled place. Michael rolls his eyes,

"There is always war going on there. Yes, the Garden of Eden is located in the very bottom corner of Iraq. It is just below the city of Al Qurnah where the Tigris and Euphrates rivers meet."

Michael turns his gaze back to the sky ahead and flies on. His spotless white wings glisten in the starlight. I'm surprised he didn't try to convince me to wait until morning. I'm tired but a mission to save the one I love and the thought of Dayton's face gives me the energy to go on.

"I thought the garden was hidden so that nobody could ever find it and enter again." I state curiously and Michael nods.

"It was hidden from human eyes. Though, I believe that because you are more Angel than human you should be able to see it. However, at the gate of Eden waits the Angel of death, Adriel. I will try to talk to him but I fear he may be... unreasonable. And the last thing either of us need is to get into a fight with Adriel. He has power over all the plagues and diseases of the earth. Many people believe him to be the Grim Reaper."

I briefly think of the black headed Grim Reaper with his creepy staff that I dressed up as for Halloween once. I remember accidentally scaring a little kid that opened the door and how I'd felt so bad afterwards. It is hard to imagine the Grim Reaper being an Angel. The sky is beginning to light up as the sun starts to ascend. The first trickles of sunlight hit the waves below us and the water sparkles. We fly for another couple hours and finally land in Al Qurnah. The city looks wrecked by war...

"We only have a few more miles until we reach Eden," Michael begins, and turns to look at me seriously, "I'm going to warn you now.

They don't call him the Grim Reaper for nothing. He's the Angel of death and he looks like death itself. Don't show fear around him, I can't stress that enough."

I don't want to know why, so I just nod and follow after him. After just a short while I see the most beautiful thing I've ever seen on earth. I take a deep breath and Michael smiles.

"It is amazing isn't it? Of course, it was meant to be a heaven on earth." He says as he begins his descent. He flies toward the eastern side of the garden where the gate is.

"Why can't we just fly straight into the garden from above?" I ask, staring down at the beautiful scenery below.

"There's an impenetrable, transparent shield surrounding the garden." Michael replies as we land gracefully.

'A *force field, got it*.'

Michael goes silent and I follow his gaze toward the entrance. Have you ever seen the scream movies? If not, you might not can picture this as easily... Imagine the scream mask, a zombies' bloodshot eyes, and the Grim Reaper get up only with wings and you should have a basic idea of what I'm looking at.

-Adriel -

Intruders! Humans cannot see the heavenly garden and it has been many millennia since any supernatural being, of any kind, has appeared before the garden's keeper. Adriel had sensed them approaching and shifted to his more menacing look, death.

'A *force field, got it.*'

He hears the younger one, the nephilim, think as the two of them land. The girl is obviously a nephilim, judging by the smell, and the older male is definitely a full Angel. In fact, Adriel thinks as he silently scans his two intruders head to toe, the Angel is one Adriel knows quite well.

"Michael of the Ark, why do you come before me? What business do you have with me? And why have you brought with you one whose blood is tainted?"

Adriel demands of the Archangel before him. The nephilim beside Michael scowls furiously and although she bites her tongue, she cannot control her mind.

'My *blood's tainted? Has he looked in a mirror lately? Some Angel he is,*
I wish I could kick his butt into the next millennia!'
Adriel keeps a straight face and an unwavering tone as he talks into the girl's head.

'Settle *young nephilim. You cannot control your tainted blood but you should learn to control your ripe young mind.*' The girl's eyes flicker with annoyance and Adriel feels a slight push against his mind.

'Hmm...' He thinks to himself, *'She is a strong one...*' He then turns his attention back towards the Archangel.

"Explain yourself Michael of the Arc."

- Aurora -

Michael shifts his weight next to me. I notice he's acting unusual. He doesn't seem exactly afraid of the Angel of death; however, he's also not his typical confident self.

'Hey, *straight up fight between you and him, who wins?*' I think at him.

'Let's *hope we don't have to find out.*' He replies without looking away from Adriel.

Adriel lets out a small growl and forms a sword in his hand. Remember when I said Michael's sword wasn't flaming but it was glowing? Well, Adriel's is really on fire. The flames licked the air but produced no smoke or smell.

"I grow impatient Angel." Adriel hisses at Michael who lets out a small grunt and says,

"I think she should be the one to explain."
I turn toward him in shock. What!?!?! Adriel turns toward me with expectant eyes.

"Well young nephilim? Why have you come?"
My throat tightens and I swallow. Why had Michael put this on me? Because it's my mission and my boyfriend, that's why.

"I have come seeking the fruit of the tree of life to save the one I love from the clutches of evil." Though it may sound cliché it's the best explanation I can come up with that sounds creditable, besides, it's true. Adriel's expression doesn't waiver.

"None are allowed entrance to the garden. I am afraid there is nothing you can do to make me grant you entrance."
The moment he says it the annoying little lie detector inside of me begins buzzing like crazy.

"Liar." I say, stepping forward defiantly.

The Angel of death raises an eyebrow, it was the first time I'd seen his expression change since we arrived. He stares into my eyes for what feels like hours, but was really only a minute, and then turns saying,

"Follow me."

Michael narrows his eyes as if he doesn't trust the fact that Adriel is just willingly letting us in, but he follows anyway. Adriel leads us through the garden and I can't help but stare at the beautiful scenery. Not even the sunrise with Dayton was this magnificent. If only he were here to see this with me. Even in this breathtaking landscape, I still can't help the twinge in my heart, as I think about the fate that will befall him if I fail. We follow Adriel silently, taking in the sights around us. The treetops overlapped the garden with a canopy of luscious, green leaves on thick branches. Soon we emerge into a small round clearing. At the center of the circle stands two magnificent looking trees.

"These are the trees of Knowledge and Life." Adriel says it without removing his eyes from the trees. I step forward but stop abruptly.

"But which is which?"

The Angel of death shakes his head.

"That is for you to decide. Choose correctly and you may go on your way. Choose wrong, well if your friend eats of it his bond will not be broken and he will either die or be tortured by his own thoughts until his time is no more. Choose wisely young nephilim."

My mouth drops slightly and Michael's face looks paler than before.

'You have got to be kidding me!' I think, to no one in particular.

As if in response to my comment an image suddenly forms in my mind's eye. In the vision I'm in Eden and I'm standing by the trees. I place my hands on them and concentrate. And then the image is gone, almost as quickly as it had come. Adriel watches me, unmoving, with his creepy zombie eyes. I ignore him and walk towards the two trees.

"Well, here goes nothing." I mumble under my breath as I place a hand on each tree.

The tree under my left hand sends vibrations up my arm, almost in a pulsing rhythm. The tree under my right hand sends a small shock of electricity through me that makes my vision blur and my headache. I yank my arms away and fall gasping to my knees. Michael dashes towards me but the Angel of death holds out his hand to stop him, offering no explanation as to why. My Guardian Angel grinds his teeth but makes no move to disobey the Angel of death. I push up off the ground and brush myself off then, without a word, I move to the tree that my left hand had touched. The fruit on the tree is shaped like a pair but is maroon in color. The fruit on the other tree has the same shape but is an indigo color. My fingers embrace the fruit and gently pluck it from the tree. I turn to Adriel and hold the reddish purple fruit out for him to see. At first, he stares at the fruit and does not react. Then he looks up at me and smiles. There's a blinding flash of light and I have to turn away for a moment. When I look back, the Angel of death has changed. He's no longer the scary, Grim Reaper looking Angel. Now Adriel is a lovely Angel with silver hair and golden eyes.

"Well done, triquarterling. May God bless you in your quest and in your life."
Then before I can reply Michael and I are suddenly transported back to my house. I'm not really sure how but I definitely don't mind not having to fly.

- Dayton -

A group of about five of Satan's best, (or is it worst?), Demons materialize nearby. Lucifer himself appears only seconds later and walks up to where Dayton stands, chained to the floor.

"I hope you understand why we're leaving you out of our little meetings. It's nothing personal, of course, but seeing as to how you're Dayton the enemy, we have to be cautious as to the information you hear."

The word Dayton drips from Satan's tongue as if it were poison dripping from the bottle. If the Devil's against it, then it can't be wrong, right?

Hope swells in Dayton and he casually replies,

"And since I don't know anything then there's no reason to fear my telling anyone. And you know I can't break my promise either so why not unchain me and let me spend one last day with the girl I love?" Lucifer is heartless and cruel and Dayton already knows what the answer will be. But it was still worth a try. An eerie laugh escapes Satan's lips,

"I'm sure a smart guy like you, Dayton, already knows the answer to a question like that. Don't you? I have no heart. Therefore, matters of the heart do not concern me. You will stay here until the war, after which, well I'm sure you knew what you were signing up for."

Then the evil one turns and walks away without another word. Dayton ducks his head; he had known what he was signing up for. Yes, he knows exactly what he is doing, what is to come, but does he regret it? No, not now, not after the war, not in the Lake of fire. No, he would never regret what he had done to save her. She is everything to him and he'd protect her, no matter the cost to him personally. He won't let any harm come to her. Not now, not ever.

- Aurora -

"You have to rest," Michael says earnestly, "Angels don't need sleep but the human in you does Aurora. You can take the fruit to him in a few hours. You need to sleep first..."

The sun is high in the sky now, it's nearly noon. I shake my head violently.

"No Michael, there isn't enough time. The war starts tomorrow; I have to save him now! Please don't try to argue with me. I'll go with or without you!"

Michael grinds his teeth, frustrated at me only because he knows that I mean it. My wings unfurl around my body and Michael mimics me, swiftly doing the same. I'm careful to keep a good grip on the fruit but not so tight that I crush it. I have the feeling, if I lose this one I won't get another. The world around me fades once again. I wonder how many times I'll have to do this before it becomes mundane, because as of now it's still a really cool, breathtaking process. This is definitely the best way to travel. And I smile as I think of seeing Dayton's face again.

I'm in hell, again. I look around as the putrid underworld comes into view. Around me I see Dayton shackled to the floor by his ankles, Satan looking alarmed at my sudden appearance, and five angry looking demons surging toward me. I glance down at the Maroon colored fruit my hands and think,

'Crap*! How can I form a sword without hurting the fruit?*'

Luckily, as it turns out, I don't have to. From behind me, Michael rushes the demons and holds them off. I dash toward Dayton but Satan howls in fury and blood red wings explode from his back. He leaps between Dayton and I as fangs slice out from his mouth and his eyes turn pitch black. I try to stop so that I don't run into him but in the process I end up falling backwards. I'm careful to hold the fruit out above me so it doesn't get squished. The devil takes a step toward me. I glance back over my shoulder to Michael but he is still preoccupied with the demons. I turn back around quickly and catch sight of Dayton struggling against his chains, desperate to come to my rescue. Satan spots the fruit in my hand and his black, snake-like tongue licks the air as he hisses angrily.

Suddenly, I'm seeing another vision. In this one I see myself holding the fruit. My fingernail pierces the fruit skin and juice dribbles down. I watched as my vision self licks the juice from the fruit and kicks out at Satan. The image disappears and I quickly repeat the actions. My nail digs into the fruit and I hurry to lick the light pink liquid that runs down the side. It is sweet tasting and delicious and I long for more. I want to sink my teeth into it and devour it here and now. Dayton yells my name and I snap out of it. My leg jerks out and I strike Lucifer right in the knee.

To everyone's surprise, including my own, he doubles over, growling in pain. Michael's voice fills my head,

'The *juice of the fruit gave you supernatural strength. Now go! Hurry*!' I leap into the air and fly to Dayton's side. I press the fruit into his hand and yell,

"Quick! Eat this!"
He bites into the fruit as I kneel in front of him to examine his restraints.
I wrap both hands around them,

'Time *to test this new strength*,' I think as I pull with all my might. I'm able to break the shackles but I cut my palms in the process. I stare at my hands in shock as they bleed. Satan is on his feet and soaring toward us but I can't seem to move, or think for that matter. My hands are bleeding pretty badly and I can feel the strength draining from my body. Everything looks fuzzy and I feel immensely weakened. Just when I think I'm going to faint, Dayton yanks me into his arms urgently and wraps his wings around us.

"Time to go!" I hear Michael yell it from somewhere in the distance but by now I'm already gone. Out like a light.

- Aurora -

"Aurora…" Someone's calling me, "Aurora…"
I force my eyes open and see Dayton standing by my bed.

"Dayton!"
I push myself up and he sits down beside me.

"Hey, welcome back."
Dayton whispers as he gently brushes my bangs behind my ears. I lay my head on his shoulder.

"What happened?"

"You passed out. Michael told me you hadn't slept in a while. Then when you cut your hand the pain and exhaustion were too much for your body so it shut down."
I look down at my hands. There is still some dried blood but the wound itself is completely gone. There isn't even a scar. Dayton lightly kisses the top of my head.

"I hate having to throw this at you the minute you wake up but…" He trails off a moment then says, "it's time."
For a second I'm confused,

"Time for what?"
As if in reply the sky outside roars with thunder. I stand and move to the window. The sky outside is burnt orange with charcoal gray clouds and lightning flashing fervently around.

"It's time for war."
Dayton says, appearing next to me in the window and taking my hand. With a flash of light Michael suddenly enters the room.

"I'm glad you're up. We have to get up there. Satan's on his way. We set up some roadblocks but they won't hold him for long so we need to leave."

I stare at him somewhat shocked but mostly confused.

"What do y'all mean it's time for the war? How long was I out?"
	Michael gives me a quick urgent response,

"18 hours. Now let's go!" The moment the words leave his lips he transports out of the room and Dayton turns me towards him.

"You're a good fighter Aurora but you're still new to this. Satan is crazy powerful so promise you'll be careful, okay?"
	He looks deep into my eyes, frowning with concern. I lean up and give him a quick, reassuring kiss on the mouth.

"I promise, but you have to promise too."
	He smiles and tenderly runs his fingers down my cheek to the tip of my lips.

"I promise."

	He pulls me toward him as if to hug me and our wings unfurl and overlap one another as we transport to heaven together. We arrive just in the nick of time. The armies on both sides are lining up. There are hundreds of thousands of angels and demons on their respective sides, all dressed in old looking battle gear. Michael is at the front of heavens army and he waves us towards him. I clench tightly to Dayton's arm; realizing now just how big of a deal this is going to be. We stop beside Michael, who looks me up and down before saying,

"You're going to have to put on your armor."
	My eyes widen and I don't hesitate to inform him that I'm completely unprepared. I don't own any armor; I wouldn't even know where to get any, so I certainly don't have a set of it on hand. Who would? Michael, I suppose...

	"Michael, I don't have…" He interrupts me before I can finish.

"It's the armor of God. You know the fruits of the spirit, right? Say each out loud and it will appear."

I think back to my Sunday school classes at church and I try to remember them all.

"Um... the breastplate of righteousness?" I say it unsure and the moment I do a big, metal breastplate appears upon my chest.

Michael nods his approval so I go on,

"The shield of faith." A large shield forms in my left hand. "The helmet of salvation, the shoes of peace, the belt of truth, and the sword of the spirit!"

My armor is officially complete and I'm surprised to find it isn't even heavy, in fact, it's really rather light.

"That's great! Although, you could have formed a sword without saying it. All right, get ready!"

"Wait!" I demand, "Dayton, where's your armor?"
Dayton sighs dejectedly.

"Aurora, I'm technically still a demon… I can't put on the armor of God. And I refuse to wear the armor of Satan. I'll be fine, don't worry about me."

I want to protest, I want to call a timeout and find him something he can use as protection, but I know there's no time. I nod solemnly as the horn is sounded. The Armies surge forward and the battle begins. Through the masses a huge seven headed, fire breathing, red Dragon appears.

"What the…"

I'm suddenly at a loss for words. Nobody told me anything about a Dragon being involved in this. Dayton's sword forms in his hand and he mutters under his breath,

"Here comes Satan."

Without another word Dayton charges into battle. I mumble a quick prayer before running after the nearest of Lucifer's troops.

-Dayton-

In Genesis Satan is referred to as a serpent, to which most people believe to mean snake. Not even close. Dayton charges toward Satan with more hatred than he could ever have felt before. Michael drops down in front of him, blocking his way. Dayton looks over Michael's shoulders at the creature, whose heads are all smiling at him teasingly.

"Move Michael." Dayton says determinedly.
Michael shakes his head and cuts Dayton a look.

"No, you know as well as I that this battle is mine to fight. Go find
Aurora and keep her safe."

Dayton growls but the thought of Aurora helps him to realize that Michael's right. He nods and flies off to look for Aurora, leaving Michael to battle the beast. Normally he could track her easily by her powers. However, when you put her in the middle of several hundred thousands of beings with equal or greater power, it's pretty much impossible to do it that way. Which only leaves him with the old-fashioned way, looking.

The problem with that is that actually searching for her will require time and concentration. Time is something he has very little of at the moment. Two of Satan's minions dive toward him and he leaps sideways before swinging his sword. It hits one but the other adapts fast, misses the blow, and twirls around to face Dayton. As far as concentration goes, well, he's kind of busy concentrating on surviving. After all, he has his own demons to face.

-Aurora-

The once beautiful, golden streets of heaven are now murky brown with blood. I look around at the armies. I can't tell if we are winning or losing. Michael is a little ways away in a fierce battle with Satan. A few yards away from Michael, I spot Gabriel holding his own with the demon that I recognize as one of the demons Michael fought when we rescued Dayton. Dayton! Where is he?

I jerk my head around frantically in all directions, searching for him. Finally I see him; he's only a couple meters away from me. He's battling a demon and doesn't seem to notice me standing close by. I want to yell to him but I'm scared it will distract him and he could get hurt. The demon he's facing suddenly slams into Dayton, sending him sprawling to the ground. I gasp and my wings burst from my back.

I'm about to fly over to help him when a sharp pain streaks through my side. I try to scream but I choke on my own blood instead.

"Hello Princess. Miss me?" Says a whisper in my ear.

Zantouron jerks the sword from my side and pushes me forward. I've gone numb and the blood spills from my wound, forming a warm puddle around me. Zantouron laughs. It takes all of my strength to force my eyes to find Dayton. The last thing I see is him dashing towards me, panicked and furious.

'I *love you...*' I think to him just before the breath leaves me and my heart stops beating.

-Dayton-

Dayton kills the demon he's been fighting and turns just in time to see Aurora, falling to the ground with blood gushing from her side. Zantouron stands behind her, laughing sadistically.

"No!" Dayton screams it out loud as he speeds toward the wounded girl.

'I *love you...*' Her voice appears, barely audible, in his head. He falls to his knees next to her, tears pouring from his eyes.

"No, no, no, no, no!"
He screeches as he gently takes her face into his hands. She's cold and no longer breathing. Dayton punches the ground next to him,

"No! Come back! Please! No! This can't happen…"
He feels for a pulse but there isn't one; she's gone. A shadow falls on him as he weeps.

"It's sad really. I'm sure she would have survived a fight with me; she was quite a good fighter you know. Too bad she got distracted by her cute, little, demon boyfriend."

Fury rises up in him and Dayton leaps to his feet and spins around. He grabs Zantouron's head with one hand and pushes the sharp edge of his sword to Zantouron's throat with the other.

"You're going to pay for this!"
Dayton growls and pushes the sword deeper against Zantouron's skin. A thin line of blood dribbles down the blade but Zantouron just smiles.

"Kill me; avenge your pretty little girlfriends' pathetic life."

A scowl forms across Dayton's face; he wants to kill him. He wants to thrust his sword through Zantouron's heart and twist! And he could, nobody would care, but there are things far worse than death. Death would be a mercy, and this creep doesn't deserve mercy. Dayton shakes his head slowly.
"You don't deserve death." Zantouron's eyes widened slightly then narrow again. He puts on a taunting tone and challenges him again.

"Poor little nephilim. She should have known to watch her back. It was

so easy to sneak up on her and run a sword through our side. And the sound she made when…"

Dayton quickly interrupts him.
"I suggest you stop. It won't help."

Zantouron smiles again, "Kill me, get your revenge. Or have you gone completely soft?"

The war is coming to an end. Dayton looks over Zantouron's shoulder to where Michael is standing, holding the end of a long chain that has Satan bound tight. Michael watches Dayton, waiting to see what Dayton will do. Dayton nods for Michael to approach and he does, dragging Satan behind him. When he's close enough Dayton asks,

"Got any more of that chain?"

Zantouron is suddenly in a rage and he lets out a slur of curse words and tries to jerk away from Dayton. His efforts are useless because Dayton just holds him even tighter while Michael binds him.

"You and Satan can burn forever in the Lake of fire. While you're there you're going to regret what you did to her."

After Dayton whispers it in his ear he releases Zantouron into Michael's grasp. Michael nods and casts Satan and Zantouron into the pit for 1000 years. Dayton runs back to Aurora's body and carefully picks her up. Since she's not full Angel her body doesn't disintegrate like an Angel's but because she's also not fully human her soul won't move on either. The last of Satan's army are now fleeing as Dayton carries Aurora's deadweight up the streets of heaven. Michael follows at a respectful distance. Tears fall from Dayton's face as he approaches God's throne. Jesus meets them there and Dayton lays Aurora down at his feet.

"Please, bring her back. Let me die instead. I'm a demon, she doesn't deserve to die, and I do."

Jesus looks at him with pain in his eyes before kneeling down beside Aurora's body and cupping her head in his hands.

"My father still has a plan for you, child. Awaken, in the name of my father."

Aurora suddenly jolts upright, gasping for breath and coughing like crazy. Dayton dives toward her and wraps his arms around her tightly. She clinches the back of his shirt, holding him close as she cries into his shoulder.

"Dayton… I was so scared! I thought I was going to die…" She whispers between sobs.

Dayton begins crying again himself, "You did. I thought I'd lost you."

Jesus smiles and steps forward, placing a hand on Aurora's shoulder to get her attention.

"It's by his faith that you were healed. Now, I believe we had a bargain."

I hold onto Dayton as tight as possible while I cry. I hate crying in front of him but I just died! So I think I've earned myself a pity party. A hand sets down on my shoulder and I turn towards the son of God.

"It's by his faith that you were healed. Now, I believe we had a bargain."

I wipe the tears from my eyes with my arm and nod. Jesus looks at

Dayton,

"Please step forward."

Dayton stands to his feet, looks at me to be sure I'm alright, and then kneels down before Jesus.

"Open your wings," Jesus instructs. Dayton's black wings come into view behind him and Jesus looks dead serious as he asks Dayton a couple of questions. "Dayton, are you sorry for the wrongs of your past?"

"I am." Dayton nods.

Jesus raises an eyebrow and after cutting a glance in my direction continues on,

"Will you now choose God over everything else?"

I watch as the question registers and Dayton stiffens. He turns and looks at me and holds my gaze. For a moment I can't breathe and all I can think is please don't let him say anything stupid! I know what Christ is asking. He's asking if Dayton will put God before me.

'Say *yes*!' I think at him. '*I know you love me. I love you! But God created me! He created both of us! You have to put him first or everything goes bad. Trust me!*'

I know Jesus can read my mind, he probably read Dayton's two, but he doesn't say anything. Dayton glances up to meet Jesus' eyes and states,

"I will."

Instantly there is a bright light surrounding Dayton and when it's gone I gasp. Dayton's pitch black wings are now shimmering, silvery white. He stands and I run towards him. He has on the biggest smile I've ever seen him have. Dayton's arms and wings circle around me as he draws me close.

"You did it! You're an Angel again!" I say as I rest in his arms. He gently lifts my chin to where he can see directly into my eyes.

"No, you did it. The Trinity may be first, but you're always going to mean more to me than everything under that. I love you more than life and I'm never going to leave you."

Then he kisses me in a kiss that sends shivers down every inch of my skin. Jesus and Michael smile but there's something hidden in Jesus' eyes, something that seems to say that things are not over just yet. When Dayton and I finally break apart Jesus asks for our attention.

"Dayton, from this point on you will take over as Aurora's Guardian." He says it and Dayton nods but I step forward.

"What about Michael?"

Michael offers me a somewhat sad grin, "Previous engagement. But I'll still be around."

I give him a quick hug that I'm pretty sure he has no idea how to respond to. When I step back Jesus continues,

"Aurora, you still have to fulfill your destiny and lead Israel. It's time for my return and I will take the Christians back with me. However, the

Jewish people are my chosen people and they have not yet accepted me. They need you to teach them." I swallow nervously but nod before hearing him the rest of the way out.

"The antichrist will be revealed in a matter of days. Things are going to get really bad and you will have to be strong and be careful. He will consider you a threat and want you dead. But stay strong and keep faith."

Dayton takes my hand and together we return to earth to pursue our destiny.

- Aurora -

Blood splatters the wall next to me and I scream as the Army rushes towards me and I run the other direction. A beautiful woman rounds the corner in front of me and yells my name when she sees me. She looks so scared… I trip and she rushes towards me. The woman pulls me to my feet and drags me along behind her. We run around the corner she just came from and come face-to-face with a group of angry people pointing guns at us. Who are these people? The woman squeezes my hand gently and whispers,

"One," I feel my body tense. "Two," she says softly. "Three!"

My wings explode from my back and… So do hers! She has beautiful white wings and I am momentarily awestruck by the scene before me. We leap into the air and she releases my hand as we fly towards the skylight overhead. The guns fire and the woman screams. I whip my head around and see her falling, scarlet red soaking her lovely white wings.

"No!" I scream in horror as she falls. There's a blur and then before I can even register what's happened Dayton is beside me, holding the unconscious woman in his arms.

"Go now!" He yells at me and we shoot out the skylight and into the sky. The image fades and I'm once again standing in my backyard. Dayton looks at me worried and questions me about my absentness.

"What's wrong?"

I shake my head, unnerved by the images   I've just

witnessed. "I don't know… The future I think..."

Book Two:
Destiny

~The Anti-Christ & Alvadenon~

There came a knock at the door and the Anti-Christ didn't even turn.

"Come in Alvadenon," He huffed as he continued to stare aimlessly out the window.

The door to the beast's office creaked open slowly and a hefty, gruff looking demon appeared in the opening.

"Sir, the media crews have just arrived and are waiting for statements." A wicked grin forms across the Anti-Christ's face.

"Good," He nods, "send them in. It's time I make my appearance."

"Yes Sir… But you do know what will happen the minute you do…"

"That is inevitable, and my time has come." The beast waves his hand as if to tell his head demon to go. Alvadenon turns to leave but the Anti-Christ stops him suddenly.

"And Crater," he says, using the demon's nickname, "make sure you give me a good introduction. This is our big moment after all."

Crater bows in response and leaves the room hurriedly. He knows that when the Anti-Christ says "Our big moment" that it was a cover. Crater isn't important to the beast. He's lucky he even has the position he does now. If Zantouron hadn't been defeated then the chain of command wouldn't have shifted as it has. Now he has Zantouron's place as head demon. But even as high a rank as he is, Crater isn't included in everything. No, it simply means he's informed of more than most demons. He's basically a lap dog for the Anti-Christ.

Alvadenon flings the front doors open and faces the crowds of people and cameras.

"Ladies and Gentlemen, you are about to meet the greatest man in all of history. I understand your skepticism. You have many questions about his rise to power and who he claims to be. However, I'm quite sure after your press conference with him you will begin to feel as I have felt for a long while... That he may be even more than a great and powerful man... Lord Talbot Desdemona may even be what he claims to be... A god!"

Reports scribble every word down in their notepads as lights and cameras flash from all directions. Alvadenon smiles and turns around to lead the crowd inside the mansion. It's time.

"Well, that's it, the world is coming to an end." Brent growls from his place on the couch. Shawna rolls her eyes as she scrambles our eggs in the kitchen. I laugh as I plop down beside Brent in front of the television.

"And what makes you say that?" I ask with a teasing smile. Brent is always claiming it's the end of the world when he's watching the news. Though, many times it's definitely believable, especially after recent events in my life… But of course they don't know anything about that.

"This idiot, Talbot Desdemona… So he's been rising up the political ladder lately and as if it wasn't bad enough that he seems to be taking over the world, now he's actually claiming to be god!" He frowns and reaches for the remote before starting up again, "In fact, I really wouldn't doubt it if he were actually the anti-Christ hims…"

Before he has a chance to finish there's a bright flash of light that fills the whole room. I cover my eyes to shield them from the light and listen as a sound blares in the distance. When the light finally deems it feels like the room is twenty shades darker than before. I look around in shock to find that both Brent and Shawna are gone!

The man on the tv stands and yells, "A new era has arrived!"

I leap to my feet in mild panic. Of course I had known this would happen, eventually, but the initial shock is pretty hard to choke back. Darting into the kitchen I flip off the stove that Shawna left and then I unfurl my silvery wings and wrap them around myself. A moment later I'm in heaven, surrounded by thousands upon thousands of rejoicing men, women, and children. Shouts ring out through the streets and I am nearly run over by several groups of dancing saints.

"Aurora!" Someone catches my hand and I spin around. I stare into two gorgeous green eyes. Laughing with delight, I leap into Dayton's arms and hug him as tight as I possibly can.

"Man, I've missed you sooo freakin much!" I whisper into his shoulder as he holds me. He tucks my hair behind my ear and I can almost hear his smile as he says, "I've only been gone a few weeks you know."

I look up at his face again. Had it really only been a few weeks? *'It felt like years!'* Dayton reads my mind.

"I know." He sighs and lifts my chin slowly, leaning forward and kissing me, ever so gently. It's a quick kiss and when he pulls away I so desperately want to pull him back.

"So your birthday is in three days right?" He asks thoughtfully.

"Yesss…" I'm a little unsure as to where he's going with this…

"So we have a trip to take." A grin forms across his face.

"A trip? What trip? What are you talking about?"

His grin turns into a mischievous smile as he suddenly wraps his wings around me. Seconds later we re-emerge in my backyard.

"Wow, great trip." I tease him.

"Very funny."

"So where are we going?" I ask, giving him a playful shove.

"We are going to meet your mother."

My mouth drops open in disbelief.

"You're joking…" I accuse but the look on his face tells me otherwise and I realize he's serious. A million different thoughts run through my head and I'm sure Dayton heard them all.

"It'll be fine," He assures me with a kiss to my forehead, "She already knows we're coming. She can't wait to meet you."

He holds his hand out to me and I nod and reach for it. I trust him. I trust him with all of my heart and I'd follow him anywhere. And with that we leap into the sky.

Down below us the world is in a panic. People are crying, screaming, and rioting. Now that all the young children and Christians have been taken to heaven the sinners left behind are at war with themselves. My heart aches for them but what can I do? The bible said there would be chaos and tribulation. *'Perhaps Brent was right about that Talbot guy being the anti-Christ…'*

"He was." Dayton chimes in from my left. Noticing my annoyed look he adds, "Sorry, I know you don't like it when I do that… but my heart aches for them too and there actually is something you can do."

I know what he means but I'm still not sure I'm ready for it… My purpose, my destiny, is to take over for my mother as queen of Israel and lead the Jews to Christ. Somewhere below a car alarm sounds and I glance down at the madness one last time. I can feel Dayton pushing his way into my head again and I block him.

"Would you please stop that?" I almost growl the words, "Just ask me what I'm thinking if you're so curious. It's less invasive that way!"
He laughs, "Okay, what are you thinking?"

"I'm just nervous…" I sigh but seeing his expression I quickly clarify, "About meeting my mom I mean." And it's true… though of course it's not the main reason I'm nervous.

Dayton nods but the look on his face seems to say he knows it's more than my mom that I'm worried about. He does his best to console me anyways…

"Don't worry. Everything will turn out just fine." He reaches down and squeezes my hand gently as we fly.

"Sure," I mumble and turn my head away, "everything will be fine…"

Just up ahead I can see the ocean. How many times have I crossed it in just the past few months? I think this will make three, which is actually less than I'd thought. Of course, this time I probably won't be coming back across it again…

Suddenly images explode into my mind like a bomb going off. The vision I'd had just after the war in heaven returns. It plays through my mind like a movie and I'm helpless to stop it. I watch myself run from the mob of angry people, a beautiful woman appears and waves me over, and I watch as we run around a corner and become trapped. The woman and I leap into the sky and I scream aloud as she's hit and falls. Then I realize I'm falling as well… Only I'm for real!

The Dayton in my vision swoops in to catch the woman, at the same time the real Dayton catches me and the vision dissipates. My head throbs and I feel faint. The visions don't usually bother me too much but it seems they are getting worse. Dayton's mouth is moving as if he's speaking to me. But I don't hear a word. He looks scared… I want to comfort him but… I'm sooo tired… So instead, I close my eyes and let blackness overtake me.

I wake to the soft sound of waves lapping against the shore. My eyes flutter open and try to focus. I'm laying on a sandy beach about 10 yards or so from the sea. A deep moan escapes my throat as I force myself to sit up and look around. The sun is setting in the sky and I wonder how long I was out. Dayton is about midway between me and shore, his back to me. I stumble across the beach and take a seat next to him.

"Welcome back." He says smiling that cocky smile I love so much.

"How long was I out?" I look out across the water. The rays of the sunset hitting the sea is mystical.

"About an hour. The sun sets sooner this far east." He tosses a yellowish fruit at me, "here, eat this."

I frown and turn it over in my hand, studying it. I'm not really sure what kind of fruit it is.
"What is it? A papaya or something?"

Dayton lets out a laugh that's nothing less than adorable. "Not quite
Angel. It's a mango. I take it you've never had one?"

I shake my head, "Does a mango flavored smoothie count?"

He laughs again as I take a big bite. My face scrunches up and I swallow hard before handing the fruit back to him.

"Uck..."

"I take it you don't like it?" He's trying so hard not to smile, I can see it.

"I think I'll just stick with the smoothies."

"Well, you need to eat something." he says, finishing off my mango for me before standing up and offering his hand, "Come on."

I take it and we walk back towards the small grove of trees behind us. It's not a very big island but as long as there is some kind of food I'll eat on it then I don't really care how big it is.

"So," Dayton starts, looking suspiciously mischievous, "Have you ever had a banana?"

"Jerk!" I tease, giving him a soft push.

He chuckles and spreads his wings. Following his lead I soar up into the banana trees overhead. We sit cuddled up next to each other on the limb as we eat.

"So I guess we're staying here tonight?" I question.

"Yeah, if we leave at dawn then we should get there around sevenish."

I nod and leap down from the tree. I have no idea where he expects us to sleep. After looking around and deciding that there really isn't a comfy looking spot to rest, I finally sit down by the tree trunk and lean back against it. Dayton slides down next to me and I lay my head on his shoulder and yawn. He gently strokes my hair as I try to relax enough to sleep. A cool breeze drifts over me and I shudder. Dayton unfurls his wings and wraps one around me. The soft familiar feathers warm me instantly. I smile and close my eyes, welcoming sleep with open arms.

~Dayton~

The sky is pitch black and owls call out in the cool night air. Dayton, being an angel, has no need for sleep. He carefully lifts Aurora's head off of his shoulder and lays it gently on the soft grass. She smiles in her sleep and he is really tempted to read her mind and see what wonderful dream she's dreaming, but he can't. He has to hurry so he can be back before she wakes. He places a small kiss on her cheek before wrapping his wings around himself and transporting to heaven.

Michael meets him when he arrives.

"Hello, Dayton. How is Aurora?"

Dayton smirks at the archangel, although Michael has tried to be kinder to Dayton since he became an angel again, he still tends to give off the 'I don't like you' vibe.

"She's fine Michael. I can protect her just fine. Thank you." He marches past Michael and over to Gabriel, who has just waltzed up.

"Gabriel," He starts, "Why have you summoned me?"

Gabriel shakes his head. "I didn't call for you. Michael did." Dayton sighs and turns back towards the stuck up angel behind him.

"Okay, What do you want?"

Michaels expression turns serious as he responds, "With the rise of the sun Aurora will have only two left. Are you sure of her decision?"

A frown creeps across Dayton's face.

"That depends," He spits out at Michael, "Which decision are you referring to? She has quite a few to make."

The archangel sighs in frustration, "Dayton, I am on Aurora's side too. I know it will be tough for her but that is why she has you."

Dayton scowl deepens; he wants to say something snarky in response but holds his tongue.

"She knows the consequences of choosing dark. I'm confident she will choose light when the time comes." He turns away to avoid meeting Michael's eyes.

"Oh I know she will choose light. You come with that choice and she's made it quite clear that she would never choose against you." Michael's voice is dripping with disgust that he just can't hide as he says it, "What
I'm worried about is her coronation."

"I can't promise you her response to that decision. She's scared."

"And with good reason. But she has to agree to take over her mother's position as queen."

"I'm doing all I can." Dayton rolls his eyes at Michael's insensitivity, though it's nothing new. "She just needs more time."

"Time is the one thing we don't have."

"I have to go." He nods to Gabriel, who hasn't spoken a word the whole meeting, and then wraps his wings around himself and returns to the island.

Aurora is still fast asleep and he carefully lays down next to her silent form. Although angels don't need to sleep, they have the ability to if they choose to. It doesn't really affect them in any way and is usually just seen as a waste of time. But typically when he's with Aurora he tries to sleep. And he had intended to do so tonight… but after that conference with Michael his mind is going in so many directions that sleep will deem impossible.

The sleeping girl mutters something in her sleep and rolls over, her head sliding onto his chest. He looks down at her lovingly and brushes the hair from her face behind her ears. The sun should start to rise in a couple hours, until then he'd just lay here and listen to the rhythm of her steady breathing.

When I wake up in the morning I find myself laying with my head across Dayton chest and my eyes looking directly into his, which are watching me intently. I smile.

"Creeper." I joke. I can hear his heartbeat in his chest and it's so beautiful I could stay there forever. He grins.

"Maybe, I mean I am a 6000 year old man Dayton a 17 year old girl so…"

He expects me to laugh but I don't. Instead, I sit up straight and stare off into the distance as a multitude of thoughts and questions flood my mind. I mean, I know how long he's been on earth but I guess it just never really hit me until now. *'How many girls has he dated?' 'What does he see in me?' 'I probably seem so young and immature to him…'* Dayton tries to push into my mind but I quickly shut him out.

"Aurora…" He whispers to me but I pretend not to hear him. That's when he sits up next to me and gently grabs my chin, twisting my face slowly to face him. I know he hasn't read my mind, I made sure of that, but it seems he can tell what I'm thinking just by looking into my eyes.

"You, angel, are the only girl for me. I will always love you, and you alone."

My built in lie detector that comes with being part angel chimes in and confirms what he's saying. But even though I know it's true, I still can't stop the nagging unease in the back of my head. Dayton looks me in the eye for a long moment, and then he stands and offers me his hand.

"Come on."

I have no idea where he intends on taking me but I don't ask. He helps me up and I follow him down to the shoreline. I watch him curiously as he reaches down and picks up a small, spiraling seashell with a hollow middle.

"Okay," He says, holding it up so that I can see it. I start to ask what he's doing but he holds up a finger as if to silence me. I hush and he looks up at me, without smiling, and says, "I love you Angel. You and only you."

He holds out his fist with the shell clutched inside. I hesitate only a moment before reaching out my own hand and letting him drop the shell into my open palm.

"Now hold it to your ear and listen."

I do as he instructs and I'm amazed to hear his voice echoing inside, "I love you Angel. You and only you."

My mouth drops open. As I pull the shell away I stare at it dumbfounded. "How did you…" I start and look up at him. Now he's smiling again.

"Angel magic. Now anytime you put that shell to your ear and hear those words you'll know that I'm still yours and yours alone. Here, let me see it real quick." He holds out his hand again and I hand my new treasure back to him. He clutches it tightly and I can see a light shine through his fingers. When he opens his hand again the shell is on a beautiful silver chain. My smile could have lit a room.

"There, now you can wear it close to your heart." He says it proudly as he steps behind me to put it on for me. I pull the hair around my shoulders, out of the way. He reaches around me and hooks the necklace together in the back. Feeling his warm breath on my neck makes my heart beat faster. When he pulls his hands away I swiftly turn to face him. I reach up and intertwine my fingers behind his neck, pulling his face closer to mine, so our noses are almost touching.

"And I love you and you only." I say informatively. He smiles and tilts his head so that his lips meet mine. And as always, a surge of electricity jolts down through my body. I swear I will never get tired of this… "Are you ready?" Dayton asks me as we finally land in front of a castle I assume belongs to my mother.

"Not in the least…" I mutter as I gaze up in wonder at the craftsmanship of the building.

"You'll be fine. Come on." He takes my hand in his and knocks on the door with the other.

A young woman opens it and looks out at us suspiciously. She's tan with light brown hair in a single braid thrown over her shoulder. She's pretty, sure, but she isn't the woman from my visions. This girl has an apron around her waist and appears to be some sort of maid.

"May I help you?" She's speaking Arabic but one of the perks of being part angel is having the ability to understand pretty much any spoken language.

Dayton smiles at her, "Yes, we're here to see Lady Shaphir. This," he motions towards me, "is her daughter, Aurora."

I smile nervously and give her a small wave. Her eyes widen some and she motions for us to follow her inside. After leading us to a large room with a couch and table, amongst many other things, she asks us to wait while she goes to fetch the queen. Then she speeds out of the room and I practically fall onto the couch. In just a few minutes I'm going to meet the woman I've been wondering about my whole life.

"Hey," Dayton starts reassuringly as he sits next to me, "It'll be great.

You're going to… Oh… She's here."

He jumps back up and looks over my shoulder. I take a deep breath and then stand and turn around to face the doorway. In the door stands a beautiful woman with dark brown hair, like mine, that's braided around her head into a bun. She's the woman from my vision… my mother…

Her face contorts into a wave of emotions that look like a blend of pain, relief, shock, and joy. She takes a step forward, keeping her eyes locked with mine.

"Aurora…"

I can't really describe my emotions at this point, perhaps mostly because I don't really understand them myself. I thought perhaps I'd feel angry, resentful, or shameful… but the moment she whispered my name it was like I'd known her my whole life and nothing mattered anymore.

"Mom?" It comes out in more of a gasp and before I know what I'm doing I leap into her arms and hug her as tight as I can.

She hugs me back and I can feel her warm tears soaking into the back of my shirt.

"I'm so sorry," She sobs and kisses the top of my head, "So so sorry…" Tears pour from my eyes as my built in lie detector informs me that my mother really is sorry… and I… well… I really do forgive her.

"I have some business to take care of; I assume you ladies will be alright without me?" Dayton smiles and nods in our direction .

My mother and I nod and Dayton wraps his wings around him and transport. The moment he's gone my mother, Shaphir, turns to me and giggles as she pulls me towards the sofa.

"I want to hear everything!" she explains as we sit.

"You first." I demand in a respectful but determined tone.

She nods, "Of course…" She swallows hard. This must be a difficult story for her to tell but it's one that I need to hear, and she knows it. "I suppose the best way to start is with my birth. My mother was obviously Queen before me and was married to the king. However, the king was not my true father."

"Did she cheat on him?" I ask curiously.

She laughs, "No, of course, I'm sure you know that my father had to have been a fallen angel and he was. He had been the angel of 'form' before he fell and therefore he had the ability to change his form, or shape-shift. He was in no way in love with my mother, he was nearly out for mischief. He shifted form to look like the king and I'm sure you can put the rest together. My mother, being human, died during childbirth."

I shake my head, "I'm so sorry." She smiles sadly and kisses my forehead before continuing her story.

"The King and his maids raised me and I never knew the truth until I was your age. Around that time the Archangel Michael appeared and explained my situation and told me how it had come to pass. At first I rejected it but then my birthday came and well, that part you will have to discover on your own."

I avert my eyes hoping she'll continue without pressing me on the subject of my so-called "choice".

She moves on, "Anyway, I chose light and got my wings and power. My power ended up being the gift of encouragement."

I smile, "encouragement?" I ask, trying not to laugh. She smiles back, shaking her head.

"I know it sounds lame. It's not though. I found that when someone was upset, if I simply touched them, they suddenly couldn't even remember why they were upset to begin with."

Okay, not so lame... She goes on, "The king and passed away when I was twenty and I was thrown into power almost immediately. The sudden addition of responsibilities and duties was a very stressful change. So to take my mind off of ruling I became very interested in art. I began making regular trips to the art museum and it was there, at age thirty two, that I met your father."

She seemed to trail off for a moment but just before I could say anything she started back up.

"I found him extremely attractive and charming but at the same time suspicious and mysterious. Michael warned me against it but I ignored him. His name was Bokim and we fell in love. Two years later we were married and soon after that you were born. Your father knew the danger you would be in, so he decided it would be best to send you away.
Michael agreed and, although it was the hardest thing I've ever had to do, I let Michael hide you."

A tear dripped down her cheek and I put my hand into hers to show that I understood. She brushed the tears aside, "After that Bokim had to leave too, for my safety. However, he comes back once a year on our anniversary. He also left me this..." She points to a small angel pin on her dress. It held a sign that says, 'my love has no end'. My hand unconsciously lifts to clutch the seashell around my neck. My mother's eyes follow it and she grins knowingly.

"Now you know my story," she says, "So… what's yours my sweet Aurora?"

I describe my life for her, excluding some of the more boring 'human' parts. I get to the part on the beach and she giggles.

"Well, that's pretty much it." I say slowly, awaiting a freaked out motherly response to all my battles and kidnappings. Instead I get a…

"I like him! You have my approval!"

I just met her and already I'm rolling my eyes at her and groaning,
"Mom…"
She laughs and stands up, straightening her gown.

"Sorry honey. I'm also sorry you've had to go through so much… And sadly, I think your troubles have only just begun. But for now let's relax. Come, I'll give you a tour."

She leads me through the many halls and chambers in the castle. Nearly every room has a chandelier hanging from the beautiful marble ceiling. The floors are also made of marble and they are such a smooth black color that it looks like still water in the dead of night. If I didn't know better I'd be scared to step on it for fear I'd sink in. In the hallway there are swords and other weapons hanging along the walls. There are also a few suits of armor lined up against the wall like you would see in movies. The dining room has a long table that can seat up to twenty people comfortably. On the wall behind the table is a strange symbol painted directly onto the wall.

"What is that?" I ask and point up at it.

"That," my mother explains, "is our family crest."

The crest has a silver knights helmet with blue and gold feathers sticking out of the top. Under the helmet is a gold shield with a single blue stripe that has three six point gold stars tracing across it. Behind the helmet and shield is what looks to be a bunch of blue and gold leafs. It's very pretty, that's for sure…

"What is our last name?" I'm suddenly curious. I'd always just gone by Aurora Shepherd since that was Shawna and Brent's last name.

Mom smiles, "Well, technically, the family crest is for the Levi family, the king before me. You can use that last name if you like but if you are asking about your father's last name, well angels don't have last names."

Hmm… that makes sense, although I'd never thought about it before. I'm somewhat surprised it had never crossed my mind before to wonder if Dayton had a last name. We continue on and mom shows me her room, the guest room the Dayton will stay in, and finally to my room. The room I'm getting is very large and consists of a bathroom, a canopy bed with gold blankets, a walk-in closet, a very large dresser, a full length mirror, and a fireplace.

"Wow…" I breathe as I walk in. The closet itself is bigger than my room back home! My mother laughs.

"Dinner is at six. Make yourself at home." She leaves the room and I take a flying leap onto the bed. This is sooo awesome!

~Dayton~

"Knock knock." Dayton calls as he rhythmically taps on the door to Aurora's room.

"Come in!" She yells from the other side. He pushes the door open and sees her laying on the bed reading a book. He walks over and sits on the edge beside her.

"What are you reading?" He asks leaning over her shoulder to take a look.

"Some fiction book I found in the library. It's called 'A fallen Angel' by Daniel Silva." She flips it back to the cover so he can see.

"Ha," he chuckles, "looks like a load of crap."

"Maybe to an angelic being but to humans it's pretty interesting." She says matter-of-factly.
He smiles and slowly pulls the book from her grasp.

"Well, you my dear, are not completely human."

She puts on a pouty face in response, "I'm still part human… Would you give me that back?"

Dayton laughs and tosses the book back to her, "Come on. Your mom sent me in here to fetch you for dinner. She's probably wondering what's taking so long and I don't think you want her to start guessing…" He smiles teasingly and wiggles his eyebrows. Her face suddenly gets red and she throws a pillow at him.

"Oh stop it! I'm coming!" She laughs and follows him out of the room. When they get to the dining room the queen beams brightly at them.

"Aurora! Dayton! Have a seat!" Shaphir grins.

Dayton pulls a chair out for Aurora and she sits. He sits next to her and grabs her hand under the table.

"So what's for dinner?" He asks.

"Schnitzel and Pita bread." Aurora's mother responds as the cook comes in and sets down platters on the table.

'What on Earth is Schnitzel?' Aurora's voice fills his head and it takes all his strength not to laugh out loud.

'Fried chicken.' He responds telepathically.

'I'm serious!'

'So am I.'

'No you're not...'

'Yes, I am. Schnitzel is chicken that is breaded and fried. It will probably look a little different but it is fried chicken. Don't worry, it's really good.'

They eat the meal and Aurora discovers she really likes it.

"And for dessert," Queen Shaphir states, "we have Malabi."

The cook sets a big bowl on the table and Dayton thinks toward Aurora, *'It's pudding with nuts.'*

She frowns, *'I can see that.'*

Dayton chuckles softly, *'Just making sure.'*

He waits for her to finish and for the queen to dismiss them, then he says, "Let's go for a walk."

Aurora looks at him skeptically, probably trying to get a read on what kind of conversation he's planning. But then she nods and they head outside.

~ The Anti-christ ~

Talbot Desdemona looks down from his penthouse window at the crowded streets below. A young news woman stands directly under the window gesturing upwards as she reports. To a human, she would probably be considered quite attractive, but to him she is nothing. She is just like all the rest of them, weak, a pathetic parasite that shouldn't even exist, let alone have the favor of the creator.

"Well Crater?" Talbot questions the demon, "How are we doing so far?"

Crater fumbles with some papers before replying. "You've already won over China, Russia, and Egypt. And Canada and England are for you also, ever since their leaders disappeared. The Korea's are close and we are just waiting to hear back from Africa and Japan." Crater smiles proudly as the anti-christ nods.

"And what of America?"

"Um," Alvadenon frowns slightly, "America is being a bit more stubborn. They aren't quite as willing to accept new leadership so quickly. Many of them still believe in their democratic system."

"Fine, play by their rules. Send someone over to start a campaign or whatever will make them happy. We will get through to them before long, or we will have them destroyed. And Israel?"

With that question the demon coughs and averts his eyes before starting,
"Sir… I'm sure you realize…"

Talbot turns around and glares angrily at his right hand before interrupting, "What Crater?! Spit it out!"

Crater runs a shaky hand through his hair, "The girl is here."

The anti-christ frowns and strokes his beard thoughtfully, "Alvadenon, put together a team. Bring me the girl, alive. I have an idea."

Crater nods in obedience and leaves the room without another word.

"You don't think a romantic stroll through the garden isn't just a little cliche?" I laugh as we enter, what has to be the biggest garden ever.

Dayton shrugs and wraps his arm around my shoulder. We walk in silence for a moment, listening to the birds sing from the treetops surrounding us. It's almost dark and the sun has almost completely set.

"So," I start, "did you just feel like a little exercise or did you need to talk to me?"
He smiles, but almost half-heartedly, and tugs me over to a small silver bench nearby.

"So how did it go with you and your mom today?"

"Really good actually," I say with a smile, "She really seems to like you by the way."

He laughs, "Well that's good to hear."

"So how did your meeting or whatever it was go?"

"Actually Aurora, that's sort of what we need to talk about…" He suddenly looks nervous.

"I'm listening…" I say, trying not to sound worried.

"Well, your birthday is only a day away for one thing."

"Oh…" My eyes drift down towards the ground. I suppose I'm going to have to think about it at some point… and it looks like that's going to be now.

"I don't mean to bug you about it Angel, but I really just have to be sure you're ready."

"You can trust me, you know. I know what I'm supposed to do. And I know what will happen if I don't. Can we please just not talk about it?" I plead with him.

Dayton looks pained at first but he finally nods without protest.

"Okay Angel. There's another thing I need to tell you though…"

"If it's about the coronation I know about that too."

For a second he looks stunned, "That's not what I was going to say but

how do you know anything about that?"

I sigh. I never told Dayton about how Gabriel keeps me updated on things concerning me in their meetings. Sometimes it frustrates me that Michael and Dayton sit around deciding my future and don't even tell me about it. Gabriel is kind enough to keep me in the loop from time to time,

provided I pretend I don't know… Sorry Gabe…

"Gabriel told me. I'm to be installed as Queen the day after my birthday right?"

"Yes, that's the plan. I'm sorry I didn't tell you Angel but I was afraid you wouldn't take it very well."

Honestly, I hadn't. When Gabriel had told me I had waited for him to leave and then very stupidly punched a brick wall… I spend the next hour screaming in pain, waiting for my super healing ability to click in and fix my three broken fingers.

"It's okay. So what else were you going to tell me?"

"Oh yeah!" He grins mysteriously, "Your father is coming to see you tomorrow."

At this point a normal teenager would.... what? Ask questions, demand answers, freak out, stare at the messenger in shock? I don't know, but it is at this moment when my future predicting vision decides to return and drag my mind into unconsciousness. How come it always chooses the worst times? The fainting thing is getting really old. I'm beginning to feel like a burden on poor Dayton, who keeps ending up with the task of carrying me.

When my eyes finally flutter open I find that I've been brought back inside and have been laid on my bed. The clock on the wall shows it's 11pm.

"You have got to be kidding me…" I mutter as my head slams back against my pillow.

I had been out for almost five hours this time. That is not good… I wonder if it will keep getting worse the closer the vision gets to coming true… I try to force myself to go back to sleep but my thoughts journey to my father. I just met my long lost nephilim mother and now I'm just hours away from meeting my demon father? Talk about a complicated home life. There are many normal kids who say their parents have high expectations because they want them to make good grades. And then there are my parents who expect me to rule a country. It's amazing how fast my life was turned upside down.

I finally decide to abandon the idea of sleep because it's apparently useless. So I slip on a pair of socks to keep my feet warm against the cold floor and slide out of my room silently. I hadn't finished the book I'd been reading earlier but I decided to go to the library anyway. Anything to get my mind off my crazy life is a welcome comfort. Passing by Dayton's room though I hear voices coming from inside. I pause and push my ear up against the cold wood.

"You're sure?" Dayton's voice rings out, his tone echoing with concern.

"Positive. It's come sooner than expected but I'm sure."

The voice is one I've never heard before. It's definitely male and sounds like what I'd imagine a guy in his early twenties would sound like. Of course, that doesn't mean much because if the guy in the room has angel blood in him, which I don't doubt, then he's most likely thousands of years old.

"Do you know when?" Dayton asks.

"No, they just said soon. I don't think he'll tell us until right at that time."

"Who's leading it?"

"Crater. He took Zantouron's place." The voice chuckles slightly.

"Crater? I thought he'd…"

"Nope. Afraid not. He's the anti-christ's little puppet now. Well, I should get back. I'll keep you posted if I can. You and your girl just keep an eye out, alright?"

There is suddenly silence behind the door and before I even have time to remove my head from it the door is jerked open and I go sprawling forward. Dayton catches me and I try not to blush at being caught eavesdropping. I expect him to be angry or at least surprised at finding me and I prepare for an argument; ready to state my case about how I should be included. However, I'm not prepared for the reaction he actually does have.

"Are you okay?!" He asks in a truly concerned manner as he looks into my eyes for any sign that I may be hurt or about to faint again. I stand up straight and nod.

"I'm fine." I insist and he grins flirtatiously.

"Yes, you are."

I can't even believe this! It's the middle of the night and he just caught me spying on him and yet he's flirting with me? I ignore the comment and question him suspiciously.

"Why aren't you surprised to find me?"

He sighs, "Aurora, remember me telling you about that energy you give off? I could feel you outside the door the whole time." He turns and moves back into his room, gesturing for me to follow him inside.

His room is almost identical to mine except that his bed isn't a canopy, but rather a normal king size bed. I watch him move to his dresser and tug out a plain white t-shirt. He pulls the one he's wearing over his head and shrugs it off. It lands in a heap on the floor. His back is to me and I can see his strong shoulder blades, his flawless skin, and the two thin slits where his wings would be if he released them. The new shirt slides over his shoulders and he tugs it down around him. I suddenly realize I've been completely transfixed by the sight and now I force myself to remember the task at hand.

"You're not mad at me for listening in?" I mutter softly.
He turns around and pauses a moment, watching me before shaking his head.

"No, I'm sorry I've been leaving you out of things. I've just been trying to protect you."

"From what then? Who were you talking to? Who's Crater? And what's coming? I need to know, this is my fight too." I cross my arms and look at him stubbornly.

He laughs and saunters over to me, "You're cute when you're determined."

"I like to think I'm always determined…"

"Exactly." He smiles and runs his thumb along my jawline. His touch is electric and I hate to stop him.

"Dayton… I am serious." I try to sound stern but it comes out sounding more like a question than a statement. He sighs and removes his hand from my face.

"I was talking to an old friend. His name is Jabez."

"A demon?" I ask in surprise.

"He's a friend Aurora. Don't worry. I trust him. He says the anti-christ has put a price on our heads and there's an attack planned. We just don't know when yet."

"Do you really think it's a good idea… trusting a demon?" I frown with disapproval.

"Did you?" He gives me a slightly hurt look and I regret the question.
Touche…

~Aurora~

I'd gone back to my room after that. I felt ashamed at what I'd said to him. Of course, Dayton had been a demon too and I had trusted him, despite Michaels objections. It was wrong of me to judge this Jabez guy so soon. I take a quick shower before climbing back into bed and finally drifting off again. I'm not really sure whether my dreams could be considered dreams or nightmares. One minute they are nice and peaceful and the next I'm surprised I don't wake up screaming.

In the morning the maid we had met when we first arrived barges into my room to wake me. She's Jewish and wears a gold necklace with the star of David on it around her neck. Apparently her name is Mara.

"Miss, it's time to wake up and get dressed." She says as she pats the edge of the bed a few times. I moan and roll over to face her.

"Look, I know I'm a princess and all but today's the last day of freedom I'll ever have and I beg you to let me spend it sleeping in…" I mumble at her without even opening my eyes.

"I'm sorry miss, but the queen insisted you come down to breakfast to meet your father." My eyes shoot open and I bolt upright. In all the drama last night I had completely forgotten about my father arriving today.

"That's more like it miss. Now, the queen says to have you wear something nice, elegant, and formal." She begins shuffling through my closet which seems to be stocked with nothing but formal dresses. *Great… I hate dresses.*

"Is he here? Already?" I ask as I throw the covers off and stroll over to her.

"Yes miss. He's already at the table. You are late."

She decides on a long white dress with straps that drape off the side of one's arm. It is straight going down and then trails out behind like a puddle of white on the floor. I admit it's a lovely dress but I feel inadequate about being the one to wear it. I doubt it will be a great match for my pathetic ponytail and ungroomed fingernails. Mara starts to lift the dress up over my head but I quickly duck aside.

"I can dress myself, thank you." I reach for the dress and she reluctantly hands it over.

"Miss, if I may at least braid your hair…"

I nod and sit so that she can fix my hair. I'm shocked when I look in the mirror after. The dress not only fits me perfectly but also it almost seems to have transformed my look completely. Mara smiles.

"You look beautiful, miss." She says before ushering me out the door.

I wonder how Dayton will react to my new look… I smile as I follow Mara to the dining room, the dress flowing behind me.

~Dayton~

Dayton is sitting at the table across from Aurora's father. Bokim had many questions and Dayton was enjoying answering them.

"So Dayton, you and my daughter have been together for how long now?"

Bokim reaches across the table for another boreka pastry as he questions Dayton.

"Well, sir, I believe it's been about…"

He glances past Bokim and has to do a double take. Aurora is standing in the doorway behind her father. She is in a white flowing gown that clings to her body in all the right places and spills out behind her feet like water. His smile falters with surprise, though only briefly before returning brighter than before. A grin spreads across Aurora's face also as she notices his.

'What do you think?' Her voice fills his head smooth as honey.

He shakes his head and thinks back, *'I'm an angel now so I'm not allowed to say all the words I'd like to. But you look too beautiful to describe in mere human words anyway.'*

He swears for a moment that her cheeks flush red but then she smiles and the color fades back to normal, almost as quick as it had appeared. Bokim raises an eyebrow at Dayton and turns around to see what he's staring at.

"Aha! There's my darling daughter! You're as lovely as your mother." Bokim stands to hug her and she seems to notice him for the first time.

Dayton watches Aurora's face curiously as he can tell she is suddenly nervous. He's surprised she didn't squirm from her fathers grip as he embraced her.

"Uh, thank you." She says softly as he releases her and returns to his chair.

The queen smiles warmly and waves her hand over the table in invitation, "Please, join us sweetheart."

When I'd met my mom all of my feelings of anger and doubt had just vanished the second I saw her, replaced by joy and relief. However, with my dad it's different… The anger and doubt are still there but they are simply joined by joy and relief. It's like I'm battling myself like two children stuck in a 'yes huh' 'nuh uh' argument. I walk around the table to sit by Dayton. He gets up and pulls a chair out for me. I can't help but grin like a giddy schoolgirl.

'You don't have to do that,' I think at him.

'Nonsense, my lady.' He tries mind speaking in a British accent and fails so terribly that I can't help but laugh.

'Who says chivalry is dead?' I respond, trying so hard not to laugh. He bounces his eyebrows at me and I shake my head, amused.

My father, a taller man with salt and pepper black hair and brown eyes, looks at me curiously before saying, "Aurora, I would very much like to hear about all of the adventures I'm sure you've been having. If you wouldn't mind that is. I love a good story."

I nod. I thought with all of my mixed emotions that talking to him would be hard, but once I start… I can't stop! He listens intently, commenting now and again on my bravery or Dayton's loyalty. I try to leave out some of the, oh what do you call them… 'Intimate' parts I guess? Like when I thought Dayton was dying or, you know, the beach… I've heard the jokes about dads going after their daughters' boyfriends... and nice or not, my dad is a demon and my boyfriend is an ex-demon. Besides, that would be really awkward to tell anyway…

Dayton notices though and raises an eyebrow when I skip the sunrise on the mountain.

'Not embarrassed by me are you angel?' He's joking of course but I do feel the need to explain myself anyways.

'Of course not. I just don't want dear ol' dad to come after you with a rifle or something…'

'A rifle probably wouldn't do much to me. Just saying.'

'You know what I mean. I want him to like you…'

'What's not to like?'

I can't even come up with a good response to that. I finish telling my dad the story and he seems impressed.

"You've overcome a lot. I'm proud of you." He states as he takes a sip of his Cafe Afuch, which is just an upside down cappuccino apparently.

"I had help." I respond, glancing over at Dayton who gently takes my hand under the table.

My father's face is hard to read as he responds, "Indeed. Oh! I have something for you!"

He pulls a blue rectangular package from his jacket pocket and passes it across the table to me. I'm a bit surprised; I hadn't expected or even suspected he'd get me anything…

"Thanks… Am I supposed to open it now? Or is it a birthday present for tomorrow?" I'm unsure as I tilt the box around in my hands.

He chuckles, "Go ahead."
I peel off the blue paper to find a book. The title reads, 'Wings of Silver.' Dayton looks at the book a bit suspiciously but I smile. My dad looks pleased, "I heard you like to read."

I hug the book to my chest, "I do, thank you." Then I lay the book on my lap and finish my breakfast.

"May I be excused?" I ask politely when I finish with my cheese filled pastry.

"Well, actually your…" My mother starts to protest but my father holds up his hand and interrupts her.

"No problem. Go on."

Mom looks at him surprised and for a moment I'm not sure who to listen to. But then she nods in surrender and I thank them and head back to my room to start reading. I know I'm still not done with 'Fallen Angel' yet but this one seems more interesting anyway. When I reach my room I find Mara in it dusting.

"Hey Mara… Um… Will I be in your way if I sit on the bed and read for a while?" I ask and she shakes her head.

"No miss. But I'm fixing to vacuum so if you need it to be quiet you may want to try the library." She continues on dusting my dresser with a duster that reminds me a lot of something out of a cartoon.

"Oh… Okay, thanks." I turn around and head back down the hall toward the library. As I stalk through the library doors I find my dad rifling through a nearby shelf. For a brief moment I consider whipping around and rushing back out but it's too late… he's already noticed me.

"Aurora! What brings you to the library? There's no way you've already finished that book." He motions to the book he gave me and laughs.

"No," I smile, "Mara is vacuuming my room so I came in here to read." I take a seat at a nearby table.

"Ah, yes. I'm sorry, I should have told you Mara does her rounds during meals. Mind if I join you?" He points to the chair across from me and I shrug. He slides into it and smiles at me.

"Do you think we might can talk for a few minutes?" Dad asks, looking at me expectantly.

'Looks like I won't be reading afterall.'

"Sure, what's up?" I try not to let out a sigh as I set my book in the chair next to me.

"I'd like to get to know my daughter better. And I figure you might have some questions as well." Well… that's true…

"Alright," I agree, "You go first."

"Hmm…" He strokes his chin thoughtfully, "Favorite color?"

"What?" Well, I certainly hadn't expected that…

"What is your favorite color?" He repeats with a grin.

I laugh, "Red I guess." His eyebrows raise a bit.

"Red? Did you know if the FBI gives you a personality quiz and you pick red as your favorite color they will consider you a sociopath?" His expression looks serious.

"Nuh uh… Really?" I laugh again.

"I'm serious! Okay, okay. How about friends? Besides the angelic ones I mean."

I frown at that one… "I don't know. I mean, I did. But… well they haven't tried to make contact with me any… I mean I'm sure most of them got taken in the rapture but even before then I hadn't heard from them. Not that I really had the chance to talk even if they'd tried to call…"

I frown and have the sudden urge to check my phone for the hundredth time since the rapture. My dad suddenly winces and I jump a bit.

"What's wrong?" I ask concerned.

"I'm okay." He states, although he doesn't look okay. He looks like someone who's just been stabbed. My lie detector comes on but something feels different about it this time. It feels like it's saying that he's both lying and telling the truth. I frown again; this is confusing…

"Umm… Are you sure?" I question uncertainty.

He forces a smile, "I think it's time I explain myself to you. Let's start with my name. My name, Bokim, given to me when I was first created in heaven, means weeper." He pauses and I jump in.

"Weeper? But I thought there aren't any tears in heaven."

My father sighs, "There aren't for humans. However, angels were created to praise the creator and to help the mortals. Sometimes mortals just need someone to care enough for them to cry over them."

"Oh, that's kind of sad…" I reply and he nods grimly.

"In heaven I would weep for the lost souls on Earth but I could turn off the sorrow when I wanted. When I fell, well, suddenly I couldn't turn it off. Everywhere I went, anyone near me who was sad, their sorrow would flood into me. What was a gift in heaven became a curse on Earth. I thought I'd never be happy again. That is, until I met your mother." He blushes and I can't help but smile. How romantic is that? He clears his throat and continues.

"I have a thing for art you see. I love how a painting can display emotions but because it isn't living I don't have to feel those feelings myself. I find self-expression through art to be fascinating."

"Do you have a favorite painter?" I ask curiously.

"Michelangelo, fascinating fellow. He once let me pose for a piece he was working on for the ceiling of the Sistine Chapel." He says it so matter-of-factly.

"No way! You not only met Michelangelo but he actually painted you on the Sistine Chapel?! That is so cool!" I'm practically bouncing in my seat.

He nods, "Of course, demons can't step foot on holy ground so I never got to see it in person. Now where was I… Oh yes. One night I was at an art museum near Jerusalem for a new Picasso exhibit. I don't care much for Picasso really, his works are a bit ugly in my opinion, but I love art so
I went just the same. While I was there, so was your mother."

"Yeah," I grin, "she told me she met you at an art museum!"

"Did she? It's true. She noticed me looking at a painting and she thought I looked sad. As I said before, I was always sad. So she came over to try her encouragement gift on me. She gently touched my arm as if to get my attention and to my complete shock, the sadness was suddenly gone. We started talking and she told me about her gift. For the first time since the fall I was happy. Soon, we fell in love and I'm sure she told you the rest."

I nod again. *It is so sweet how she's the only one in the world that can make him happy.* I think to myself.

"So," I wonder aloud, "when you're not around her do you go back to being sad?" This time he nods. I guess I can't be as angry at him for leaving my mom all the time then… He really must be doing it to protect her because it's got to be the hardest thing for him to leave behind the one he loves, the only one who can make him happy.

Suddenly my mom bursts into the library, panic flashing across her face.

"Bokim!" She screams and he leaps to his feet and dashes over to her.

"What is it?" His face is suddenly dead serious. I stand up timidly but make no move towards them.

"We're being bombed again!" She cries out in fear and he kisses her forehead lightly but swiftly.

"I'll be back." He assures and turns towards the door.

Dayton suddenly appears and says, "I'm going with you." Before I can even comprehend what is going on the two of them disappear out of the room, leaving my mom and myself behind.
~Aurora~

Bombs? Again? I'm going with you? Wait! Going where? What are they going to do? Now my mother stands here gesturing for me to follow her. But I can't. In fact, I can't move at all! The vision swirls in again and I drop to my knees. My mom screams and darts towards me. I'm laying on the floor paralyzed, but I'm not unconscious. Strange… The images flash through my mind but this time it's somewhat different. This time the colors in the vision are distorted. They are sharper, more intense, and almost seem to be rising off the images as if they are being sucked right off.

The vision drains from my head and I realize that I have been carried from the library to the living room and placed on the couch. My mom is crouched next to me as if she'd been trying to wake me but her eyes are not on me. I follow her distraught gaze to the large television on the wall. It takes a moment for my mind to comprehend what it's seeing.

My moms, Daytons, and my face are all plastered across the screen. Along with the words: 'Wanted, dead or alive.' I groan and my mother startles and turns back towards me.

"Aurora! Are you alright?" Concern dripping from every word.

"I'm fine, at least I didn't pass out that time." I try to smile but the thought of our faces on the wanted poster comes to mind and smiling feels like an impossible feat. I make a gesture towards the tv and begin again saying, "is that…" She finishes my sentence glumly.

"The Anti-christs doing."

I frown, "What are we going to do?"

"We can't do anything. Not until the bombing has stopped anyway."

"How much time do we have?" I ask but I have a feeling I know the answer.

"Not enough…" She avoids my eyes solemnly, "Nowhere near enough."

<h3 style="text-align:center">~Dayton~</h3>

Dayton squints his eyes, trying to see past the smoke. Somewhere in the midst of the screams Bokim yells instructions to him.

"You got a heavenly bow kid?" Bokim asks as he draws a smoking black bow from thin air.

Dayton nods in response and his own bow materializes in his hand. He pulls a flaming arrow from his back and lets it fly. It hits its target and a large black bomb explodes in midair, before it can get low enough to hurt anything.

"Sure do. You need an upgrade Bokim." He smiles and aims towards another bomb as he soars. Bokim laughs.

"If only it were that easy." Aurora's dad shouts back as he shoots a pitch black arrow toward the nearest device. Dayton shakes his head, looses another arrow, and starts to holler back.

"You know it's actually not th…" He's suddenly out cold before he can finish his sentence and someone yanks a bag over his head and throws him over their shoulder.

2o minutes later…

Dayton wakes up, "What the heck…" He mumbles and lifts his hand to rub the back of his head, where he'd been hit. That's when he notices the shackles. Forget the migraine, he's in a dark room and somehow shackled to the floor. He strains against the chains but to no avail. *'What kind of restraints can hold an angel?'* This is not good… A thought hits him out of the blue… *'Where's Bokim?'* He looks around as his eyes start to adjust to the dark.

Besides himself in the middle of the floor, the room is completely empty. He's sitting on his knees with his arms and feet chained to the concrete beneath him. There's a door about ten to fifteen feet in front of him. On the door is a small window with cell bars cutting through it. Just outside the door there's a guard; a guard with a smoking black sword.

"A demon. Of course…" Dayton sighs.

He needs to get the guard to come inside the room, or even better, to come right up to him. If the guard were human that would be easy. All he'd have to do to get a human to come in is to insult him. A demon, however, is a bit smarter. This guard won't fall for something like that. In fact, he'd probably find it amusing.

There's only one way to seriously tick off a demon, and he knows from experience. If he wants to make the guard angry enough to burst in here, he's going to have to remind him of his future. And the best way to do that is to sing. Not just any old hymn though… No, it'll have to be straight from the bible, straight from God himself. So something like psalm 77… No, exactly psalm 77. David had some seriously depressing thoughts in that chapter. And they should be perfect for the situation at hand.

"You kept my eyes from closing; I was too troubled to speak. I thought about the former days, the years of long ago…" Dayton starts singing and the guard bangs on the door. It's already starting to work; so he goes on.

"I remembered my songs in the night. My heart mused and my spirit inquired; will the lord reject forever?" The guard slams his fist into the door again, harder this time.

He yells from the other side, "Shut up traitor!" But Dayton just grins and starts up again.

"Will he never show his favor again? Has his unfailing love vanished forever?"

The guard looks through the bars, his face a deep red color. "I said shut up or I'll make you!"

Dayton sings all the louder, "Has his promise failed for all time? Has God forgotten to be merciful? Has he in anger withheld his compassion?"

The guard lifts his sword to the bars, "I'll kill you! You hear me Angel? I.
WILL. KILL. YOU!"

Dayton smiles daringly, his songs over but he just needs one more thing

to push the guard over the edge.

"What? Jealous that I get a free pass outta burning for eternity? Is that it?" Dayton asks with false curiosity and watches as the color drains from the demon's face and then returns with a flare.

"That's it! You're dead!" The demon flings the door open and charges into the room. Perfect. The guard wields his sword as if it were a baseball bat. He rushes at Dayton with, literally, steam coming out of his ears, nose, and mouth… He is one ticked off fallen angel… Just as the demon swings the sword towards him, Dayton thrusts his arm toward the guard at the same time, pushing the rest of his body back as far as the chains will allow.

The guard doesn't realize what he's doing until it's much too late. The sword strikes the chain, freeing just one of Dayton's arms, but it's enough. Dayton's own weapon forms in his free hand and the shocked demon has no time to react. The blade pierces through the guard's chest, sending heavenly flames straight through the demon's blackened heart. The body discentigrates around the sword and the keys from his belt clamour to the floor.

Dayton quickly frees himself and runs out the open cell door, sword in hand. He makes his way down a long corridor until he hears voices behind a door up ahead. He plasters himself against the wall next to the door to listen in.

"There, I gave you the Angel. Now leave my family alone. That was the deal." The voice belongs to Aurora's father. Dayton scowls and shakes his head in disbelief. Then a second voice chimes in.

"You should know better than making deals with the devil Bokim. I need that girl of yours out of the way. And to be honest, you're starting to bug me as well."

The tone changes and it doesn't sound good. "Idiot…" Dayton breathes softly before throwing open the door and barging inside. The room isn't anything like the cell he'd just escaped. This one looks like a cozy office, except for the whole part where the anti-christ has a sword to Dayton's girlfriend's dad's throat. His entrance manages to startle the anti-christ just long enough for Bokim to leap away from the blade.

"Hell!" The anti-christ curses furiously.

"Not quite…" Dayton retorts as he bolts across the room, slamming into Bokim and sending them both sailing out the large glass window at the back of the room.

They extend their wings and soar off as quickly as they can.

"That a boy!" Bokim yells excitedly. Dayton frowns angrily and a metal pole forms in his hand. Before Bokim has a chance to protest Dayton bangs the pipe over his head and catches his unconscious body. Soon after Dayton finds a safe place to land. They are in what looks to be the middle of nowhere, surrounded by nothing but dirt and trees. Dayton sets Bokims body against a tall pine tree and produces a large chain.

After chaining the unconscious demon to the tree he sighs and says, "You're staying here until I can figure out what to do with you. Making a deal with the devil is stupid… Trust me, I know." Then he flies off, leaving Aurora's knocked out father behind.

~Aurora~

After changing I begin packing. If you can call tossing two books, my cell phone, and a jacket into a small backpack packing. I also throw my toothbrush in there, although I'm sure dental hygiene will probably be the last thing on my mind for a while. We are supposed to be ready to leave the second my father and Dayton get back. The doorbell chimes in the distance and I grin. He's back! I quickly grab my bag and rush out of my room.

Suddenly I hear Mara let out a scream, followed by a loud thud. My chest tightens and for a brief moment I can't breathe. Then around the corner a man appears. He's stocky and has charcoal colored hair and a gleaming silver tooth showing through his evil grin. The smell hits me like a train and I spin on my heel and race as fast as my feet will carry me. My mom appears and calls for me to follow her. We run around a corner and come face to face with an angry mob. It's mostly composed of humans but a few demons are scattered amongst them too.

'Oh no…' I think as it dawns on me. My visions are finally happening. My mother takes my hand.

'Wait… something's about to happen… something bad…'

My mind draws a blank and I can't remember the next part of the vision. Mom points upward towards the glass skylight above us. Something in me screams to wait but my mother starts counting down. She leaps up and I do the same. Our wings burst out and we soar upwards. At that moment I remember the last part of my vision. I gasp but even as I turn towards her I see the bullet pierce her skin.

"Nooo!!!" I scream as she starts to fall. Just then, like in the vision, Dayton swoops out of nowhere and catches her as she falls. He yells for me to go and I obey. We burst through the glass above and shoot out across the sky. I follow close behind Dayton. I'm not sure where we will go now but I am content to follow him anywhere.

'Will she be okay?' I ask him in my head so that if she is still awake she won't hear. I can't help but stare at the blood staining her beautiful ivory wings.

'I can't say for sure, but most likely. It only hit her wing so it shouldn't do too much damage.' He doesn't even turn around to look at me as he replies. I suddenly long to be in his arms. I'm so shaken up and all I want is for him to hold me close… Then a thought occurs to me and I stop following him and just fly in place. He seems to sense it and stops as well, turning to face me with a questioning look on his face.

'Dayton…' I start nervously, *'Where is my dad?'*

I watch his face contort into a painful expression and I get a bad feeling in the pit of my stomach… Please don't tell me my day is about to get even worse…

Dayton tells me the whole story in mind speak so that my mom wouldn't have to be troubled by it as well… When he finishes I am in shock. I don't even know how to respond to this. Anger rises up in me and I fight to keep from yelling out loud. I just met my dad; I've barely even gotten to know him, and then he goes and hands my boyfriend over to the anti-christ?! Why can't he just threaten him like a normal dad? Not hand him over to the devil incarnate! And to what? Protect me? Doesn't he know that I'd rather die than live without Dayton?

Maybe he was trying to protect my mom and I but it was stupid to make a deal with the devil. Mom drifts in and out of consciousness, occasionally muttering my dad's name. It pains me to wonder how she'll respond when she finds out what he did. Would she thank him for betraying my trust to protect us? Would she be angry or hurt? She begins to shiver in Dayton's arms and he frowns with concern. I fly up next to him and place my hand gently on her forehead. It's hot.

"Dayton, why isn't she healing yet?" Panic escapes with my words but instead of offering me comfort or even an answer, Dayton says, "We need to land. Right now!"

His usual calm demeanor has fled and the idea of something making him so anxious scares me. I follow his lead and we land in the middle of an Israeli street.

"What about people?" I whisper with alarm but he just shakes his head.

"The bombing drove them underground. They won't come back out for a while. But we should hurry."

Hurry with what I wonder? Most of the buildings are small and made of wood or clay. The first word to come to mind to describe it is poor… Dayton carries my mother into a building with a sign on the door that reads doctor in arabic. I watch as he lays her down on a small wooden table and goes digging frantically through some drawers nearby. My mother lets out a groan of pain and I feel utterly useless to help.

"What's going on?!" I demand urgently, taking my mom's hand in mine. "I thought a human shot her…" He sounds angry with himself. I watch as he pulls out something that resembles a scalpel and sets it on the counter.

"Was it not?" I frown, confused. Dayton sighs in frustration.

"No, it was a demon."

"A demon?" I start with surprise, "I thought angels and demons only used swords and things like that."

Now he has an armful of medical tools that he carries over and sets down on the table next to my mom.

"The gun was created during what you know as World War two. Adolf Hitler was possessed by a demon known as Merikh, meaning death or slaughter. He was very vengeful and wanted revenge on God so he possessed Hitler and made him slaughter God's chosen people, the Jews." He pauses and in his hand he materializes a jar of glowing gold liquid. Then he continues…
"The seven archangels of heaven decided to create a more modern weapon to destroy him. They called it 'The gun of Emmanuel's glory'. What they didn't realize is that not only can it kill demons but it can also kill angels and anything else as well. It's the all powerful weapon." He rubs some of the gold liquid onto my mom's wing and she gasps but doesn't cry out.

"That's what shot my mom?" I ask, fear rising up in my chest.

"I'm afraid so… We have to get the bullet out. Here," he hands me a small rag, "put this in her mouth between her teeth."

I don't ask why, I just do it. A tear runs down my cheek as I think
of the pain she'll have to face before the bullet is removed. Dayton grabs
the scalpel and goes right to work. My mother tries to scream but the rag
muffles the sound. I turn away; I can't stand to watch. Tears flow down
my face as my mom squeezes my hand in pain. I want to know more
about the gun but I don't want to distract Dayton and make him mess up.

When he finally sets the scalpel down and wipes his forehead
with his arm, my mom has passed out again. I turn back to him and ask,
"So what happened? How did the demons end up with the gun?" He
shakes his head and collapses into a chair against the nearest wall.

"I have no idea! I didn't know they did! The demon made Hitler
kill himself and then fled before the gun was ever used. I'd always
thought the archangels had it destroyed after the war." He suddenly looks
furious. He stands and punches through the wall. I stare at him in shock.
There are few times when Dayton actually gets angry…

"I was one of them! They had that freakin gun the whole time?"
He yells, then stops and jerks his head up. "Wait!" He starts, the anger
fades and is replaced by a mix of curiosity and confusion, "If they've had
it the whole time… Why haven't they used it before?"

"Maybe they were saving it…" I offer, trying to help. His eyes
widen slightly.

"We need to go!" He rushes over to my mom and lifts her easily.
His wings expand and I let mine unfold as well. The urgency in his voice
and the panic on his face tell me not to question him. Something is very
wrong and I'll just have to trust him. Though I've never had a problem
with that. I trust him with my life… With all our lives.

~Bokim~

When his eyes finally flutter open, Bokim finds himself chained to a tree. He sighs; he brought this on himself. Why had he agreed to a deal with the anti-christ? That had to have been one of the stupidest decisions he's ever made. The chains wrapped tightly around his body and the tree, leaving marks on his skin. Had that boy really left him here? How long has he been here? Bokim struggles against his restraints but to no avail.

"Angel magic." He breathes aloud in frustration.

What will his daughter think of him for giving her boyfriend over to the anti-christ? He frowns. She's going to hate him… and all he wanted was to protect his family. The flutter of wings draws his attention and he lifts his head towards the sky. His daughter lands first. She looks scared at first but upon seeing him her expression changes to one of betrayal.

"Aurora I…" He is about to explain himself, or at least apologize, until Dayton lands with Shaphir in his arms. The color drains from Bokims face.

"What happened to her?!" He demands and Dayton and Aurora both suddenly look sympathetic.

"She's been shot." Dayton says and gently places the queen's injured body on the ground.

Hope rises in Bokims chest. A gun wound should heal easily. But one look at his daughter's tear streaked face and the hope drains out of him. He looks to the boy for an explanation. Dayton hesitates a moment before looking him in the eye and asking,

"Bokim, did you know the beast has the gun of Emmanuel's glory?"

Shock hits him like a tidal wave to the gut. Bokim looks down at his wife, covered in dried blood.

"No…" He whispers softly. A tear flows from his eye and drips down onto the chains. He's used to sorrow; feeling others sorrow is his curse.
But this time it's different, this time the sorrow is his own.

"Unchain me… NOW! Let me loose! LET ME LOOSE!" He screams in
pain and rage as he twists against the chains. Dayton rushes over and sets him free. Bokim falls to his knees at his wife's side, grabs her hand, and weeps more intensely than he ever has before.

$$\sim\textbf{Aurora}\sim$$

I watch my father weep for my mother. There is something wrong…

"What's going on…" I ask, tears in my eyes. Dayton turns to me, a sad expression across his face.

"Aurora… She's not... " He stammers for the words and I shake my head violently. No… He can't be about to say what I think he's about to say. The tears break free and fall onto my cheeks.

"No… You got the bullet out! You did it! You saved her! She can't… I mean… She isn't…"

Pain. My whole body suddenly aches. Dayton steps towards me and I fall into his embrace and sob into his warm chest.

"I'm so sorry angel…" He starts as he rubs my back tenderly. "She lost too much blood. Her body doesn't have the strength to heal."

His words cause me to sob harder. I just got her back only to lose her forever?

"Aurora…" My mothers faint voice drifts over to me and I pull away from Dayton's chest. I rub my eyes with my arm and move towards my mom. My dad moves aside and I sit down next to mom and take her hand in mine.

"I'm sorry…" She says in a voice that's barely audible. I know she means for giving me away and I shake my head.

"It's okay mom. You did it to protect me…"

"I love you…" She slowly lifts our hands up together until my hand is touching my shell necklace that Dayton gave me. Then she whispers, "Follow your heart. And happy birthday."

She coughs and my dad sits back down. I feel Dayton's strong hands on my shoulders and I stand back up and turn around towards him again. His arms envelope me and he gently kisses the top of my head as I cry.

Mother passes and my dad holds out his arms to invite me for a hug. I may be angry with him but I rush into his embrace without a thought. It's weird, this is the first time I've ever hugged my dad. I pull away after a second and rub my eyes. I frown as I stare at my mother's body in confusion.

"Umm… Why is she… umm... " I try to ask but I can't bring myself to say out loud what I'm wondering in my head. I can feel the slight pressure of Dayton trying to probe my mind and this time I let him. He sighs.

"She's still here because she's not fully angel. She still has a lot of human blood so her body stays." He explains and I nod to show I understand.

Dayton and my father dig a grave and gently place her body in it. I walk away and sit on the ground, pulling my knees up against my chest so as to hide my face while I cry. A moment later I feel someone sit next to me. I turn, expecting to find Dayton, but instead I find my dad.

"What do you want?" I try to sound accusing but it comes out sounding more pathetic and choked.

"Your mother wanted you to have this. And I do too."

He holds out his hand and in it I see the small angel pin my mother had told me he had given to her. My eyes widen slightly and I hesitate before reaching out for it. I flip it over in my hands and examine it silently. My dad takes this moment to talk.

"All I wanted was to protect the two of you. I had no idea…" He frowns and a solemn tear travels down his face, "I'm so sorry… so so sorry…"

He puts his hands to his face and begins to weep. I realize two things in that moment. One: he's telling the truth… and Two: without my mom, he may never be happy again. So I place my hand on his shoulder lightly and whisper,

"I forgive you daddy…"

He looks up at me, both of our eyes brimming with tears, and I lean forward to hug him again. And then… we mourn together.

"You know Alvadenon, you're to be my false prophet in the coming years." The anti-christ says softly and Crater's eyes widen. Talk about a promotion… The false prophet is said to have incredible powers and privileges. He's not sure what to say but he understands where the conversation is heading… Talbot Desdemona sighs at the look on Craters face and continues.

"Yes, but three and a half years is plenty of time for me to find someone more competent for the position."

Talbot turns to see what Crater's reaction will be. Crater tries his best to keep his face expressionless as he replies.

"You won't have to wait that long. I will succeed in my mission and bring you the girl." It comes out somewhat defensive and he inwardly scolds himself. The anti-christ pulls open a drawer in his desk. He reaches inside and draws out a small hand-held pistol. Crater can't help but grin as he looks at the small weapon in his master's hand. It's incredible how much power is in the small device. It has the potential for so much evil. The anti-christ turns the gun over in his hand, examining it carefully. After a moment he says,

"I should hope so. Kill the others, starting with the traitor. But bring me the girl. Also…" he pauses, a thoughtful look in his eyes, "Send someone for the child."

The request surprises Crater but he doesn't dare open his mouth in opposition.

"Yes, sir." The demon nods obediently as he exits through the broken window at the back of the room.

~Dayton~

"What do you know about Talbot's plan for the gun?" Dayton begins to drill Bokim while Aurora lay asleep, wrapped up in his jacket nearby.

"I didn't even know they had it! I mean, I've heard rumors but…" Bokim trials off and Dayton raises an eyebrow.

"What rumors?"

"Just that they may have the gun…"

"Any about what he's using it for?" A frustrated scowl forms on Dayton's face.

"Not that I can… Well, there was something about a kid."

"A kid?"

"I don't know. Some kid with some power. They've supposedly been keeping an eye on him. Waiting."

"Waiting for what? What power?" He raises his voice slightly and Bokim frowns in anger.

"I said I don't know! If I did I swear I'd tell you!"

"Would you?" Dayton gets even louder as his anger builds.
Aurora stirs slightly and Dayton sighs, trying to calm himself down. She needs her sleep; she's been through a lot today. Bokim shoots him a look but says nothing.

"Fine," Dayton starts again, "we need to find some answers. In the morning we'll fly to Damascus. My buddy Jabez lives there, he's been helping me out."

Bokims eyes narrow in suspicion.

"Jabez? Can you trust him?"

"Can I trust you?" Dayton shoots back and Bokim frowns again.

"You can trust me to protect my daughter." He says as he turns to walk away. Dayton shakes his head as he watches him go.

"Well... we have that in common anyway."

Dayton gently shakes my shoulder and I wake up instantly.

"Sorry," he apologizes, "but we gotta head out." I give a small moan and sit upright.

"Oh, and happy birthday Angel." He says and plants a soft kiss on my lips. I frown against his mouth. My birthday… right… I sit up and try to comb through my frizzing hair with my hand.

"So," I start, "Do you know when I can expect this birthday thing to happen?" I'm standing now and I hand Dayton back the jacket he let me sleep with.

"Sorry, that's more of a nephilim thing." He shrugs and gives me a sympathetic look.

"Happy birthday sweetheart!" My dad lands beside me and pulls me in for a hug.

"Thanks…" I mutter, "Where have you been?" I step back and look at him suspiciously.

"Oh you know, selling you out, setting a trap…"

"WHAT?!" I yell and turn to Dayton. He shakes his head and sneers but doesn't look worried.

"I'm joking darling." My dad sets a hand on my shoulder and gives a small laugh. I frown and pull away from his grasp.

"Look, dad, it's a little too soon after betrayal to joke with me okay?" My face is heating up and I'm not sure if it's anger or embarrassment. Dayton notices right away and slips his arm around my waist, letting me know he's got my back. I immediately relax upon his touch and let out a long sigh.

"So where are we going now?" I ask. My dad makes a face that seems to suggest he's not happy about the answer before responding.

"Damascus. Your boyfriend says he's got a contact there." He looks at Dayton with mild disgust. So much for them liking each other… I glance over at Dayton next to me.

'Contact?' I ask in mind speak.

'Jabez.' He sends back simply. Jabez… right. I feel Dayton trying to push into my head again. Probably curious on how I feel about meeting his demon friend… I push him out; he doesn't want to know.

"Well, we should get going then." I say and let out my wings.

My dad scans my wings with interest for just a second before releasing his own. They are black, of course, and look just like Daytons used to; except they are a bit longer. It's the first time I've seen my dad's wings and I can't help but stare as they extend. Dayton pulls his arm away from my waist and his own wings appear. For a brief second I think I can see jealousy cross my dad's face as he sees Dayton's cotton white wings. But it's only a split second and it's gone. Dayton slips his hand in mine and we all leap into the air. Only about 135 miles to Damascus.

~Crater~

Crater kicks the door to the small, square shaped house inward with little effort. The second he steps in Jabez leaps at him, sword in hand. Crater jumps to the side allowing Jabez to fly right past him and lose his footing. Crater spins around, grabbing the falling Jabez by the shirt collar, and throws him backwards against a wall. A thin trickle of blood glides down the back of Jabez's head where it had smacked into the wood.

"Jabez, old friend. How have you been?"
Jabez's sword dematerializes as Crater's hand encircles his neck. Jabez scowls at Crater silently.

"I've heard you've been in touch with our former pal Dayton. You wouldn't be willing to replay that conversation for me would you?" Crater grins maliciously and Jabez grits his teeth in obvious refusal.

"Hmm… I suppose you leave me with no choice then."

Jabez's eyes widen and he tries desperately to look away but it's too late. Craters' eyes peer into the demon's mind and suck out the memories. The process Crater has used thousands of times before. It kills the victim but if you don't need them alive then it's an effective means of information retrieval. And when he finally pulls his hand away from Jabez's neck, Crater knows everything he needs to know. The girl is on her way here now… and he'll be waiting. Jabez's lifeless body slides back down to the floor in a heap, and after a moment, disappears.

We're about halfway there when we decide to stop in Tiberias for some food. My dad wanders off to a nearby market to buy us some fruit, leaving Dayton and I alone.

"I have something for you. For your birthday." Dayton says and pulls a folded piece of paper from his jacket pocket. I lean forward curiously as he unfolds it.

"What is it?" I ask with a smile.

"It's a poem. And I suck at things like this so you have to promise not to laugh at me… Okay?"

"Oh whatever, I won't laugh. Just read it."

He clears his throat and recites the words without even reading it. It's as if he's rehearsed it a thousand times…

"The sun itself cannot outshine
her For her light is more than radiant.
Can you say one has stolen your heart
When you have surrendered it willingly?
She is my souls true hope
When the darkness pierces my
faith. And as I love with love
unmatched My heart soars with
only her. She's my angel in the sky,
My hope, my love, my life."

When he finishes I'm speechless. My heart beats faster and I'm too shocked to say a word. Small dots of pink appear on his cheeks and he shifts his weight and says,

"Told you I suck…" he tries to laugh but he looks uncomfortable. I shake my head but I still can't think of words to say. It was beautiful and it was the most romantic thing I've ever heard. So instead of saying anything I reach up and grab the sides of his head lightly, lean forward, and kiss him passionately.

'It was beautiful and I loved it. I love you. Oh how I love you.' I think to him as he kisses me back.

I run my fingers through his hair and after a moment we both pull back for air. I gaze at him intently, taking in his smell as I study his deep green eyes and the way his hair hangs over his forehead. Something's different…

"You smell weird…" I state abruptly and he looks taken aback.

"What?" He looks embarrassed and I giggle at the face he makes.

"No, I mean, you don't smell like smoke anymore. I haven't noticed until now…" I frown at the thought but he looks relieved.

"Oh, smoke is the smell of a demon and I'm an angel now. My smell will change to a heavenly scent. Just as my hair will eventually get lighter and my eyes will most likely turn blue." He shrugs as if it's no big deal. I however, find it to be a very big deal.

"No! No, I like you just the way you are!" I make a pouty face and continue, "I love everything about you…"

He laughs and says, "Well, I hope that won't change when my hair does."

Okay… I'll admit I'm a bit distraught over the idea of Dayton with any other color of hair… but I shake my head.

"Of course it won't… I'll always love you. No matter what."

As soon as the words escape my lips he reaches for me, one hand flies down grabbing me behind my knees and the other grabs my back as he sweeps me up into his arms. I let out a small yelp of surprise as he lifts me up and holds me to him.

"You know, the phrase 'sweep a girl off her feet' isn't meant to be taken literally I don't believe." I say, laughing, as I wrap my arms around his neck. He shrugs and grins at me.

"But It's more fun this way."

~Dayton~

"Bokim is taking a long time buying food." Dayton mutters nervously as he gently sits Aurora back down. She grins mischievously at him, grabs him by the belt loop on his jeans, pulls him closer, and says,

"Let him."

Dayton looks at her surprised for a moment. Is she not worried? Bokim has betrayed them once before, he could do it again. She sighs, obviously sensing his fears.

"I don't fully trust him either," She starts, her fingers still twisted in his belt loop, "but if he does betray us again, I won't forgive him. But we can worry about that later. I have a feeling we aren't going to get much alone time after this, so let's just focus on now okay?"

Dayton gazes down into her eyes and he can see her innocence, her longing, her spirit, and her beauty all glowing like embers behind them. He smiles, this is the girl he fell in love with. He leans forward and kisses her deeply and she kisses back more forcefully.

For a moment, he loses himself in her kiss, in the way her body feels against his, in the feeling of her breath on his cheek, and her touch… Oh no. He has gotten so lost in the moment that he hadn't even noticed when she'd slid her thumbs just under the waistline of his jeans. The soft skin of her thumbs brushes lightly against his waist. He leaps back, away from her, but it's too late. She'd felt it, his one flaw… the one thing he's tried to hide for decades… his one scar.

~Dria~

"You wouldn't hit a lady would you, Bokim?" The nephilim girl tries to sound seductive but the fear creeps into her voice.

Bokim steps menacingly up to her and she backs up as far as she can against the bricks behind her. Walking down an alley alone isn't usually a problem when you have supernatural powers, but she guesses it doesn't really help if the person jumping you has them too. And more powerful ones at that…

"It was you! Wasn't it?" Bokim shoves her against the wall and puts his sword to her throat.

"Always thought I'd die by an angel's hand, not a demon's. Who woulda thought?" She tries to struggle but the blade dips into her skin and she stills.

"It was you! It was you Dria!"

"What was me? You're crazy!"

"You gave the freaking gun to Talbot!"

Dria pauses, surprised, then says in a silky tone, "No, I gave it to Satan. A century ago."

She gives him a triumphant smile and he releases her neck. She rubs it gently and watches him as he paces.

"What were you thinking?" He asks softly.

"Uh, I was thinking I was dying! I was left to die and even if the wound hadn't 'miraculously' healed I still would have died eventually. I am half-mortal you know. Satan cut me a deal and I was grateful. He took me under his wing. He got the gun and I got the closest thing I've ever had to a dad and immortality." Dria shoots Bokim an angry look and he seems to soften some.

"You should never make deals with the devil…" He says quietly. She looks into his eyes, searching them.

"Like you've never made the same mistake?" She catches a flash of pain cross his face before he replies,

"Come on. You're coming with me. I may need you."

"And if I refuse?"

"I'll kill you. Immortality won't protect you against a demon blade... or a fathers protective nature."

She gives him a curious look, shrugs, and follows him out of the alley-way.

"Dayton?" I stare at him as he pulls away. What was on his hip? It felt like a scar but how could that be? Dayton shoves his hands into his pockets and angles his body away from me. I feel a little hurt, whatever happened to him, he obviously doesn't want me to know.

"No, I don't." He mumbles and I'm taken aback. Somehow he managed to get into my head unnoticed, like he used to.

"Why? Don't you trust me?" I frown, my gaze traveling to his waist where I'd felt the unknown mark. He twists his head to face me and pain flickers in his eyes. I can see that the story behind the mark is extremely painful for him. If I love him, and I do, I shouldn't force him to remember whatever it was. I step forward and wrap my arms around him slowly.

"It's okay, you don't have to tell me. As long as you're okay." I whisper, my head resting lightly on his chest.

He lets out a soft groan and gently pulls away. He takes my hand and pulls me down so that we are both sitting side-by-side on the soft green grass.

"No," he breathes a deep breath and continues, "you have every right to know. But just know it's not an easy story to tell any more than it's an easy one to hear." He sighs and his hand seems to shake. I place my hands on his and they stop shaking almost instantly. Then I listen as he tells me of the horrible events that transpired to give him the scar on his hip.

"It started with world war two, the same time Merikh had possessed Adolf Hitler and began recruiting his army. Satan was all for Merikh's plan, slaughter the Jews and tell the world he was doing it for God. He kills God's chosen people and makes God take the blame. Genius is what Satan called it. But with Satan in on it he demanded all demons fight. Because I was on my own, an outcast, I had no intention of joining any war with Satan…… but…… I had, at the time, become….. well….. umm…..”

Dayton shifts uncomfortably on the ground beside me. He clears his throat then continues.

“Very good umm… friends with a nephilim that insisted on fighting, sort of, and I didn’t want them to fight without me. So I joined as a Nazi. Well, pretended to be one for a while anyway. The archangels made the gun of Emmaniel’s Glory but as I’ve already told you, Merikh killed Hitler and fled before it was used….. but I didn’t tell you that it was used after he fled…”

I can’t keep my gaze from traveling to his hip. I gasp involuntarily and ask, “they shot you?” He shakes his head and a tear slides down his cheek.

“No, the Archangels captured my friend and I. They assumed we knew where Merikh had gone. We didn’t of course, but they didn’t believe us….. When we couldn’t give them the information they wanted they shot my friend. While the gun was still hot they placed it on my hip. The pain was like none I’d ever felt before. I don’t know why they didn’t kill me, but they didn’t. They unchained me and transported back to heaven as I slumped to the ground in pain and sorrow for my friend. When the pain finally subsided I fled. I never should have been in that stupid war… Now I have the scar to remind me of my mistakes.”

His voice fades and I’m dumbfounded. He was tortured? By angels? My heart aches for him and I long to make him feel better, to ease the pain. I lost my mom, and that was hard, but I hadn’t known her long. Dayton was obviously very close to his friend and I can hardly imagine how hard it must be for him….

“What was your friend’s name?” I ask it softly, I’m sure it brings him painful emotions and the last thing I want to do is hurt him more…. but I also want him to know that I care and I want to help. He looks surprised at the question. He hesitates a second then starts to open his mouth when suddenly my dad lands in front of us. We both jump and I let out a small yelp of surprise.

"Dad!" I say accusingly. He smiles and sets down a bag of groceries.

"I have something for you." My dad says as he kisses my forehead lightly.
I raise an eyebrow curiously. "You really didn't have to get me anything……"

"Nonsense. You're my daughter and it's your birthday of course I got you something. Here, watch closely."

He puts his hands together slowly and Dayton and I watch curiously. I have no idea what he's doing. My dad pulls his hands apart at about the same speed he had put them together. Only, when he does, an object begins to form between them. An object I instantly recognize and a smile peaks across my face, growing as the object does. When his hands are about two feet apart the thing has been completely finished. It's my skateboard.

I leap to my feet and rush toward him. "No way!" I yell as he places the board in my hands.

Dayton looks at it skeptically but says nothing. I've been so caught up in the supernatural lately I haven't noticed that I'd lost the human part of myself along the way. The crazy, risk taking tomboy I used to be has been hidden by my new careful, angelic, responsible princess side. Not that I don't love this side of me too, but it feels good to be holding something so normal again.

"How did you do that?" I ask as I look at the skateboard I'm holding.

Bokim grins proudly. "I may be old but I still got some magic in these bones. It was easy as pie." He says with a laugh. Suddenly a figure lands just behind him. It was a girl I've never seen before.

"Hey old man! You didn't do it alone. Give me some credit."

The girl laughs and pushes a loose strand of her raven black hair behind her ear. Her hair was perfectly straight and cut in a short choppy style just above her shoulders. I couldn't find a single blemish on her face and her silver eyeliner only made her gray eyes shine brighter.

My dad laughs as the girl glides up next to him with a walk that's both graceful and challenging at the same time. She folds her black wings back up and my dad begins to introduce her.

"I'm sorry. This is……" He doesn't finish because Dayton finishes for him.

"Dria….?" His voice cracks and I whip around to face him. His face has gone white as ash; he looks as if he's seen a ghost.

"I thought you were dead…." His hands are shaking as he says it. I turn back to the girl, confusion flowing through me like ice water in my veins. Dria looks both sad and relieved at the same time.

"Hello Dayton…" She mutters. Then she turns to me and smiles, although for some reason I see something in that smile that looks almost threatening.

"And you must be Aurora. Bokim's daughter?" She asks in a sweet enough tone yet it seems venomous. Maybe I'm imagining it but I'm not stupid and I feel the need to clarify something.

"Yes, and I'm also Dayton's girlfriend." I try to smile but I don't think it looks like a smile. Maybe it's childish to say but I don't like the fact that this chick not only knows Dayton but also keeps giving him that look. The universal look for…. well, I don't even want to think about it. Who the heck is this chick anyways? There's an awkward silence as we all take each other in. I rack my brain to figure out who she is. There has to be some….. Suddenly it hits me. I turn to Dayton and start to ask him about it when my dad coughs and says,

"Alright, well, now that we're all acquainted I guess it's time we get a move on huh?"

Dria nods and her wings unfurl behind her. Dayton stares at her as if he's remembering something. I frown.

"Good idea," I say as I intertwine my fingers with Dayton's, effectively snapping him out of his trance. He glances at me in surprise for a brief second before giving my hand a gentle squeeze.

"Yeah, ugh, let's go. Jabez is probably waiting on us." He says and releases my hand as his wings spread out and we all leap into the air.

Dria glances over at Dayton curiously and I shoot her a 'back off' look. Dayton focuses his attention on the sky ahead. I think he's afraid to look at anyone. And that's probably for the best right now.

My dad is leading the way about ten feet ahead and our newest member is taking up the rear about the same distance behind. I'm by Dayton's side in the middle. Every so often I glance back at Dria, to make sure she's not staring at Dayton or something. Although… what would I do if she was? But every time I turn her gaze is fixed, not on Dayton, but on me. She doesn't bother looking away when I turn either, no, she stares me down with a confident glare and mocking smile. She's messing with me…. I feel like the mouse the cat has trapped but isn't bothering to kill yet.

"That's going to cause problems." Dayton says suddenly and if it's possible to trip in the air I believe I just did.

"What?!" I ask nervously. I'm hoping he hadn't been referring to my feelings about Dria….

"Your skateboard. You shouldn't be carrying it with you. It will weigh you down in the battles."

"Oh," I mutter, relieved. Then I hug the skateboard to me.

"But I…."

"I completely agree." My dad says ahead of us. He has stopped and turned toward us. He motions for me to come to him and says, "Come here and I'll show you what to do." I frown and look at Dayton, then Dria, then Dayton again. He nods and I reluctantly fly toward my dad. Out of the corner of my eye I see Dria soar up next to Dayton and I try to hide my scowl as I reach my father's side.

"Well, she's definitely your type, isn't she?" Dria says with a laugh.

Dayton frowned.

"What do you mean my type?"

"You know, undecided nephilim, free spirit, high connections……. Did you tell her about me?"

"She's not like you."

"And is that a good thing? Or a bad thing?"

"What happened to you? I thought you died in Dresden." His eyes filled with concern.

"Obviously not," she said venomously, "I don't know how I survived. All I know is I did. I only had a bit of strength left but it was enough to lure those blood thirsty angels back. I used my power to morph into Merikh and when the angels noticed they hightailed it back down here. I managed to get the gun from them, after surprising them by not being dead, then I transported to Hell. I passed out and when I came to I had an eager Satan sitting next to my bed holding the gun. He healed up my
wound and took me under his wing. End of the story." Her look softened a bit but Dayton's only got harder.

"You're the one who gave Satan the gun?"

"Don't you dare judge me. You left me."

"I thought you were dead!"

"Did you miss me at all? How long did you mourn me? Huh? Or was I nothing to you?"

"Stop it Dria. You know I cared for you! I never forgot you." He sighed and she glanced ahead at his new girlfriend.

"Yeah, I can tell. You know," she said, still looking at Aurora, "I had heard rumors in the underworld about you working for heaven again…." She faces him and studies his expression, looking for any sort of reaction, but there was none. "I didn't think it was even possible but I guess you proved that wrong." She sighed.

"Dria….. why are you here?" Dayton asks sternly.

Dria feels as if she's been struck. After all this time, out of all the things he could ask, he only wants to know why she's here?

"Well it wasn't by choice and it wasn't for you. If that's what you're asking. Bokim didn't even mention you were here. He said we were going to meet up with his daughter and her boyfriend. He didn't say that boyfriend was you. Imagine my surprise huh?"

She can feel the anger rising up in her and her face goes red. She once again turns to look toward Aurora and Dayton's eyes light up with concern once more.

"Dria please don't make this harder than it already is."

"What happened to you anyway? You used to be so independent. You didn't need anyone. You didn't take orders from anyone and thought rules didn't apply to you. That's what I loved about you. So what changed?" A tear slid down her warm cheeks.

Dayton turned to face Aurora like she was still doing. Dria looked at him as he watched Aurora next to her dad. Then she nodded and turned away. "I understand." She said and flew back a few feet.

"It's quite simple," Bokim stated as I slowly glide up alongside him, "you see, to form the board you pull your hands apart. To store the board you do the opposite."

"So I push my hands together?" I ask curiously and place one hand on each end of the board.

"Exactly. But I would advise doing so slowly. The board is solid so if you push too quickly you might just bruise your hand." My dad instructs me and I nod.

I slowly push inward on my skateboard and it begins to dematerialize.
My dad smiles as the board disappears completely.

"Great job. Now you can pull it out and put it back whenever you want." I hear him but I'm not really paying attention. I can hear Dayton and Dria whispering and I strain to make out the words but I can't. I hear something about hell and Satan but that's about it. My dad clears his throat and waves a hand in front of my face. I jump.

"Umm… Sorry dad."

"It's alright I suppose I can get pretty boring."

"No, it's not that, but umm… Dad? Did you know they knew each other?" I ask softly.

"Who? Oh… No sweetheart. I'm afraid that was just as much a shock to me as it was to you."

"Oh… I frown and turn to look at them. Dria turns in my direction and I turn back around, only to see my fathers sad expression. Crap. I forgot he feels all the sorrow around him.

"Dad, I'm sorry! I didn't mean to make you feel, well, you know…" Think happy thoughts I tell myself. Why am I letting this chick get to me anyway?

"It's okay Aurora. There's no need to apologize. But if it makes a difference, that boy of yours obviously loves you an awful lot and I don't think you have anything to worry about."

Those words should have been comforting but for some reason they only made me feel queasy. My dad must have been able to tell it hadn't helped because then he sighed and pointed to my necklace.

"Isn't that thing supposed to reassure you of something?"
I reach for the shell, I had almost forgotten I was wearing it. It almost feels like part of me now. I close my eyes and let the memory of us on the beach flood back in. I remember it so perfectly. The sound of the waves as they beat against the sand, the cool salty air, and Dayton's words encased in this shell. I lift the shell to my ear as I had that day on the beach.

"I love you angel. You and only you."
A lone tear escapes down my cheek and I rub it away with my sleeve. My dad floats quietly in front of me and I give him a quick hug.

"Thank you dad." I mutter as I pull away.
I turn back toward Dayton and notice he's already watching me. Dria is a few feet behind him avoiding eye contact with everyone it seems. **~Aurora~**

We hadn't been flying long when Dayton, who had been dead silent the whole trip, suddenly points down and says, "We're here." To be honest I think I may have jumped a bit. He kinda startled me. Of course, these days there isn't much that doesn't startle me….

Dayton lands first, then me, then my dad, and then Dria bringing up the rear. I follow Dayton as he heads toward a small hut that is so old and rundown I wonder how Jabez can stand to live here.

'Beats Hell.' Dayton says in mind speak. I don't reply. There's only a jaggedy curtain where the door should be and Dayton pulls it open and walks in; I follow close behind. This place gives me the creeps. My dad places a hand on my shoulder before I go in. I turn toward him, sensing he has something to say. He does.

"Dria and I will stay out here and watch. You shouldn't have anything to fear from Jabez but stay alert just the same. I nod and head inside. The room is empty and dark, not so dark that I can't see, but still dark. There's nothing more than a dirty mini-fridge and an old wooden table in the room.

"Where's Jabez?" I ask softly.
Dayton narrows his eyes and scans the room. Suddenly, black smoke begins to appear all around the walls of the room, surrounding us. Dayton steps back in front of me, an angry expression on his face. The smoke disappears and in its place is a whole room full of demons. And the one directly in front of us I recognize immediately. It's the demon from the castle, the one that chased me.

"Crater!" Dayton hisses and throws his arm out in front of me protectively. I slide my fingers into his and I can feel his tension ease up slightly.

"What did you do to Jabez?" Dayton asks although I have a feeling he knows the answer. Crater, as Dayton called him, smiles and turns toward me.

"Hello again, Aurora is it?" Crater turns back to Dayton, "You know, I'd been told she was quite the looker but when I saw her in the castle I was like dang, the stories didn't do this one justice." The demon's smile looked so evil it sent a chill down my spine. Dayton looked enraged.

"Yeah, and she's mine. Stay away from her." Dayton snarled and his grip on my hand tightened a little. Crater laughed.

"Don't be so testy Dayton. Once you're gone she'll need protection. Don't worry, I'll take good care of her." Crater took a step toward me and Dayton let go of my hand and stepped in Crater's way.

"Keep your filthy hands off of her! I'm not going anywhere and I've had enough of your crap Crater!" Dayton's sword formed in his hand and Crater smiled, seemingly amused. He made a clicking sound with his tongue and his own sword began to materialize. The curtain door opens and two gruff looking demons pull my father inside and throw him toward us.

"Look what we found." One of the demons says proudly.

I help steady my dad as he stumbles toward us. Dayton never loses eye contact with Crater. I glance toward the door then I turn to my dad and mouth, "Where's Dria?" He slowly shakes his head and I frown. She probably ran off to save her own skin. I look around the room and try to count the demons. There looks to be about fifteen or sixteen and all of them have their swords out and ready. We are clearly outnumbered but Dayton's look is one of pure determination. We've faced more than this before but still, these demons look more powerful than the others we've faced.

I draw my sword and my dad does the same. We all stand back to back and wait for someone to start this blood bath. That someone, as it turns out, is Dayton. He leaps at Crater and all the other demons run forward together.

I would like to say that I'm holding my own pretty well, but unfortunately that would be a lie. While my dad has already killed about four of the seven demons that were around him I have killed one. Dayton had rushed toward Crater but about three of the other demons cut him off. Crater, it seems, has no interest in fighting Dayton. Instead, he made a beeline for me. So now while Dayton and my dad are all tied up with their matches, I am being shoved to the floor and held down by three demons while Crater leans over me with a smug grin and a smoking sword. My sword has dematerialized and I'm reduced to kicking and squirming.

"Dayton!" I scream out as I try to kick the demon holding my feet. Dayton spins around and his eyes go wide. He tries to run toward me but the two remaining demons he'd been battling cut him off. Crater pulls a glass vile from his pocket and kneels down beside me. He grabs my wrist and I realize what he's going to do. I yell and thrash but he doesn't lose his grip on my arm.

I hear Dayton yelling from across the room for Crater to get off of me, but Crater acts as if he didn't hear. He places his sword against my wrist and pulls back. I scream in pain as blood pours from the wound into the vile. Once Crater is satisfied with the amount of blood he's obtained he stands back up and looks around. The demons my dad had been fighting had him at knife point and Dayton was backed into a corner by the demons he'd been facing plus the ones that had been holding me down.

"Kill them all." Crater said calmly as he tucked the vile of my blood back into his pocket. Suddenly, the curtain door burst open and Dria appeared.
The demons all stared in shock, including Crater. Crater's face went pale.

"Dria? What are you doing here?" He asks in a shaky tone. Why does everyone react that way when they see her?

"Let them go." She says in a serious tone.
Crater looks confused and unsure for a moment.

"We were ordered by the anti-christ to kill them when we were done." Crater narrows his eyes at Dria.

"Well, I'm ordering you to let them go." She said confidently.
Ordering? What the heck?

"I'm sorry Dria but your 'daddy' told us only to obey the anti-christ while he's gone so I'm afraid your orders mean nothing." Crater shakes his head.

The blood is still draining from my slit wrist and I'm feeling weaker and weaker by the second. I want to understand what they are talking about but I can barely think. Dria looks uneasy and she mutters under her breath, so quietly that I'm not sure if I heard her right when she said,

"I'm going to regret this."
Next thing I know the world is spinning and I'm losing consciousness.

Dayton kneels over Aurora's body in a panic. Dria and Bokim stand and watch silently as Dayton pulls his shirt over his head and begins tearing it into long strips. He quickly ties them around Aurora's bleeding wrist. She is losing too much blood.

"She should be healing! Why isn't she healing?!" He yells at no one in particular. Dria doesn't say a word, Bokim on the other hand decides to state the obvious.

"It's a pretty deep wound."
Dayton punches the ground beside him. "It should still heal!" He says frantically.

"It will but it will take time." Bokim tries to encourage him but they both know if the bleeding doesn't stop it won't matter.
Dayton's shoulders slump forward and he sits beside Aurora looking defeated. Dria looks at him as if he's lost his mind, but at the moment he doesn't even care. The only thing that matters is Aurora.

"Why did Crater want her blood anyways?" Dria asks thoughtfully.

"That's a good question." Bokim nods.

"I don't know," Dayton says softly as he gazes at Aurora's limp form, "but I do know one thing, I'll make him pay for this." His hand clenches
into a fist and Dria raises an eyebrow. She's never seen him act like this before. Not even for her.

~Aurora~

"Aurora?" Someone is shaking me. I'm so tired… so weak.

"Aurora, sweetheart, wake up now." It's a woman's voice… I swear I've heard it before.

"Please darling, there's not much time."

The voice is soothing but urgent and so familiar.
I try to force my eyes open, they are so heavy. I manage to open them just a slit and I search for the source of the voice. A few feet beside me I can see the bottom half of a beautiful gown. It's dazzling and also familiar. I've seen this dress before…. But…..

I force my eyes open the rest of the way and shoot up into a sitting position. Which, I might add, was a terrible idea because I am now incredibly dizzy and seeing double. Two lovely dresses, two heads of luscious dark brown hair, and four loving eyes, all of which eventually settled back into one person… my mother.

"Mom?" It came out more as a choked cry than anything and I could already feel the warm tears filling my eyes. Great, more tears. She smiled tenderly and moved toward me to offer her hand. I took it and she helped me up. The moment I was standing I threw my arms around her and hugged her as tight as I could without squeezing her to death… Okay that wasn't the best phrase to use in this particular situation…. even if it is an exaggeration, not meant to be taken literally. I think there's a fancy name for that… hyper… something.

"Mom, am I dead?" I mumble into her shoulder.

She's quiet for a moment and I pull away to look at her expression. She looks sad…. Maybe I am dead.

"No, you're not dead sweetheart…" She says softly.
I let go of her and rub my eyes with my arm.

"Then, is this a vision? Or a dream?" I ask and she shakes her head to both. I frown and think for a moment.

"I'm hallucinating." I'm not sure I meant to say it out loud but I did. My mother's eyes lit up and she actually let out a soft laugh that even managed to make me smile.

"No, you're not quite that crazy yet." She said, still laughing. "Let me explain. Have you ever heard of a place called limbo?"

I don't have to think about it for long. "Isn't that something Catholics believe in? It's supposed to be some kind of in-between right?" I'm confused about what that has to do with anything… she nods.

"Right, but not for humans, like the Catholics believe. Limbo is a place for nephilim. You see, when we die the angel in us wants to disappear but the human in us wants to go to an afterlife. So, for the time being the nephilim ends up in limbo." She pauses to be sure I am following along.

"So that's where you went?" I ask, intrigued.

"Yes, and that is where I will return to after this until the battle of Armageddon is over. Then the angel side will win and I will leave." Her expression once again turned to sorrow and it hurt me to see her this way.

"Is that what will happen to me when I die?" I didn't want to ask but I had to. The question had been burning inside me through most of the conversation.

Her expression changed again, this time to one of shock.

"Do not even think of that!" She yelled. Her tone startled me and my face must have shown it because then her voice softened and she tucked my hair behind my ear.

"You shouldn't worry about things like that. You are so strong and so brave and I am so very proud of you. You are a survivor and you need not fear death." She kisses my forehead and I find myself wanting to cry again. I don't though; I hold it in, even when she looks behind me and informs me it's time for her to go.

I give her another hug, knowing it will be the last, and after that she disappeared. I suddenly become aware of a presence behind me and I turn around quickly, anticipating trouble. The figure standing behind me is none other than Adriel, the angel of death. Well, after that interesting conversation with my mom about death, this is a tad bit awkward....

"Aurora, daughter of Bokim and Shaphir, the time has come." Adriel says, although I can't tell if he said it aloud or in my head. I frown.

"The time has come for what?" Oh my gosh! I. am. going. to. die. He's here to take me! My mother said not to fear death, but that's easier to agree to when it's not staring you in the face!

"For you to choose."

~**Aurora**~

"She's fine! I swear you are acting absolutely ridiculous!"

When I come to I see Dayton pacing back and forth….. shirtless? Dria, it seems, is the source of all the yelling. She glances in my direction and points.

"See?" She puts on a triumphant expression and Dayton spins toward me. Upon seeing me, struggling to sit up, he rushes to me.

"Aurora! Are you okay?" He puts a hand on my back and helps me to my feet.

"I'm fine…" I assure him. I find myself unable to resist staring at his bare chest and I can feel the heat rise in my cheeks. Dria, nearby, rolls her eyes but I can see flames leaping behind them.

"How's your wrist?" Dayton gestures toward my hand and I look down. It's been wrapped up in cloth. That explains why Dayton's shirt is missing. I untwist the bloody strips and let them fall to the ground, revealing my bloody arm. Blood, but no cut…

"I guess it healed…" At those words Dayton looked relieved. My father, who has mysteriously appeared, has a very different expression.

"How? I had estimated such a cut would not heal for another half hour in your condition…" He seems both amazed and suspicious.

Well, I have an idea. I decide this is perhaps as good a time as any to tell them. So instead of answering him, I release my wings. The moment I did all three of their mouths dropped. Dria, however, was the first to close hers and feign disinterest.
I could tell she hoped I hadn't noticed, but I had and I couldn't help but grin. Dayton smiles and pulls me in for a hug.

"Congratulations!" He says into my ear, but not quiet enough. Dria's look of disinterest suddenly turns to one of complete disgust. He releases me and my dad nods.

"You did the right thing." He says softly.

I smile and suddenly wish I had a mirror. I know what they are seeing, but I wish I could see them for myself. My gray wings are now pure white. White as snow.

~Dria~

Wow, things just keep getting better and better don't they? Dria is practically seething with anger at this point. Watching Dayton pacing like a caged animal had been bad enough but then the girl had to go and wake up.

So what if her little scratch healed? That's what cuts do! Especially given the fact that she's some kinda super powerful triquarterling or whatever. So Dayton and Bokim are quaking at that and little miss show off decides to go ahead and bust out her perfect little white wings.

It's at the moment that Dria realizes two things. One: she hates Aurora with everything in her. And two: she envies Aurora. As much as she hates to admit it, Dria envies Aurora because Aurora has both God's favor and Dayton's heart. Both of which used to belong to Dria.

Now what does Dria have? A seat reserved for her in the lake of fire. Yep, right next to dear old Lucifer himself. And after the stunt she pulled today she probably won't even have that anymore. And so far she hasn't heard one thank you from any of these three idiots she just saved.

"Bokim, is it safe to go back or not?" Dria asks in a vicious tone.
Bokim nods and Aurora suddenly looks around, confused, before asking,

"Go back? Where are we? How'd we get away?" Dria smiles, pleased to know more than the girl.

"Alternate dimension. Remember your skateboard? Yeah, it's kinda what I do." She flips her hair and transports everyone back to Jabez's house.

~Aurora~

One minute we're in some alternate dimension, which had basically been one big open field, and the next we're back at Jabez's house. I have to admit, Dria's power is pretty awesome, but of course I don't have to admit it out loud.

"So why'd you bring us back here?" I ask nervously.

The little hut gives me the creeps now. Dria's smug grin instantly disappears.

"Really? Not even a thank you for saving your life?" She turns and stomps out the door in a rage.

I suddenly feel slightly quilty… I may not like her but she did save my life… our lives.....
Dayton notices my shocked expression and checks to see if Dria's out of earshot before explaining.

"Dria can only transport people back to the place they left. It makes her power great for hiding but not for running. She's tried to transport to other places but it never works. She gets frustrated by it easily. The only reason your skateboard can reappear other places is because you're out here telling it to. If you were in there with it, and had her power that is, then you could only return it to where it came from."

"Oh…." It's the first thing I can think of to say.

I wonder if I'll ever get to the point where people don't have to explain everything to me. It's like information overload ever since Zantouron first kidnapped me and this all began. I decide to change the subject and ask another question, even though I'm sure it will just lead to another explanation. Oh well.

"So, umm… what did Crater do to Jabez anyway?" I remember when Dayton had asked Crater that... Crater had simply smiled and changed the subject. Dayton, however, had looked as though he knew. I hate to hurt him… I feel like that's all I ever do lately is hurt people, but still, I ask.

Dayton grinds his teeth together in anger.

"Crater's real name is Alvadenon. He got the nickname Crater for two reasons. First, was because when we fell from heaven during the original fall, he landed so hard that he actually made a crater in the Earth." Dayton looked like he was picturing the event even as he said it. I tried imagining it in my mind and I can kinda see it I guess… Dayton's voice comes out in almost a growl as he continues.

"And secondly, for his power. He can suck out all your memories, leaving a crater in your mind. All he has to do is hold you down, look you in the eye, steal your memories, and as soon as he's done, well, I don't know anyone who has ever lived through it…." His voice trails off and the last line hangs in the air.

"I'm sorry…" I mutter, understanding that this must be what Crater had done to Dayton's friend. I want to step forward and comfort him but before I can do anything he sighs and heads toward the curtain door.

"We should get out of here." He says as he pushes the curtain aside and disappears beyond it.

My dad must have slipped out at some point too. I take one final look around the room before exiting myself.

I step out into the cool night air. It's later than I'd expected but I don't mind the dark. I'm just glad to be out in the open again. Honestly, I think I'm becoming claustrophobic. I like being outside where I can fly away at the first sign of danger. It may sound cowardly but I just feel more secure this way.

"So what now?" I ask as I walk up to the others.

"Now," Dayton says in a serious tone, "I'm going to send word to Michael and Gabriel. We need to call an emergency meeting right away.

There's an old wheat barn not far from here, and I'll tell Michael and

Gabriel to meet us there as soon as they can. Let's go."

He plucks a feather from his wings and lets it go. Dria gives a fake yawn and a small stretch.

"Yeah, you guys have fun. I'm gonna find some place to hit the hay." She starts to turn but Dayton reaches out and grabs her hand.

"You need to be there too." He says.

He still has a hold of her hand and I know my face is going red. Dria notices my face and a slow smile glides across hers.

"Whatever you say babe," she pulls her hand from his and places it on her hip, "lead the way."

I'm so angry I can't even think straight! Babe? What the heck is wrong with her?! Dayton looks a bit uncomfortable but only for a second. Then he points over to the East.

"The barn's this way. Follow me." He turns and walks off toward the barn and we hesitate only a second before falling in step behind him.

Michael and Gabriel step out of the shadows as we arrive. They must have been here for some time already. Of course, that would make sense considering they were only a transport away.

"Michael!" I rush over to him and wrap my arms around him. His body immediately stiffens and I decide to stop torturing him and step away. He clears his throat and nods at me.

"Good to see you Aurora."
It is good to see him again. It's been a while, I mean, I know he's been busy but I did really miss him. I say hi to Gabriel and then the meeting officially begins.

"What is so important Dayton?" Michael only looks slightly concerned.
He mostly just appears annoyed. He still isn't on the best of terms with Dayton and he keeps giving him some really irritated looks. Though the looks Michael is giving Dayton have nothing on those he's shooting at Dria. It appears Michael dislikes Dria about as much as I do. Dria grins back and blows a kiss in Michael's direction. The shocked and disgusted look on Michael's face would have been comical under different circumstances. However, in this particular moment I think I'm probably making the same face he is.

Dayton recounts the events of the last couple days and my dad occasionally adds something or elaborates a bit. Dria and I are never even addressed. I begin to feel unnecessary. Dria apparently had the same idea because she wanders off and finds a pile of hay to rest by. She settles in and makes herself comfortable and watches the others talk for a while. But eventually her attention turns towards me.

She looks at me with a strange look in her eye, almost as if she's sizing me up. A chill races down my spine and it's all I can do not to physically shiver. But I refuse to give her that satisfaction. I glance over at Dayton and the others to find they are still engrossed in conversation.

So I decide now is as good a time as any to confront Dria. I'm not sure how she'll respond to my coming over and sitting by her. I figured she'd at least be a bit taken aback but unfortunately no such luck. She doesn't seem surprised at all, in fact, she almost seems pleased…

My mouth twists into a nervous frown. The look in her eyes almost makes me wonder if I'm doing exactly what she wants me to. I take a seat on the floor next to her but I'm quiet for a minute. How exactly do I even start this conversation? Should I just be straight forward and say 'stay away from my boyfriend'? I hardly think that would work… I'm trying to decide how to word it when Dria breaks the silence.

"He still loves me you know." Her sudden proclamation both startles and angers me at the same time. I almost can't believe what I just heard and I'm sure I must have heard wrong.

"What?!"

"Oh, don't get the wrong idea sweetheart. He loves you. There's no denying that. But he still has feelings for me, even if they aren't as strong as those he has for you."

I'm not really sure how to respond to that. On the one hand she's saying he loves me most, but on the other hand, she's saying I only have part of his heart… I want to be mad… I want to deny every word of it. The problem is that she's telling the truth, or at least she believes what she's saying enough to fool my lie detecting powers. And yet, I can't just accept that. I can't.

"Maybe he loved you once but he's light now and you're still dark. I'm sure his feelings have changed." I wanted it to be a strike, I wanted to hurt her, but instead of sounding confident I sounded more like I was trying to convince myself than her.

She sighs and wraps her arms around her knees.

"You're right. I am dark. Do you know why I chose dark?" The question makes me somewhat suspicious but my curiosity gets the best of me.

"Why?"

She rests her chin on her arms and fixes her eyes on Dayton.

"I chose dark for him." She says it softly and I don't know what to say. I sit quietly trying to process it but she continues with a small laugh.

"Not that he appreciated it. He never told me how he felt about my choice. I literally sold my soul to the devil to be with him and he didn't even seem to care."

A single tear glistens down her cheek and drips onto her arm. I'm once again speechless and I almost feel sorry for her. She suddenly lifts her head, rubs her face dry, and flips her hair back before putting on that daring smile she's worn almost since I met her. Anyone who wasn't a part of the previous conversation, like I was, would never be able to tell that anything had been wrong with Dria at all. She covers up weakness better than anyone I've ever met. I'm actually a bit impressed by how easily she can hide her true feelings. Sometimes I wish I had that ability…

"But now I'm back from the dead sweetheart and Romeo there doesn't know what to think. You may have him right now but that doesn't matter to me. I'm pulling out all the stops. You're not so bad but we are not friends and as far as I'm concerned Dayton is a prize we're both playing for. That makes us rivals. I'm not a loser either honey. So I'd suggest you just stay out of my way."

Dria stands up and dusts herself off as I stare open mouthed at her in utter shock. So much for poor broken girl. She's evil to the core and I'm not letting her have Dayton! I start to go off on her but before I can get one word out she walks off towards the others without a final glance. I leap up and follow after her. She slides in between Dayton and my father so I move around to Dayton's other side, next to Michael. I shoot a glare in her direction but by this point she's completely ignoring me and listening in on the conversation.

Dayton sighs dramatically and shakes his head.

"That's great but we still don't know anything about that mystery kid he has."
Mystery kid? I have no idea what they are talking about… However, the same can't be said for Dria apparently.

"You mean Vadim." She says correctively and the others all spin towards her. They look like they've just been slapped across the face. I'm suddenly feeling very left out of the loop and I start to ask who Vadim is but I'm interrupted by Michael.

"You know of this child they speak of?" He steps towards her just an inch and she almost seems to recoil a bit. I wonder if I simply imagined it… But then, it would make sense. Good and Evil are like the opposite ends of a magnet; they tend to repel from one another. Michael seems too determined to get answers to notice or care though.

"Tell us what you know!" He insists and Dria snarls her lip at him.

"Fine, I'll tell you, gosh. Just back out of my bubble Ark." She's looking at Michael like he's something sticky on the bottom of her shoe. She hasn't even looked at me like that before… Wow, she seriously hates him…

"He's nephilim, obviously, but when he was born, and his human mother died during childbirth, he had no other family. His father, being a demon, gave the kid to some scientific research facility in Russia. They experimented on him and engrafted several different unknown serums into his DNA." She states it all so matter of factly but I suddenly feel queasy.

"That's horrible!" I exclaim, mouth agape. Dria rolls her eyes and continues her tale.

"The serums had a strange effect. They brought out some of his lesser powers early, at age two. Satan took an interest in the boy and had him removed from the lab before destroying it completely and killing those that worked there. He had the child's father drop the kid off with a family of atheists nearby. The family took him in and raised him as their own, not knowing anything about the boy's real identity. Satan has had demons guarding Vadim ever since. He said the kids' powers are unique and he plans to use them during the tribulation. But he never told anyone what for as far as I am aware." She shrugs as she finishes, as if to inform us that we won't be getting any more info than that out of her.

The others are quiet for a moment but Michael finally speaks up.

"That is impossible. You surely must be lying."

"No Michael," I sigh and shake my head, "I'm afraid she's not."

The Archangel turns to me and looks as if he's about to question me but then seems to remember my gift and goes silent before turning his attention back to Dria.

"How can that be?" He mutters softly, "We would have seen." His frown deepens and Gabriel rests a hand on his shoulder.

"If it was all taking place in the company of demons and atheists then it would not have been our jurisdiction, my brother. Satan could have easily hidden such a thing if he did so at the right time and with the right distractions in place." Gabriel is not usually a big talker but I think he's probably the wisest of us. He's definitely the brains while Michael is the brawns.

"How old is the child now?" Michael tries to move the conversation along. Probably frustrated knowing they had been blind to this scheme.

"Last I heard he's seven now and his powers are almost fully developed. The only thing missing is his wings." Dria actually sounds impressed as she discusses the boy's progress.

Everyone had seemed so interested in me when I got my powers at 17… I can only imagine the attention this kid got or is going to get…

I decide to take this time to offer my opinion for once.

"Well if this kid is so important to Satan don't you think we…" Unfortunately my moment is stopped mid sentence when I suddenly slump to the floor with a scarring headache before, as usual, passing out.
I could hear shouts of alarm ring out around me as I fell into darkness. But soon all of that was gone and the darkness was replaced by images of swirling color.

'Well,' I think, 'what does the future hold this time…'

Darkness. All around me there is darkness. The sky is black and a terrible thunderstorm is raging as far as the eye can see. I watch myself below, as if I'm having some kind of futuristic out of body experience. Of course, that's how all of my visions seem. The me down below is hiding around the edge of a building, crouching next to Dayton. Both Dayton and I peer around the corner cautiously and watch three figures standing huddled together. One of them is Crater, there's no doubt about that. The next is a small child, a boy… probably the one Dria told us about. And the last being below I recognize instantly from what I had seen on tv back at my moms palace. It's the Anti-Christ.

The boy is holding onto a small metallic object… a gun. The gun! Dayton suddenly cries out in alarm, spins around, and pulls me towards him. He holds me in a tight protective grip as the world begins to shake. There's a great explosion of light and I can't see anything. I can hear a loud, methodic ringing in my ears as everything goes black…

I expect to wake up. Isn't that how it's supposed to work? I have the vision, then I wake up. But instead, the images come back, moving in reverse as if being rewound on a dvd player. then the scene starts over and plays through a second time. My first thought is 'well this is different' but after the fourth time… I begin to wonder…

'Will I ever wake up again?'

Book Three: Armageddon

~ **The False Prophet** ~

Crater marches into the Antichrist office confidently. The beast watches him curiously.

"Did you retrieve it?"

Crater says nothing but he places the vial of blood on the desk before him. The Antichrist grins and picks up the vial, studying its contents.

"And the child?"

This time Crater answers, "Taken care of. He is in a room down the hall."

"Perfect. You have done quite well. That is why you shall be my false prophet from this moment on." The Antichrist pauses, obviously to let his words sink in, then continues, "Do not make me regret this decision."

Crater gives a short nod and says, "You won't." It's a known fact that there will be only one false prophet under the Antichrist rule. This means Crater is now irreplaceable. He can't help but smile at the thought.

The beast suddenly looks serious and Crater's smile disappears, He waits silently for orders.

"As for your next assignment, Alvadenon, I need you to disrupt the balance of nature."

After a moment of thought Crater asks softly, "Which element?"

"All of them."

At that Crater almost laughed, that is until he saw the beast's face and knew he was serious. In his head Crater was thinking 'You're crazy!' But from his mouth came the words, "Which should I start with first?"

~ Dayton ~

"Does she do this often?" Daria moans, annoyed.

Michael shoots her a look and she backs off. Dayton picks up Aurora and gently pushes her hair aside. He always feels so useless when she has visions.

"We need to find some place to rest for the night. And something for her to eat…" he sighs.

"Me too, I'm starving!" Dria groans, holding her stomach and slumping back against a wooden pillar, seemingly in pain. The others ignore her as they discuss a place to stay.

"There is an elderly woman that lives nearby. She is strong in the faith and often hosts weary travelers." Gabriel suggests hopefully.

Michael nods in agreement, "that is our best option at this point."

Dria looks confused and makes her way over towards them again. "Hold up. If she's so good in the faith then why wasn't she taken up in the rapture?"

Gabriel and Michael share a look before Michael answers. "That is a good question, you see, she has always struggled with doubt and sometimes her doubt overran her faith. It took her missing the rapture to realize she had slipped away."

"Okay, whatever you say. So lead the way Ark. I've got to get some food in me or I'm going to die!" Dria gestures to the door and Michael gives a soft grunt before exiting.

"I am afraid I must return to heaven." Gabriel begins reluctantly, "If you require my assistance you know how to reach me. I will wait for your contact."

Dayton nods in response then follows Dria, Bokim, and Michael outside. He holds Aurora firmly, yet gently, as they make their way, on foot, to the old woman's home. They can't exactly land on the front lawn wings and all... The poor old lady would have a heart attack!

It's about 10 minutes later when they arrive at a little wooden house with a few pots of wilted flowers set out in front of the door. Michael starts to knock but pauses and glances back at Bokim and Dria.

"Behave." was all he said to them before knocking on the door. A light came on behind the door and it slowly cracked open just an inch. A little silvery-haired lady peered through the crack cautiously. Dayton could see the fear in the poor woman's eyes and he couldn't help but pity her.

They had agreed that Michael should do the talking partly because he gives off such a heavenly essence and partly because his face isn't plastered on every wanted poster across the country.

"Excuse us for bothering you ma'am, but you see we are very tired and hungry and have nowhere else to go. Someone mentioned that you are a very kind lady and we humbly ask of you refuge for the night." Michael actually sounded convincing. Dayton couldn't help but grin and surprise.

She studies Michael, obviously I'm sure whether to trust him or not. Her eyes drift past him and land on Dayton. She looks at Aurora in his arms and her eyes grow wide. There's no doubt in Dayton's mind that this lady recognizes them. He expects the door to slam shut and he tenses up as he awaits the coming thuds. But it never comes. Instead, the woman opens the door and ushers them inside.

"Quickly! Quickly now!" She hurries them in and locks the door behind them.

"Thank you so much." Dayton says as she turns back around to face them.

"You all are the bunch that Talbot devil is after aren't you?" She questions curiously. Dayton nods solemnly and the little old lady smiles.

"Well, in that case, welcome to my humble little home. If that bloody beast is after you then you must be all right. My name is Anna. What are your names?"

Michael steps forward and offers his hand. "I am Michael. It is surely a pleasure Ms. Anna."

Anna takes Michael's hand in hers and pats it gently with her other.
"What a nice young man!" She exclaims and Michael's face contorts. Dria can't contain herself and cracks up laughing. Anna turns towards her.

"And you are?" She asks accusingly.

Dria instantly stops laughing and says, "I'm Dria, sup?" She flips her hair and hardly looks at Anna at all as she speaks to her. It's apparent from the look on Anna's face that she and Dria are not going to get along very well.

Bokim then smiles and steps forward. "My name is Bokim. It is lovely to meet you."

And his eyes fill with pity as she replies, "Bokim? My, what a sad name…"

"So I am told." Bokim nods and Anna moves on to Dayton.

"Hello, I'm Dayton, and this is Aurora." He nods down towards his unconscious girlfriend in his arms.

"Oh, the poor dear! She looks absolutely exhausted!"

"Um... Yeah," Dayton frowns, "She hasn't gotten much sleep the last few days…"

It is sort of true but obviously Anna doesn't know Aurora is not sleeping. It probably would not be a good idea to correct her though... Or there would be a lot of explanations going on tonight.

"Here, follow me," Anna insists, "let's find you all a place to sleep."

She leads them to a small guest room, the only extra room in the house. "The two ladies can share this room. One of them may have to sleep on the floor. I'll go fetch some quilts."

Dayton watches Anna leave the room then places Aurora gently on the bed. Dria raises an eyebrow and Dayton half expects her to complain about not being the one to get the bed. However, to his surprise she bites her tongue. Bokim peers at Dria nervously, certainly thinking the same thing Dayton is. But out of the three of them it's Michael that says it out loud.

"Dria I understand you and Aurora are not exactly the best at friends so I would suggest just ignoring one another. I do not want to have you starting trouble while we are here."

Dria's mouth falls open and she puts on a glow of false innocence. "Why
I have no idea what you're talking about Ark."

Everyone ignores her sarcasm and Anna then rushes back in with an arm full of homemade quilts. She hands Dria a light blue one and a small square pillow. Dria looks at it in shock and starts to protest but Bokim notices and clears his throat. Anna turns towards them and hands each of the guys a quilt of their own.

"You young men can sleep in the living area. One can have the couch the other two will have to make do on the floor. Sorry it's not more." She says but Dayton just smiles and assures her that it's perfect. Michael and Bokim follow Anna out of the girls room but Dayton hesitates a moment.

He walks back over towards the bed and places a kiss on Aurora's forehead before turning to leave. Dria is clenching her teeth angrily. She's trying to look as though she hadn't noticed Dayton kiss Aurora but her face is red with anger. For a brief moment Dayton regrets having done it while Dria was in the room. He is by no means trying to hurt her. Dayton sighs as he exits the room, all he ever does is hurt people these days it seems…

~ Dria ~

"Oh the trouble I could cause…" Dria states as she stands over the bed watching Aurora, who as far as Dria can tell, is still unconscious. Dria suddenly morphs herself into an exact copy of Aurora, a skill only Dayton and the devil himself knows she possesses. She glances at her reflection on the windows glass and thinks to herself.

'It would be so freaking easy to sneak into the living room, wake up Dayton, and…'

Dria sighs and shifts back into her normal self again. She is by no means soft hearted and the idea of tricking Dayton into kissing her doesn't bother her at all as far as the ethics of it go. However, even if it did work, and Dayton didn't figure it out, he still technically wouldn't be kissing her anyway. He would be kissing Aurora. Because when you love someone you kiss them with your heart, not just your lips.

Dayton's heart no longer belongs to her. Tricking him would be pointless because the kiss would mean nothing towards her. She could always just leave... She stares out the window and ponders this idea moment. No, she can't leave, if there's even the slightest chance that he could ever love her again then she has to stay.

She snarls at Aurora's limp, pathetic, form on the bed. This girl may be
3/4 angel but she is not immortal. Dria is so obviously superior to Aurora. But it seems Aurora has everything Dria could ever want. With every passing moment Dria hates her more and with every moment she envies her more.

"Sleep tight, Princess." She growls before laying down on the floor across the room and dozing off.

Much to his surprise, Dayton noticed that Michael had stayed with them all night. He had expected him to transport back once Anna fell asleep but he hadn't. Of course, he hadn't slept, but he had stayed. Dayton, on the other hand, had slept. Another surprise. He had not planned to sleep that night, in fact, he had planned to stay awake in case Aurora came to and needed him. Yet somehow he had dozed off.

Of course, it's not like staying up would have done him any good anyways because now it's 6:30 in the morning and Aurora is still out cold. She's been unconscious for the past 8 and 1/2 hours and Dayton is starting to get somewhat anxious. The longest she's ever been out for a vision is 5 hours.

He thinks back to the first time she'd ever passed out. It had been just after she'd saved him in hell and she had passed out from exhaustion and the cuts on her palms. She had been out 18 hours that time but that wasn't for a vision. Dayton knows he needs to stay calm, for Anna's sake at the very least.

The living room and kitchen are the same room and Anna is standing not too far from where he's sitting on the couch. She is leaning over a small stove and suddenly announces that she has made breakfast. Dria walks in yawning and reaches past Anna toward the pastries Anna has just made. Anna sweats her hand away and scolds her.

"You don't eat until everyone's here!"

Dria Looks shocked and turns to Dayton and speaks into his head.

'Tell this old bat she's crazy! I need to eat and there's no telling when sleeping beauty will rise!'

It's weird for him. Dayton hasn't had anyone mind speak to him other than Aurora in nearly a century... Especially not Dria...

"Um…" Dayton starts, trying to think of an excuse for Anna to let Drea eat, "It's all right Anna, you know what... I'm not hungry so she can go ahead and eat and there will be plenty."

Anna shakes her head stubbornly. "Oh no sir. Breakfast is the most important meal of the day! Why don't you go try to wake that girl up then come eat."

Dayton sighs and heads towards Aurora's room, even though it will do no good. He hasn't quite reached the door yet when Dria suddenly yells in alarm.

"What the hell?!"

Dayton spends around just in time to see Anna Dria on the butt with a rolling pin.

"Youch!" Dria is more embarrassed than hurt and she yells at Anna,
"What the heck was that for?"

Anna crosses her arms and scolds Dria. "What's your mouth young lady!"

By this point Dayton, along with Bokim and even Michael, is doubled over laughing hysterically. Dria's Face turns a dark shade of pink.

"Shut up and look out the freaking window!" She demands hostility.

They stop laughing and march over to the window she's next to. Anna steps up behind them as they pure out the slightly fogged glass. Outside it is raining, but there's something wrong with this rain. The rain is falling up!

"Oh my stars…" Anna mumbles as they watch the rain. There's not a closed mouth in the room and not a one of them can pull their gaze from outside.

That is until a voice behind them suddenly asks in a shaky tone, "What's everyone staring at?"

All five of them jump, startled by the break in the silence. Dayton spins on his heel and rushes towards Aurora, embracing her tenderly. She grabs hold of his shirt and lays her hand against his chest as he wraps his arms lovingly around her.

"Are you all right?" He was first in her ear. Her body trembles lately against his and he notices she's breathing heavily.

"What happened?" He asks softly so no one else can hear. She replies in his head rather than out loud.

'I was so scared… I thought I'd never wake up again. The vision just kept replaying and replaying. I can't do that again... I just can't.'

He can feel her warm tear soaking through the shirt and I'll let him from her belated husband's drawer.

"It's okay. You're all right. I'm here." He holds her tighter and tries to comfort her but her words trouble him. What if she hadn't woken back up?

Anna steps forward and lightly touches Aurora's shoulder. "What's wrong honey?"

Aurora slowly pulls away from Dayton and wipes her eyes. She looks at Anna with confusion and Dayton realizes that she doesn't know who Anna is.

"Aurora this is Anna," He introduces her and then addresses Anna, "She had a nightmare. I think we've all had a few of them lately."

It's a lie, angels and demons don't sleep very often and when they do they don't dream. He hates to lie to Anna but it earns Aurora a sympathetic look and it ends the conversation. So it was sadly necessary. Aurora gives him a grateful look and Anna insists that they sit to eat.

They start to take their seats and Dria looks at Aurora and asks, "So, your 'nightmare' didn't happen to include any upside down rain by any chance, did it?"

She said it in a smart alecky tone but the guys turned to Aurora, awaiting her response. Her brow wrinkles and she asks, "upside down the rain?
What?"

Dayton ushers me over to the window and I peek out it uncertainly. It almost appears as if the rain is coming up from the ground and floating up into the sky. I back away from the window slowly, unsure what to think of this. At this point there isn't much that can surprise me but this is... Well, supernatural. I shake my head and turn back to the group.

"No, that definitely was not in my… Um… dream. Michael, what do you think it means?"

Anna gazes at Michael curiously, no doubt wondering how this young man expects to answer such a question. Michael glances towards Anna and sighs. He must have decided that there's no point in skating around her any longer because he answers the question.

"It means something's very wrong. The balance of nature has been disrupted."

Anna narrows her eyes, "Oh nonsense!" She exclaims with a wave of her hand, "I don't tolerate negative thinking around here. Toms are hard enough without thinking that everything that happens is a sign of doom."

I'll look around the room and wait for someone to respond to Anna's little pep talk. The silence drags on and I begin to wonder if anyone will. Did they ever plan on telling her who we really are? Michael, unfortunately, reads my mind and responds in mind speak.

'I would like not to, however, it seems we may have to.' When I don't respond Michael sighs again and turns to Anna.

"Ma'am, I wish I were only being negative... But sadly I am quite serious. I believe it's time that you know a bit more about your house guests."

The old lady looks around the table but no one else has a word. I would think it's probably best that Michael explains this... Cuz I sure have no idea how to do it!

He continues, "You see Miss Anna, we are not your ordinary travelers.
We are... Well…" now it seems that Michael is having a hard time deciding how to tell her himself.

Dria, being extremely impatient, decides to take matters into her own hands. "What he's trying to choke out is that he's an angel."

Everyone's heads whip around to face her in shock. Anna goes deathly silent and I can only imagine what she might be thinking. I'm sure she doesn't believe her, and maybe she thinks Dria is crazy, But none of us deny the exclamation. So if she does think Dria has lost her mind, she must be considering mass hysteria by now.

Michael reaches to place a hand on Anna's arm but she falls away. She still won't say a word, she just stares at Michael with suspicion in her eyes. Michael sighs and slowly stands to his feet, unfurling his wings inch by inch behind him. As they appear Anna's eyes go wide and once they are completely showing, Anna begins muttering a prayer beneath her breath. She looks somewhat terrified but maintains her composure pretty well.

"I do apologize. I had no intention of frightening you, however, I felt it was necessary for you to know." Michael says it softly and there's a long silence before Anna finally responds.

"Are you all angels?"

Dayton answers this time. "Michael is the archangel of the Bible. I am a warrior angel. Aurora is a nephilim of light."

Our hostess looks at me curiously for a moment. "You are a child of human and angel?"

I make a face and shift uncomfortably, "Well… um… Not exactly. My mother was also nephilim." I glance over to Bokim, "and Bokim is my father." I decided not to say anymore on the subject. But it doesn't matter because then she nods and turns to my father.

"And you're an angel also then?" My dad's face goes red and he runs his fingers through his hair, obviously uncomfortable with the question. Dayton notices and takes it upon himself to explain.

"Um, I'm afraid that Bokim is not exactly an angel of sorts... He is... One of the fallen."

Anna's face contorts in what I can only assume is fear before she exclaims, "You're a demon?!" Her voice catches on the word and Dayton comes to the rescue once again.

"Yes, he's a demon. However, not all of the fallen are as evil as the demons you have been taught about. Bokim has been helping us on our quest."

Anna swallows but nods in acceptance, "I suppose it's not for me to understand the workings of the spiritual realm," She then turns to face Dria, "let me guess, your demon too?"

Dria grins, "nope. I'm a nephilim, just like Aurora."

I frown and jump in to clarify that statement, "Only I am a nephilim of Light and you're a nephilim of dark!" My announcement does not seem to shock Anna in the least bit.

She puts on a satisfied look, "I knew there was something about you I didn't care much for." She shakes her head and Dayton gives a small smile.

We take the next little while to explain everything that's happened so far and Anna is completely entranced by the tail. After that Michael sends a message to Gabriel and a moment later he appears in the living room with us. The reaction Anna has is absolutely hilarious. It's like she's meeting a childhood hero for the first time. She goes all fan girl on Gabe. After she finally calms down we are able to start our little meeting. Turns out, Gabriel's already aware of the rain and he knows the reason.

"Crater has killed the cherub from the first of the four corners of the earth and destroyed the wheel of the element of water." His expression is very serious and Michael looks more than concerned as he thinks it over.

Anna is the first to react to this, "The what of the what?" She pretty much spoke out loud the very thing I was thinking. I'm just glad I'm not the one having to ask this time. Gabriel explains further...

"There are four elements of nature. Water, earth, fire, and air. They are kept in balance by their guardians, the chair of angels. The Bible describes the cherubs as having four heads, many eyes, and a wheel that goes with them wherever they go. What isn't recorded though, is that in each of the cherubs wheels there is a power source for one of the four elements. The cherubs stand at each of the four corners of the earth and guard their particular element with their lives. It is nearly impossible to kill a cherub…"

At this point Michael takes over for Gabriel and finishes the explanation. "And that is precisely why they were instructed with the elements. Crater must have used the gun to do it because I can think of nothing else that can kill a cherub. The fact that he has waited so long to do this must mean it's part of the Antichrist's plan for Aurora's blood and the boy. Vadim. I only wish we knew exactly what he was planning…" Michael throws off thoughtfully and Gabriel frowns.

"Brother, I do not suspect he shall stop with water. If my suspicions are correct Crater will kill all four cherubs."

Michael raises an eyebrow and stands to his feet. "Then we must go to the chair of Earth immediately!"

Dayton, my dad, and I all stand and after a string of complaints, Dria finally follows. Gabriel turns to the elderly woman as the rest of us prepare to leave. "You will no longer be safe here. I have orders to return to heaven with you. It is your reward for opening your home to my friends." Gabriel offers her his hand and Anna cries tears of joy as the two transport to heaven.

"Umm… Michael?" He turns towards me as my question forms on my lips, "how do you know that Crater will kill them in order?" As soon as I've asked it he stops in his tracks and frowns thoughtfully.

"You are correct. We will need to split up. Bokim and Dria, The two of you head to the second corner and stay with the Earth cherub. Dayton, you and Aurora head to the cherub of fire in the third corner region. I will make my way to the fourth to warn the cherub of wind and air."

We all nod in order to show that we've understood our assignment before flying off in different directions. I have no idea where the third corner is located but I assume Dayton does.

"So, where exactly are we heading?"

"Cape Horn. South America." He responds.

Well, I guess the other day wasn't the last time I'd be crossing the ocean after all…

~ Bokim ~

"Remind me again why it is that we care if these freaky looking angels die?"

Dria's unruly remarks are officially driving Bokum up the wall. He has been trying to ignore her as much as possible but it's become more and more difficult since they landed in Sweden. And despite his refusal to answer her nagging questions she continues to ask on.

"Seriously! Why should we care? Whatever it is that the Antichrist is planning, I'm sure that its success will only stand to benefit us in some way. Like it or not we kinda are on his side you know…"

This would be a very good point if Bokim only had himself in mind. However, that's not the case, and never has been.

He sighs, "Dria, whatever he is planning may benefit you and I but it will surely hurt my daughter." Bokim notices her look of indifference and adds, "and Dayton as well."

Her face drops briefly before she sighs an annoyance. That had gotten through to her. "Whatever, fine. Let's go save this stupid cherub."

Bokim nods as they approach the dome. It is hidden from the human eye and can only be opened by an angelic being.

"I'm assuming you know how to get into this thing right?" Dria raises an eyebrow and he steps forward and places his hands on the side of the clear force field.

"Well, I'm a bit out of practice but I can definitely try."

We are still a ways out to see but it's not hard to tell we are too late. Blaming boulders sell through the air, escaping from massive volcanoes that may or may not have already been around the edges of Cape Horn. People are running for their lives with nowhere to go but into the ocean. Dayton and I take in the horrible scene before leaking into action. It's obvious there will be no stopping the volcano but we can at least save some lives.

We swoop down, grabbing as many people as we can and flying them as far away as possible before going back for more. They're screaming continues as we fly them through the air and I wonder if they are still screaming because of the volcano or if they are screaming because of us. I suppose we hadn't really thought about the fact that we would be seen, the only thought I had was that we had to do something...

The volcano rages on and won't let up, and honestly I don't think it ever will. But we managed to get all the people to safety, well all the ones that were there when we arrived. Who's to know the casualties before we intervened? I look down at the soot covered faces of the people we just saved and I watch as they cry and embrace one another. They don't know
Christ or they wouldn't be here…

Dayton tries to pull me away from the scene. "We have to go…" He tries to insist but I refuse.

I land in front of the crowd below and they all go silent and watch me closely, unsure how to react. I start to say something but stop myself, realizing that I have no idea what language they speak. One of the women in the crowd steps forward and chokes out a thank you in her native tongue. My angel receptor automatically translated so I still have no idea what language it was to begin with.

My gauge drifts over the crowd and then turns back to Dayton, just behind me. He answers me before I even ask.
"They speak Portuguese."

The smile on my face serves as my thank you before I turn back to the group. Of course I, as a human, don't speak Portuguese. However, my angel side does. In the end it takes me about 20 minutes to give a very very short explanation of Christ and the rapture to the crowd. When I'm finished the water works start up again. I want to stick around a while and tell them more, I want to lead them in the sinner's prayer, and see the joy on their faces as they accept Christ's love. However, unfortunately, it's about that time when Gabriel shows up...

There's a blinding flash and the crowd of people screams, I try to yell to them and calm them but it's no use. Gabriel appears and a woman, not the same one that thanks me, thanks into the arms of a man I assume is her husband. The first two angels don't bother you but the third one shows up and then you pass out? Well, I guess I shouldn't really be the one to talk…

He is not one to cry, not to say he doesn't because he certainly has, but tears are few and far between for Gabriel. Come to think of it, Gabriel cries even less than Michael does. But the scene he has come upon nearly brings a tear to his eye. If only Shaphir could see her daughter now. Aurora has not only just led many people to Christ but she has done so under extreme circumstances and during a time when God has removed his hand from the Earth.

Gabriel raises an eyebrow as a woman nearby faints at the side of him. It is not the first time it has happened but it still always manages to catch him off guard.

"Fear not," his voice thunders out to them and a man in the group thanks us as well. Gabriel sighs and turns to Aurora and Dayton. Dayton is trying hard to control himself and keep from bursting into laughter.
Apparently humans passing out at the side of an angel is amusing to him. Aurora, on the other hand, looks shocked by the unconscious bodies behind him.

"They'll be fine. I can't begin to tell you how many times that has happened before." Gabriel shakes his head and Aurora snaps out of her trance.

She suddenly looks nervous. "Gabriel, we were too late. How are the others?"

Gabriel sighs, oh yes, he'd nearly forgotten the reason he'd come in the first place. "I'm afraid you two weren't the only ones that were too late. Michael got to Antarctica just as Crater and his crew were fleeing. He tried to chase after them but he lost them along the way. He has no clue where they escaped to but Michael went up to Sweden to wait with Bokim and Dria. Crater still hasn't killed the earth cherub so we assume that is his next target."

That effectively stopped Dayton's laughter. "Then that is where we need to be also." He looks at Aurora as he says it, waiting for her to agree. She frowns and looks past Gabriel to the group of wide-eyed men and women behind him.

"What about them?"

It is a shame things have changed, she would have made a wonderful queen. She doesn't know about the change yet and sadly Gabriel is not at liberty to tell her either.

"They will be fine. I will find someone to help guide them. There are other nephilim of light still in the world that can help teach them until the end arrives. You must go." He holds out his hand pointing in the direction that they should head.

Aurora nods in understanding and takes Dayton's hand as they prepare to take off.

"Oh, and Aurora," Gabriel calls out and she turns back to face him, "Your mother would be so proud."

"So are you in or not?" Crater growls as he asks the other demon for help. He hates that he needs help. Everything was going fine until Michael showed up. If only Zantouron had succeeded in killing the archangel in the first place. That would have made everything go so much easier. Crater still has one more cherub to kill and this one will be guarded now that Michaels caught him in the act.

"What's in it for me?" The dark figure hits his back. Crater despises this particular demon for so many reasons. If he weren't necessary for the plan then he might would just kill him now. Just because they are both demons does not In any way mean they get along, after all, not all humans get along either. Cain and Abel were brothers but, well, they didn't quite see eye to eye now did they?

"If the Antichrist plan succeeds it will tip the scales. You can work out the details for yourself." Crater doesn't bother trying to hide the impatience in his voice.

The other demon doesn't reply for the longest time. Crater scowls and starts to wrap his wings around him to transport back to Earth. For some odd reason hail seems a bit less hot without Satan there. It also feels empty, despite the thousands of demons that roam the fiery halls.

"Wait," The other demon says softly, "I'll do it. Who doesn't enjoy a family reunion?" At that Crater actually manages a smile. That wasn't even a thought in his mind but If that's the other demon's goal then this is going to get very interesting.

"What is this thing?" I stare at the dome before us and I hope that Dayton knows how to open it.

"It's a shield to guard the cherubs. Humans can't see it, so they can't try to open it."

"Did the other cherubs have shields too?"

"Yes, they all have a shield guarding them and their element." Dayton says as he begins to examine the dome's exterior as if searching for something.

"Well, a fat lot of good it did the other cherubs against Crater…"

"Yeah, well, it was built so that anyone that speaks the heavenly language and knows the secret code can enter. Only angels are supposed to have the codes but I'd imagine that Satan had them tucked away."

"Right, well, do you have the code or should we knock and wait for an answer?"
Dayton raises an eyebrow at me, not incredibly thrilled with my sarcasm. He steps forward and places his hands on the clear dome.

From his mouth the angelic language comes forth and he says to the shield,
"Four cherubs, four wheels, amidst one wheel, the Earth revealed." The dome shakes and slowly a watery door appears where Dayton's hands are placed.

"Awesome…" I mutter under my breath, "Hey, so is there a different code for each dome?"

Dayton shrugs, "Not really. The only difference is the part where it says 'The Earth revealed' would be changed based on the element. Like to 'water revealed' or fire or air…" He gestures his hand around in a circle next to his head to emphasize his explanation. Then he opens the door and I follow him through watching as it closes and disappears behind us.

"There they are." Dayton points off ahead of us and I follow his finger.

Michael, my dad, and Dria are all ahead standing next to an unusual figure that I assume is the cherub of Earth. The cherub has four faces consisting of a man, a lion, an eagle, and the main face, which I assume is the angel's actual face. He has four wings and four arms and under each arm and wing are hundreds of little eyes. One might would say the cherub sounds horrifying, however, he's surprisingly beautiful to me. Dayton and I make our way over to them and introduce ourselves to the cherub of Earth.

"Hello," I belt out as we approach, "I'm Aurora. You must be the cherub of Earth."

He nods, "I am. Good to meet you nephilim of light. Cherub of Earth is my title, true, but you may simply call me Dyzek. If you wish."

"Um, okay, sure… Dyzek is definitely less of a mouthful…" I giggle, unsure how else to respond.

"And you, young angel, who are you?" He asks. I'm suddenly very confused because he has not turned away from me yet but surely he's no longer talking to me…

"I'm Dayton." I turn and realize Dyzek was addressing Dayton this time. I had forgotten that with four heads you really don't need to turn. The one head is still facing me, sure, but one is facing Dayton as well.

"Dayton?" The cherub questions curiously, "surely you are not the Dayton that fell alongside Lucifer?"

I expect the question to bother Dayton, to bring back bad memories, but instead Dayton just smiles. "I am." Every brow of the cherub's four faces wrinkles in thought for a moment.

"Very well. The Lord's mercy knows no bounds I suppose." I can't tell how Dyzek feels about the idea but I get the feeling he doesn't approve. I frown, I'm trying so hard not to judge this cherub based on this assumption.

Michael suddenly steps forward, "Did you have any trouble getting here?"

"No, like what?" Like what? Really? I don't even know why I asked that. Like what couldn't happen to cause trouble these days? I'm feeling really stupid for asking that question In times like these but Michael answers it anyways.

"Well aside from the rain, there's tornadoes everywhere now that Crater has killed the cherub of wind and air. And I'll assume you know the effects of the death of the cherub of fire. Correct?"

I grimace at the thought, "Volcanoes…" My mind wanders back to the people we had saved. I hope Gabriel has found someone to look after them.

"Of course. We need to…" Michael starts to say something but Dyzek suddenly points towards the wall of the dome and announces, "They are here."

We all leap into action, forming a protective circle around Dyzek. "What if he just shoots all of us?" I ask, as I draw my sword. I hate to admit it but I'm scared. Crater doesn't even have to get close to shoot us, honestly, it doesn't look like we stand much of a chance. Michael, on the other hand, displays incredible confidence.

"He won't waste the bullet. The gun has seven silver bullets and one gold spare. He's already used it four times, that's four of the eight."

Dria steps forward to add, "Not to mention the one that shot me during the war. That means there's only three left. Michael's right, he won't risk wasting a shot."

Doors begin appearing all along the walls of the dome and through them come demon after demon. My eyes are all around searching for Crater. I can't find him.

"You ready?" Dayton whispers next to me. Honestly, no, I'm not. I'm so tired of fighting and worrying about being killed or Dayton being killed. But I guess now isn't the time for a therapy session.

"I guess." I sigh and we all take off, swords in hand, towards the oncoming demons. After fighting off a few I get a break in their attacking. My head whips around and I spot the cherub. He has a sword in each of his four hands and is killing a ton of demons with great ease. His skill is incredible and I marvel at the rate in which he's moving. That is until I spot a familiar figure moving towards him. Crater.

Everyone else is busy fighting and I know there's no way they can go to the cherub's rescue. So it's up to me. I race at Crater and leap between him and Dyzek. He stops and dawns a creepy smile.

"Aurora, come to stop me I suppose?" He laughs and draws his sword. There's something different about him... I'm not sure what it is exactly, I mean he looks the same but he seems like he's carrying himself differently. He lunges at me, catching me off guard. I leap back, barely avoiding the tip of his blade.

Once I regain my balance he's already diving at me again. He reaches me and swings but I manage to side step and thrust my sword towards his side. It doesn't make contact however because he spins with such amazing reflexes and blocks the strike with his own sword. The force of the impact causes a shriek so shrill that it catches the attention of everyone on the field.

Is it that moment, with the metallic ringing still in the air, that a gun fires. At first I'm in shock, Crater has the gun right? But he's fighting me and... There's a third behind me and I risk turning my head to look. The cherub falls to the ground and his body disappears. Behind the spot the cherub had been is... Crater?

'But how?!' I whip my head back around and where Crater had been standing moments before, sword still against my own, is a demon I have never seen before.

"How? Who are…" my stammer, at a loss for words, and the other demon smirks.

"Who am I? I am your grandfather."

~ **Michael** ~

The cling of metal rings out through the air and both Michael and the demon he's fighting turn to search for the source. Metal on metal always makes a sound but this sound is almost deafening. Aurora is neck and neck Crater, but something isn't right... No, this demon doesn't give off the same energy as Crater. But then…

A shark sounds and everyone spins in shock. Dyzek hits the ground hard and disintegrates as the figure behind him beams. Crater had fooled them all. Michael quickly turns back to Aurora and the Crater look alike, who has more back into his original form. Michael should have known, the demon is Aakar. Aurora's grandfather, Shaphir's father.

The demon Michael had been fighting before swings his sword and Michael was forced to look away from Aurora again. Aakar is a very powerful demon and could easily beat her, she doesn't stand a chance on her own. But despite his desire to dash to her rescue, if he runs for her now this demon will stab him from behind and that wouldn't do either of them any good.

"Dayton! Aurora!" Michael yells as he fights off the fallen. Hopefully Dayton will have a chance to get over to Aurora in time. Aakar will not go easy on her just because they are related. In fact, he would probably consider killing a ¾ nephilim a great achievement.

~ Dayton ~

Michael yells to Dayton to help Aurora but Dayton's already on his way. He had not even turned when the gunshot went off because he had already known what had happened. He had realized the moment Aurora's sword struck the demons and he turned towards them that this demon wasn't Crater. And it wasn't hard to guess where Crater was, but the thing he was most interested in wasn't the death of the chair of... It was the safety of Aurora.

He had watched as the demon posing as Crater shifted and the second he recognized the demon's true identity he had broken into a run. Dayton leapt over wounded demons that had yet to die as he dashed towards Aurora. Even if Aakar doesn't plan to kill her just yet he will try to talk to her, confuse her, or hurt her emotionally. And he would likely succeed.

Dayton tries to push into Aurora's head but she pushes him right back out. He can't see her face but he knows she's curious. It's her nature to be curious. She wants to hear what he has to say, she wants to know her family history even though she knows it will only hurt her. But she doesn't realize just how dangerous he is. He isn't like Bokim. He may be related to her but he'd gladly run his sword through her for a laugh.

Aakar has no feelings of love left. He's as evil as Satan himself. Even his fellow demons despise him. The only reason one of them hasn't run him through yet is because his skills and powers are so useful at times. Just as Dayton slides up to Aurora's side Crater gives a loud whistle and one by one the remaining demons transport to hell.

"Think about it." Aakar flashes Aurora one less smile and transports. Dayton's face drops as he turns to Aurora.

"What did he say to you?"

"Nothing…" The word comes out but it's obvious she's lying. Why would she lie to him? Her face looks nervous and she refuses to look him in the eye.

"Aurora, I'm serious, you have to tell me. Whatever he told you was a lie!"

Suddenly looks at him with narrowed eyes and his skin crawls slightly with the intensity of her glare.

"I'm a freaking lie detector!" Then she sighs, "It's no big deal. Don't worry about it. We should go." She marches past him looking defeated and he honestly has no idea what to do. Whatever Aakar told her, true or false, had scared her and she won't even tell him what it was. How can he protect her if he doesn't even know what he's protecting her from?

~ **Aurora** ~

I walk past Dayton and I'm holding back tears. I can't help but feel like I'm betraying him by not telling him what my grandfather told me. Which was what exactly?

I am going to die.

He had said something about how the Antichrist plan involving my blood would result in my death. And as far as I could tell he was telling the truth or, at least, he believed his words enough to make my lie detector believe it. How could I possibly tell Dayton? We still don't even know what the Antichrist is planning so how can we stop it?

I could tell Dayton, but I know if I did he would only become frantic and he wouldn't think straight. If we have any hope of stopping this thing, whatever it may be, then everyone needs to be completely focused.

Dayton is walking a little ways behind me and I suddenly feel terrible for the way I'd talk to him earlier. I stop and wait for him to move to my side. He doesn't say a word, he just stands beside me waiting for me to do or say something. I turn and slowly wrap my arms around him and rest my head on his shoulder. He lays a hand on my back and squeezes me gently.

"I'm sorry for reacting that way." I mumble into his shirt sleeve. "It's okay, I'm sure you'd tell me if you thought it was important." I can tell by the way he said it he's fishing. A wave of guilt washes over me but I keep my mouth shut.

Instead of assuring him, because I don't want to lie to him, I simply say, "I love you."

He starts to respond but suddenly the earth begins to shake and tear apart. Michael nearby starts yelling for us.

"Earthquake! Let's go! Quickly!"

We'll leave into the air as the earth below crumbles into a bottomless pit.

"We need to find where they are holding the boy!" Michael exclaims and the others all nod. Everyone looks relatively unharmed aside from a few bumps and bruises.

Hi, however, clear my throat and offer, "Well, I don't know if it will help but in my vision I saw the Antichrist and Vadim next to a big building with a bunch of empty crates and things beside it…" everyone is now staring at me as if I'm holding the winning lottery ticket.

"Did you notice anything else?" My dad asks curiously. I frown and think back, you would think after watching it so many times I would have noticed everything there is to know.

"Um, well, I think it had some metal storage rooms next to it with red numbers on them… and maybe a red symbol of some kind… like a hammer and an anchor or something like that…"

Dria raises an eyebrow at that and speaks up. "That sounds like the old warehouse is in Moscow, Russia. One of Satan's henchmen showed them to me once when they were setting up a drug deal for some low life humans."

"So demons are drug dealers?" I ask it with a smirk just to get a reaction from her. She flips her hair and shrugs.

"Satan is a father of all sin is he not? So how do you think humans come up with all of these ideas and things?" It's a good point and I shut up.

"Fine. Lead the way Dria." Michael spits it out, hating having to hand Dria the reins. She can obviously tell and she's eating it up.

"Sure thing Ark, follow me and try to keep up." Her teeth sparkle in the sunlight and she flashes a smile and sores off, the rest of us close behind. I'm frightened by the thought of us heading to the warehouses. If that's where my vision took place then that is where it will come true. Can I stop it? Can I change the future? Or is the future set in stone with no way around or out? And if I can't stop it, will it kill me, or was my grandfather wrong?

Dria leads us to the building and we land. My body shakes involuntarily at the side of it. I remember the vision, and I remember the fear it instilled in me. Dayton notices my shivering and slips his hand into mine.
It helps but not enough, I need to feel secure in his arms. He reads my mind and I don't try to block him. He glances at Dria up ahead and then wraps his arms and wings around me tightly.

His warmth emanates through me and my breathing slows. After a moment I stopped shaking but I'm suddenly aware of the exhaustion that has been building up inside me over the last few days. More than anything I long to curl up in his arms and sleep. A series of emotions triggered by my worn state, float through my mind draining my strength.

'I love Dayton.'
'I'm going to die.'
'I'm so tired.'
'My mom is dead.'
'I'm not human.'
'Dria wants Dayton.'
'Dayton is conflicted.'
'I wronged him.'
'I feel so lost...'

The energy drains out of me and I don't want to go on but it's at that moment when Dayton releases me and turns to Michael.
"What's the plan?"

"We need to split up. It does not appear as though they are here yet but if Aurora's vision is correct," Michael nods in my direction, "as I do not doubt that it is, then they will be here, and likely soon."

"Right, I'll go with Aurora." Dayton holds my hand again and Dria literally growls. I wonder if she saw the hug earlier... Dayton doesn't seem to have heard her just now though. I don't even have the energy to smile at her anger. I just stand here feeling rung out.

Michael nods in agreement and pairs Dria with Bokim again, volunteering himself to go alone just as before. Then he turns and disappears into the building. Dria And my dad stroll over to the warehouse, leaving Dayton and I to search outside. He turns to me and his eyes sweep over my face, searching. He knows something is wrong and it's killing him not knowing what. I can feel him inside my head, digging for an answer and I start to block him but I'm just too weak. 'Don't… please…' I think it towards him and his face softens as he pulls back from my thoughts. He respects my wishes even though it hurts him to do so. I feel so terrible and I open my mouth to explain but the home of voices stops me. Dayton hears them too and quickly places a finger to his lips. I go silent, suddenly on edge.

Dayton grabs my hand and pulls me to the corner of the building and peers around cautiously. I don't want to look... I know what's there... But I do anyway. Around the corner lies the Antichrist, Crater, and Vadim, with the gun. My stomach drops and I'm growing queasier by the second.

'Not again... No... Please not again...'

The Antichrist pulls out the vial of blood, my blood, and pours it down the barrel of the gun.

"No…" I groan and Dayton looks at me confused before spinning back around.

Talbot then passes the gun to Vadim and says almost inaudibly, "Take us to the future."
Crater smiles and Vadim slowly raises the gun into the air.

"NO!!!" I scream as the gun fires. There's a blinding light and Dayton whips around and wraps himself around me protectively as the world begins to spin.

Blackness. All around me there is darkness. I don't know where I am, I don't know where Dayton is, and I don't know when I am… The Antichrist had told Vadim to take him to the future. Is that possible? Did he really time travel? And am I dead? Maybe my grandfather was right, maybe it did kill me. Perhaps that would explain the darkness around me. Is this limbo?

I look around for any sign of light... Or my mother. If this is limbo she'd be here, wouldn't she?

"Mom?" I moan as I try to push myself to my feet.

"Aurora?" I hear my name being muttered nearby and I freeze. It's not a woman's voice, it's not my mom. No, my heart speeds up as I recognize the voice.

"Dayton!" I call out in excitement, I guess I'm not dead.

"Well, I'm not your mom I'm afraid."

"I'm glad, where are you?" Turning circles in the darkness I search for the direction his voice is coming from.

"Right here." He says, as his warm hand grasps mine, making me jump.

"How can you see me?"

"I can't, I just guessed based on the sound of your voice." I'm sure if I could see him right now he'd be shrugging as if it was no big deal. Funny cause I was trying to do the same thing and was having no luck whatsoever.

"Well you better be glad you managed to grab my hand then…"
I'm trying to say it jokingly but honestly if he could see me right now he
would see how bad I'm blushing at the thought.

"Glad?" I can almost feel his devilish grin gleaming on his face
through the darkness.

"Oh quit it," My face is now burning hot and I'm actually grateful
for the dark, "where are we?" I try my best to change the subject and
luckily it works.

"Not sure…" He sighs next to me, "I'll send word to Gabriel and
see if he's heard from the others.

They're suddenly a sharp pain in my wing and I wince, "Ouch!
That was my wing!" There's a short moment of silence after my
complaint before he finally apologizes.

"Sorry…"
"It's okay just send the message." I can still feel the stinging
sensation but I'm trying to ignore it.
"Already did."

A brilliant glow appears, lighting the room for a brief second,
hardly long enough to notice anything about the room. Gabriel can be
seen during that brief second before the room goes dark again.

"Gabe, mind giving us that light again?" Dayton asks hopefully
before the room is once again illuminated in a small glow. The source of
which turns out to be Gabriel's sword.

"Thanks, have you heard from the others? What just happened?"
Dayton drills Gabriel for answers while I take the time to look around the
room. There's some old totes in the corners covered in dust and cobwebs.
The walls appear to be made of metal and on one of the walls there is a
small handle at the bottom, almost touching the floor.

"The others are fine. The Antichrist used Aurora's blood to get her vision powers. The ability to see the future. That mixed with the powers of the archangels in the gun and Vadim, whose powers it appears are the ability to teleport and to take on the powers of other angelic beings he's in contact with, gave them the ability to basically warp time." Gabriel sighs.

"So he fast-forwarded time?" I asked, turning my attention back to Gabriel, who suddenly looks upset.

"Yes, and we also know why. The Antichrist intends to kill the two witnesses using the gun."

Dayton looks suddenly shocked by the news. "But they…"

Gabriel responds solemnly, "They cannot be resurrected if they are killed by that gun. It will completely even out the scales and it may even cost us the war."

"We have to stop him!" Dayton rushes towards the handle on the wall, he must have noticed it when I had. He yanks on it and it comes up with loud clinking noises. It's evening outside and it appears we are still at the warehouses.

Gabriel nods to us, "The others are already in pursuit. You'd better get to the gates of Jerusalem quickly."

We race outside and soar into the sky. Their storm clouds all around and lightning flashes in English streaks across them. We shoot out across the sky as fast as our wings can carry us, and I try to ignore my screaming body as it complains with each stroke.

~ The Antichrist ~

The two men lie just ahead, loudly declaring the gospels for all to hear. A beaming grand forms across Talbot Desdemona's face as he thinks of the event soon to occur. It is clearly stated in the Bible that these two witnesses will be killed and then resurrected. Of course, the Bible did not account for the use of the gun.

'Who knew such a small measly thing could change the course of the future so powerfully?'

The Antichrist entertains this thought while spinning the gun slowly in his hand. Heavenly fire swirls around over the heads of the two men and seems to flare up as the Antichrist steps towards them.

"Moses, Elijah, how are you?" Talbot smiles wickedly and the two witnesses eye him suspiciously but make no attempt to flee. either they believe he can do them no real harm or they know they are going to die and choose to do so without showing fear. One may say the second one is Noble, however, to Talbot both possibilities are simply stupid.

"Farewell gentlemen." The Antichrist pulls back the trigger and watches the bullet embed itself into Elijah. His body evaporates until it points the gun at Moses. There isn't an ounce of fear in Moses's eyes, which only succeeds in further infuriating Talbot. The gun fires again and Moses is gone a moment later, along with the flames that had been above.

There's a sudden thud behind him in the Antichrist turns apathetically towards the sound. Michael is already charging at him, sword in hand and anger burning off his face. The Antichrist raises an eyebrow and smiles, amused.

"Michael? Whatever happened to punctuality? I'm afraid the party is over and I really must be going now." His wings twist around him and Michael's sword lashes forward striking the empty air where he had just been. Now to prepare for the after party…

~Michael~

Michael couldn't remember his wings ever carrying him as fast as they just did before. Of course his effort was in vain. The gun shots could be heard in heaven as well as on Earth, there's no doubt in his mind about that. He's too late, again, and again lives are lost because of it. He lands just as the Antichrist pulls the trigger on the second shot.

Within seconds Michael's sword is in his hand and he charges at the Antichrist in a blind rage, tears swelling up in his eyes. The beast mocks him with a smile and mutters something that Michael doesn't hear. Talbot's wings twist around him just as Michael bears down on him with the sword. Too late. Always too late.

The Antichrist is gone and there's nothing left but dead silence and the shells of the fired bullets. Michael's shoulders slump into feet as the tears break loose. Nothing is going according to God's plan and Michael was the one who was appointed to make sure it did. The cherubs and now the two witnesses they all died because Michael, the seemingly perfect angel, isn't as perfect as he believed.

Michael finally forces himself to wipe his tears and turn around. Behind him stands a weary Bokim and his judging conrad, Dria. He hadn't even heard them arrive. Dria has a smug looking smirk on her face but there's a slight hint of pity in her eyes as well. Even she can tell that the event that just occurred is nothing to make light of. They stand in silence for several long minutes before Michael finally finds his voice again.

"We need to find Dayton in Aurora. Especially Aurora."

"Why especially Aurora?" Dria demands, her voice dripping with disgust.

"Because her blood was the key to this time jump and I have a bad feeling about it."

Bokim frowns with concern as he considers Michael's words. "What kind of feeling Michael?"

Michael's eyes glaze over and he shakes his head. "I am unsure. I just feel like traveling through time and space should not have been so easy for Talbot. There has to be more to it…"

Bokim nods uneasily and Michael points off in the direction they had all come from. "I am sure that they are on their way here from the warehouse already. We should try to meet them."

Michael waits for Dria and Bokim to acknowledge this before shooting off into the sky.

Screaming. I can hear it so clearly, so loudly, it's as if it's emanating from close by but Dayton and I are the only ones here. My body aches worse by the second and I can't think straight. My mind is empty other than the thought of the pain. The screaming gets louder and I cover my ears with my hands as I fly.

I have a headache... Make it stop! Make the screaming stop! I squeeze my eyes shut tightly and when I open them again I see Dayton staring at me and horror. His lips are moving but I can't hear him over the screens. The screens, I now realize, are coming from me. My body convulses in pain and although I try to close my mouth I can't and thus my blood curdling screams continue.

Speaking of blood... The pain I'm feeling is like none I've ever felt and it makes me think that something unnatural is occurring within me. It almost feels as though my blood has suddenly changed direction and is now flowing backwards throughout my circulatory system. It hurts... Oh how it hurts... And for the first time in my life I actually beg myself to pass out.

I'd rather be in a coma than feel what I am feeling right at this moment. Dayton reaches for me, unsure how to respond. His fingers connect with my arm and a searing heat flares on my skin in the spot they made contact with. I gasped through the screens and my body grants me my wish. My mind falls into darkness as my body falls from the sky.

I'm so scared. Even as I slowly drift into unconsciousness there is a steadily growing sense of terror rising through me. It appears my grandfather may have been right. Maybe whatever the Antichrist did with the gun and my blood will kill me. I've been dead before and honestly when you are resurrected from the dead you have some very conflicting feelings afterwards. On the one hand you are thankful to be alive but on the other hand you feel as though you have cheated death and thus death feels more like a joke.

If you can just come back from the dead easiest pie then death suddenly doesn't seem as serious. Up until this point the prospect of dying hasn't phased me a whole lot. Now, of course, the thought of people I love possibly dying gets to me but the idea that I may die hasn't crossed my mind and much until my grandfather told me this. But now it's all too real and all too close... Turns out I'm not immune to death, no one is, and no one can escape it's cold heartless fingers when they determine it's your time to go. My eyes closed, my breathing shortens, and I fall gracefully to the earth below with Dayton hot on my heels.

"Aurora! What's wrong? What's happening? Aurora! Can you hear me?

You have to tell me what's happening!" He's yelling as loud as he can but Dayton's words are lost on her. His adrenaline is racing but he has no idea what Aurora is screaming about. Her eyes look distant and terrified and she shows no sign that she comprehends anything he's saying.

Could she be having a vision? This has never happened before and Dayton doesn't know what to do so he simply lays a hand on her arm. Aurora's face constricts in pain before her eyes roll back in her head and she drops from the sky. Dayton dogs after her at an incredible speed and catches her only about 15 ft from the ground. Unfortunately the excess speed along with the added weight made slowing down a difficult feat and stopping... Impossible.

They hit the ground with a massive force, Aurora landing on Dayton, sandwiching him between her and the rough desert sand below. Dayton moans in pain as he rolls Aurora off of him gently and tries to sit up. There's no doubt in his mind that something, if not everything, in his body is broken or at least severely bruised. Of course, he will heal in an hour tops, he's more concerned with Aurora and the cause for her sudden screaming.

He drags himself up next to her and shakes her gently, hoping she will respond, but of course she doesn't stir. There's no way this was just a vision. Her face when he had touched her arm floats through his mind and he knows this is something much worse than just a vision. He has to do something to help her but considering he still has no clue what's wrong with her that could be very difficult.

He runs his thumb along her cheekbone and notices the heat immediately. She's burning up, dangerously so. Dayton's eyes cloud over with concern and he leaps to his feet, ignoring the pain in his limbs. It takes a lot of effort but he eventually manages to scoop Aurora up into his arms. There's no way he could possibly fly in this condition, not for the next hour anyways. His wings encircle them and he tries to transport to heaven. Nothing happens.

"What the heck?" Dayton groans and tries again but the result is the
same. Something is seriously wrong… Gabriel had transported to them just moments earlier so there's no way it's the time travel thing that's causing it. Dayton sets Aurora back down carefully And plucks a feather from his wing. Only a minute after releasing it Gabriel appears in a swirl of light and sand.

He doesn't say a word, rather he moves swiftly to Aurora's side. Gabriel checks Aurora's forehead with his hand then leans down to listen to her breathing. Dayton watches silently as Gabriel examines her. Finally, the angel stands up and shakes his head.

"I have no idea what's wrong with her. Aside from the fever she shows no sign of injury or illness. I, however, I'm not the one that is best to ask."

"Who do I need to take her to? Gabe, I can't transport! I don't know why but there's something blocking me every time I try…" Dayton throws his arms up frantically and immediately regrets the decision moaning and pain and lowering them slowly. Gabriel looks at him curiously before responding.

"When you tried to transport, was it with Aurora in your arms?"

"Yes, I was trying to get her to heaven so someone could figure out what's wrong with her and heal her!"

"Try it now." Gabriel commands softly.

"What?" Confusion washes over Dayton as he tries to comprehend the angels command.

"Try to transport without her."

Dayton remains confused but obeys in a moment later he's in heaven. He quickly transports back and finds Gabriel once again examining Aurora curiously.

Realization hits him. "So... It's Aurora? I can't transport with her. But why?"

"That, young warrior, I do not know." Gabriel stands back up shaking his head.
"Well, who do I need to take her to that will know?"

"First, you need to get to Michael and the others. Michael can lead you to Errapel, his powers can better examine Aurora's body. He can use his abilities to check her internally as well. Because it is obvious that whatever the problem is, it is not external. Errapel is also a healer, find him and find him fast. I fear the final battle is upon us." With that Gabriel transports and Dayton once again tries to lift Aurora into his arms.

~ Dayton ~

Dayton had nearly forgotten how useless walking is for long distances. He'd been carrying Aurora for the past 20 minutes and he feels as though he's made no progress whatsoever. anger boils up in him and he yells in frustration. Who knows how much time Aurora has left. Whatever is wrong with her could very well be killing her this very instance and there's no one here to help her.

"Aurora wake up... Please…" He begs as he nuzzles his cheek against hers. Her face is on fire, indicating a severely high fever. The color has drained from her also, leaving the surface of her skin pale and lifeless. Her breathing grows steadily softer as date and trudges across the sand.

"Crap... stay with me... Come on... Whatever this is, you have to fight it!" Dayton tries to leap up and fly but he barely makes it two feet off the ground before landing again and stumbling to regain his balance, Aurora clutched tightly against his chest. In the distance he can make out a group of large birds heading towards them.

'Great…' He thinks to himself, *'now the buzzards are gonna start circling…'*

"She's not dying! Go away!" He yells up at the oversized birds as he drags his feet across the hot ground. "I won't let her…" He whispers. The birds get closer, ignoring his command. Only as they get closer he realizes, they aren't vultures, it's Michael and company.

"Thank the good Lord…" Dayton lets out a sigh of relief as they land.
"Michael, I could just about kiss you right now!"

Michael's face distorts in a clearly repulsed manner. "Please refrain from doing anything of the sort. What happened?" He inquires as his gay's lands upon Aurora and Dayton's arms.

"There's no time, I'll explain on the way to Errapel's."

"Errapel? Good heavens, you don't think she's…" Michael's face goes white. Bokim looks equally as stricken.

"Michael!" Dayton shouts at him and he snaps out of it.

"All right, this way." Michael starts to fly off again and Dayton groans.

"Michael, I can't fly. You're going to have to carry Aurora. And at this point, for the next 40 minutes or so, someone is going to have to carry me as well…"

Michael turns back and holds out his arms as Dayton slides Aurora into them. Dria flips her hair and smiles wide, like a predator that just found her prey trapped and helpless.

"I can fly you there Dayton."

He glances in her direction and gives a nervous smile before nodding in acceptance. He knows she has a hidden agenda but he can't really be too picky right now. Aurora doesn't have time for that. Dria wraps her arms around his waist and they take off, Michael leading the way.

~ **Michael** ~

Michael Land suddenly without warning the others. They will figure it out easily enough. Aurora skin is beyond hot. a rough estimate may put her fever at 106, far too high... It was roughly a 30-minute flight from the desert they met in to Jerusalem. The others land with soft beds on the cracking soil behind Michael. He glances back and does a quick head count. It appears everyone made it all right and Dria actually managed to avoid dropping Dayton.

"Errapel takes up residence at the wall of prayer. We need to get there as quickly as possible... Aurora isn't doing well. I can sense her life force draining."

Michael instantly regrets the statement, seeing as to how both Dayton and
Bokim's faces have just bled out of all color. They are almost paler than Aurora at this point. He considers saying something to calm them but he fears he'd only make things worse. So he closes his mouth and nods in the direction of the wall. They will have to walk the remaining distance due to the massive amount of people roaming the streets.

The level of immorality has grown beyond imagination. Oddly, this produces a slight physical pain in Michael that he can't fully understand. As far as he knows human sin should have no physical effect on himself or any spiritual being. Yet the site causes him unease and sins uncomfortable sensations through his chest. He grounds his teeth as he leads the group through the streets.

"Where's your mark, pretty boy?" a growling voice rumbles somewhere behind him and Michael spends around to assess the situation.

Bokim and Dria stand off to the left, looking tense, and Michael immediately spots why. Dayton is positioned in the middle of a triangle of three rough looking men with demonic grins. Although demons they are not. simply some evil humans that have no doubt fallen under the Antichrist spell.

Under ordinary circumstances Dayton could easily fend off all three alone, unfortunately with his wing not fully recovered the pain would surely lower his odds. The men each have a symbol that looks almost embossed onto their skin on their foreheads. It's obvious that this is the mark of the beast. Three sixes loop together to form what, at first glance, would appear to be a circle filled with three smaller circles.

The men step in a foot closer to Dayton with a threatening look in their eyes. "I asked, where. is. your. mark?" Each word from the brute's mouth comes out like a sin it's all of its own. Dayton scales at them and Dria's face clouds over with rage. Michael shakes his head, aware of her intentions. Why they single Dayton out is a mystery, though perhaps it's because he's hurt, his slight limp being a dead giveaway. But it's apparent that if they lay a hand on him Dria we'll be on them in a nanosecond.

"We don't tolerate rebels around here so I suggest you roll up that sleeve and show me a mark or I may just have to put one on there myself!" The biggest of them growls.

Dayton remains silent, never taking his eyes away from his confronters. The leader of the three, the one that's been talking, lashes forward and grabs Dayton's right arm. No sooner had he latched on to Dayton than Dria bolts towards them, followed close behind by Bokim. Michael glances around to be sure they would not have more attackers randomly join in.

"Dria, Do not kill them." The command exits Michael's lips softly yet sternly. Bokim already knows better but he has the feeling Dria May need to be reminded.

The assailant lets out a raspy laugh as if the thought of Dria harming him or a joke. "Whatcha gonna do babe?" He mutters as he sucks Dayton in the gut and tosses him aside. Dayton hits the ground and dust flies up around him causing him to let out a stream of hacking coughs. Michael's brow rises, as does his anger. If Aurora weren't in his arms he would likely dive into the bra without hesitation as well. However, it appears Dria and Bokim will have it covered.

Dria kicks the leader's feet out from under him before kicking him straight between the legs and once with a move that he never saw coming. The man balls up in a cradle position and lets out a deep moan. He won't be getting up for a while after having a ticked off nephilim kick him in the groin. He better be glad that's all she did… These men chose the wrong people to mess with, and at the wrong time. There's not a human on Earth that can put the same force behind a kicker a punch that a nephilim, demon, or angel can.

Michael supervises as Dria does a roundhouse kick to the second guy's chin, effectively knocking him out cold. Bokim has the last guy stumbling backwards. Michael didn't quite catch the fight that went on between them but the human has two black guys and a busted lip that's lending way to a steady stream of blood. He's likely to have also suffered a concussion as well.

"We need to go, grab Dayton and let's move on before there's more trouble." Michael demands after a brief assessment of the scene. Dria rushes to date inside and scoops him into her arms, whispering something to him and she does so. Her head is so close to Dayton's that Michael could have sworn her lips brushed against his for the briefest moment. And if Dayton's slightly startled expression says anything then it's likely she actually did kiss him.

Michael's eyes narrow with disapproval, even if it wasn't necessarily Dayton that committed the offense. Dayton does not appear upset by the gesture, surprised perhaps, but not upset. This annoys Michael and that he fears for Aurora's feelings. With all she's been through the last thing she needs is a broken heart.

"Do you think you can walk or are you helpless?" It's Bokim that addresses Dayton and judging by the edge in his tone he must have seen the exchange as well. Dayton glances up at Dria, aware of the reason for Bokim's anger. He gives a quick nod before rolling out of her arms and grunting softly as his feet hit the ground.

Michael turns back around without a word and they follow him to the wall, leaving the three men behind to ride in pain on the cold, hard ground. They've already wasted too much time and Aurora could have very little of that left.

~ Bokim ~

Bokim trails behind the group, keeping a close eye on Dayton and Dria from behind. The wall of prayer, also known as the wailing wall, looms ahead and Michael ushers them into a nearby hut. The moment they enter they are greeted by the barrel of a long shotgun.

"Don't move or I'll blow your faces off!" The other end of the shotgun is held by a little old man whom Bokim immediately recognizes.

"Errapel! Good to see you old friend. It's been like 5,000 years!" The gun lowers an inch as Errapel's eyes shift from Bokim to the others and back.

"Bokim? Michael?" The hermit questions them suspiciously. They nod and Dayton clears his throat.

"Not forgetting me are you Errapel?" He asks in a low tone. The old geezer turns his attention to Dayton and frowns.

"Now how could I possibly forget you Dayton? I believe you owe me some very rare herbs you stole back in... 33 AD? Don't you think I forgot about that! Also, congratulations on your reinstatement or whatever." Errapel waves a hand in the air as if his words hold no sentiment or value whatsoever.

Dayton's face falls but he's quick to perk back up with a soft grin. "Thanks Errapel, It means a lot. And I'm truly sorry about that herb incident, I'll do whatever I can to make it up to you."

Bokim glances over at Dayton curiously, wondering why he would steal herbs from Errapel. Herbs of all things! Of course this boy never ceases to surprise him, and that is not always a good thing. He suddenly has the urge to give Dayton the 'If you hurt my daughter' speech. But then, he's not really sure if he qualifies as a father… He shoots stating a look that he hopes says it all. Dayton quickly looks away, unwilling to meet his gaze.

"Errapel," Michael addresses the healer, "Please, we need your help right away." He lays Aurora down gently on the couch and Errapel moves swiftly to her side. He places a hand over her forehead and gasps before darting around the room, frantically piling random herbs and concoctions into his arms. Once he's satisfied with his findings he returns to Aurora's side and lays everything out on a small wooden stand at the end of the couch.

"Tell me everything!" He insists as he begins working on Aurora.

Dayton gladly fills him in on everything that has happened so far. Errapel places a small purple leaf on Aurora's tongue before reaching for a jar containing a curious looking silver goop. He dips two fingers into the jar and scrapes out a thick portion of the substance that he then spreads across Aurora's forehead.

"What is that? What does it do?" It's very difficult for both of them to stand by and watch as his daughter's beautiful skin is cloaked in unknown mixtures.

"It's a big fat none of your business! You want her to live or not?" The old man shakes a finger in Bokim's face and he holds his hands up and surrenders.

It's hard not to think that Errapel has gone somewhat senile in his old age. He was simply a nephilim for the longest time but at the age of 90 the
Lord decided to grant him immortality so that the charlatan could use his 'gifts' for generations to come. But then, perhaps his craziness has less to do with old age and more to do with all the shrooms and spores he's been inhaling around here. Bokim's eyes skim the room, noting all the odd shaped fungi in jars on the shelves around the walls.

Errapel spreads different oozes down Aurora's cheeks and neck, occasionally changing the leaf on her tongue out with another. He lays one hand on her stomach and one on her side and with his eyes shut tightly he hones all of his powers towards her. No one in the room makes a sound as he concentrates on saving her. Dayton reaches for Aurora's hand but Errapel seats it away without ever even opening his eyes.

Dayton backs away in defeat and moves to stand next to Dria. Bokim glances in their direction and notices Dria's hand slowly slipping into Dayton's. He waits for Dayton to shrug her hand off and step away from her, he doesn't. Heat rises up in Bokim's chest at the sight. He's angry with Dayton, but then he can't help but feel partially at fault himself. After all, he is the one that dragged Dria along with them.

"She has gone." Errapel says it as a fact, emotionless, and the whole room goes cold. Dayton starts to say something but Bokim cuts him off.

"What do you mean, she's gone?" He asks it but he fears the worst and he can already feel the swell of grief burrowing inside him.

"She has passed on. She is in limbo but it was not her time to die. Now it is up to her whether she shall return or not. We shall wait." Errapel stands up and brushes himself off as though this were nothing at all.

Bokim lets out a choked cry and falls to his knees. Dayton drops Dria's hand, his face wider than a ghost. He looks lost as he saunters over to the bathroom and shuts the door behind him. Michael's face streams with tears and his head raises to the heavens in a silent prayer. Dria remains silent and eventually she walks outside, no doubt uncomfortable around the emotions and doors. Heaving sounds emanate from the bathroom and bochum can tell Dayton is literally sick with grief. Seeing and hearing these things spark something in Bokim and he realizes that there's no need for any of this.

Errapel said Aurora could choose to come back. That means there is still hope. Aurora is her mother's daughter, if there's a way back she will find it. Bokim forces himself to stand up and wipe his eyes. Michael watches him through tears, wondering how he could possibly stop crying so soon after his daughter's death. Bokim can't bring himself to give an explanation, but he moves to the bathroom door and bangs on it violently.

"Get out here now!" He yells at Dayton through the wood of the door until it finally swings open. Dayton stairs out at Bokim with a zombie-like gaze that is laced with sorrow and confusion. Bokim grabs him by his shirt and yanks him out, and not for a hug either.

"Quit your pity party, she'll be back. You on the other hand may not be around when she wakes up."

After this Bokim shoves him in the chest, fairly hard, and Dayton snaps back into reality. His eyebrows pinched together in a threatening manner.

Michael's eyes go wide and he mumbles something about checking on Dria before rushing out the door.

"Don't break nothing! And don't get blood on the carpet!" Errapel warns before following Michael's lead and making a break for the exit.

"What the heck did I do? My girlfriend just freaking died! Your daughter! Have you lost your mind?" Dayton screams in Bokim's face And it takes everything that's left in Bokim Not to punch the crap out of the already injured angel that stands before him.

"My daughter is strong and she'll be back. I don't know when but I know she will. I'm her father, I'm supposed to protect her! I may not could have protected her from this but I sure as hell can protect her from the sorry likes of you!"

"What are you talking about? I love Aurora and would never do anything to hurt her!" Dayton looks completely exasperated at the insinuation.

"Oh is that right?"

"Yes, that's right! Whatever you think I've done or I'm going to do I didn't and I won't!"

"So you are telling me you didn't kiss Dria after that fight earlier? That you weren't holding her freaking hand as your girlfriend lay dying before you?" Bokim's words sliced through the air like a knife and Dayton's mouth arches downward in a frown that has guilt written all over it.

~ Aurora ~

"Mom?" It's peaceful here, for some reason I would have thought limbo would be, well I'm not sure what I thought... I didn't expect this though. There's just a beautiful blue sky and a ground made of clouds as far as the eye can see. This is aside from the people of course... Souls roaming around aimlessly, staring into the vast blue distance, lost to reality…

"I'm here." My mother appears on the cloud beside me and surprisingly her sudden manifestation doesn't phase me.

"Then I am dead…" I mutter as she embraces me. I don't bother wrapping my arms around her, no, I simply stand there as she hugs me to her chest.

"You can't be here…" She says it so quietly, and with a certain sadness, as if she almost wished I could stay with her. And oddly, I want to.

"Can't I stay here with you?"

She gives a small gulp and she shakes her head no. "In theory, yes, but I can't allow that. You have people on earth that love you so much. They are mourning you, you must return."

"I'm sorry, I failed you... The wars almost here and I didn't stop the Antichrist, I didn't become Queen, or save the Jewish people. I feel like I haven't accomplished anything…" I feel as though these statements should cause me tears but instead I felt almost nothing…

"You have not failed me. You can do no such thing. I am beyond proud of you. Aurora, you let a whole village in South America to Christ after saving them from a volcano. You chose light and stayed true to your faith despite the toughest obstacles. And it's not over yet. Now you're going to overcome the greatest challenge of all, death. Go back and win that war sweetheart. And never forget how much I love you."

I nod into her chest until I feel her begin to fade away. The sky around me begins to shift in and out of focus until it's gone entirely and in its place is the blurry shape of a room and a small table.

Arguing. That's what I wake up to. I don't think whoever it is realizes that I'm awake, or alive even for that matter. Being the curious person I am, I decide to stay still and quiet and listen in.

"Oh is that right?" The voice belongs to my dad, I recognize it immediately.

"Yes, that's right! Whatever you think I've done or I'm going to do I didn't and I won't!"

Dayton. My heart quickens with the sound of his voice. The wait, I just died, what the heck are they yelling at each other for?

"So you're telling me you didn't kiss Dria after that fight earlier? That you weren't holding her freaking hand as your girlfriend lay dying before you?" My dad accuses and my heart nearly stops for the second time today.

'What? No, it can't be... He wouldn't...' Dayton doesn't answer, I wish I could see his face, it can't be possible... It just can't.

"That's what I thought." My dad growls and I blink back tears as I roll off of the couch and stand to face them.

I don't say a word, I just wait for them to notice me. My dad starts to open his mouth to yell some more but his eyes catch sight of me and he stops short. His face floods with pain, mine I'm sure. Dayton turns so fast he's almost a blur. His gaze hits me and a blade through my heart would have hurt less. He looks guilty, just plain guilty.

"Aurora!" He rushes towards me with concern but I back away from him.

"Is it true?" I choke out and he looks helpless.

"Yes… but no… Aurora I…" He starts to explain but I can't bring myself to hear it. I turned to exit the small hut I've somehow managed to end up in. Michael is seated on the ground outside but he leaps to his feet the moment I appear.

"Aurora! Thank the good Lord you're alive!" He rushes over and I fall into his arms. Michael pulls me in and that's when I lose it. I'm crying so hard I'm shaking and I'm beyond thankful to have Michael here. Footsteps erase the doorway but I latch onto Michael and refuse to turn around even when Dayton calls out to me.

"Please, let me explain! It's not like that! Aurora I swear! I love you!"

Michael goes rigid and I can sense that he knows what's going on.

'Tell me.' I pushed the thought out, directed to Michael. I know I can trust Michael to tell me the truth, mostly because even if he didn't I would know. And I can't bear to hear it from Dayton. Michael says and I can feel his chest rise and fall with it.

'Dayton was injured upon catching you after your blackout. On our way here he was cornered by several men looking for a fight. The leader punched Dayton and threw him to the ground. Bokim and Dria fought them off and afterwards Dria kissed Dayton.' Michael explains the situation to me in mind speak as quickly and efficiently as he can. I can tell he's uncomfortable but I appreciate his honesty.

Dayton continues to plead with me but I ignore him, focusing instead on
Michael's thoughts. I asked him, hopefully…

'So Dria kissed Dayton? He didn't kiss her?'

'Yes...' But the way he says it does not imply that this is any more a good thing than if it had been Dayton. I swallow hard.

'But he didn't stop her... Did he?' somehow I already know the answer and it breaks my heart. Michael shakes his head sadly but responds nonetheless.

'Not that I saw. But Aurora, I can tell he does love you and I believe you should at least try to hear him out. Perhaps there's more to the story.'

'I heard my dad say Dayton held Dria's hand while I was dying. Did you see that?' I can feel my stomach turning within me.

'No, I didn't. But I was more focused on you at the time. I did, however, see Dayton reach for your hand at first. Errapel wouldn't let him though, it would have interfered, or so Errapel believed.' Michael releases me and I run my arm across my face. It comes away wet and covered in some kind of nasty goop. Great, there's just no end to the humiliation this world has to offer me. I wipe my face again and then my neck, doing my best to rid my skin of the strange oozes. My hand eventually brushes over the shell at the base of my neck. I hold it a moment and let out a long, deep breath, before slowly pivoting around to face Dayton.

I take you in his gorgeous features as my gaze lens on him. His raven black hair now tipped with gold and his strike and green eyes that now hold a splash of blue. He's even better looking now than when I first met him. Of course, the look of shame and regret across his face aren't doing him any favors at the moment. Dria stands off to the side, silently taking in the scene. Knowing her, she's probably getting a kick out of the whole thing.

"Talk." I demand it as I stand before him, clutching the necklace like it is the key to everything.

"I didn't kiss her." Dayton doesn't even glance in Dria's direction as I had expected. Instead he keeps his eyes locked on mine securely. Dria raises an eyebrow as if she's actually surprised he didn't admit to the heinous crime.

"I know."

"She kissed me…" He nervously runs his fingers through his hair.

"Yes. But you didn't stop her." I let go of the shell and cross my arms.

"She caught me off guard! I swear I didn't even have a chance to stop her!" He tries to defend himself.

Dria suddenly looks ticked off, like she's fixing to blow a fuse or something. But she remains silent as I continue my questioning.

"And you had no reaction afterwards? Like say, telling her to stay the heck away from you?"

"Aurora I'm sorry I hurt you but I swear it meant nothing!" My lie detector chimes in, soft and pathetic, as if it's not even sure how to interpret this particular statement. In fact, I'm not even sure Dayton knows whether or not that statement is true or false. Dria, however, takes the statement very seriously.

"What?! It meant nothing? Nothing at all to you?" Her eyes are brimming with tears but I can't say I feel an ounce of pity for her. Dayton gives her a sad look before facing me again and waiting for my judgment to fall.

"Why did you hold her hand? While I was dying?" I wouldn't want him holding her hand at any time but something about him doing so while I lay on my deathbed just sickens me to the core.

"I... I was scared," He admits dejectedly, "I needed some comfort and she... She was just there."

My mouth falls open at this and I glance over at Dria. She looks equally stricken and honestly I do feel a tiny spark of pain for her now. truthful as it may have been, Dayton's last few words were some that could have chilled the bones of any girl on the planet. Dria was… just there. He used her and nothing more. She's worthless to him. But then deep down inside I can see that isn't completely true. He does care about Dria, just not enough to make a difference.

Dria walks over to Dayton without a word. She runs her finger seductively down his right cheek before suddenly slapping him with massive force. His head jerks from the impact but he quickly straightens back up until it's his head to stare at the ground. Dria's eyes rain tears as she marches past Dayton and into the hut.

I can't help myself and I race after her with every intention of comforting her. She can no doubt hear my budding footsteps running up behind her and she spins around to look me in the eye.

"Dria, I… I didn't want…" I studied my words, searching for something I can say that may ease her pain, but she cuts me off.

"You can have him." It's all she says before speeding off into the hut and slamming the door. I start to follow her but think better of it and head back to the others. A little old man suddenly hobbles into my path and nods at me.

"Oh good, you're not dead anymore. Nice to meet you. I'm Errapel. Now all of ya get lost!"

~ **The Antichrist** ~

It's ironic really, that Nazareth is to be the city in which the war shall be fought. The Antichrist surveys the town as he arrives. Jesus was known as Jesus of Nazareth so it is funny that this shall be the town where the forces of good and evil will have their final battle.

Crater lands dutiously by his side as if on cue and the Antichrist addresses him without a glance. "Did you return the child?"

The false prophet nods absolutely in response. They could have just killed the boy, after all, his family wouldn't have known the difference since he's gone three and a half years already anyways. But after tonight it won't matter who is dead and who isn't.

"Did you call for the others?" Talbot inquires. Crater hesitates merely a moment before answering.

"Yes sir, we are all set. Every legion of fallen from around the world is preparing for battle. Along with the nephilim of dark. They should arrive before sunset."

"Good, and the humans?"

"There is not a country that is not devoted to you. Your mark is upon the wrist or forehead of every law abiding citizen across the globe. Any who refuse the mark are beheaded or burned at the stake upon capture."

"Yes, but will they fight?" The Antichrist glances over at his false prophet impatiently.

"Fight? The humans? But sir, only angelic beings are allowed to fight in the war of the realms." Crater grimaces even as he says it.

"Under whose authority?" Talbot raises an eyebrow.

"Um… God's sir?" Crater gulps.

"And do we follow God's authority?"

"No sir. Yes, the human shall fight. I'll make the call."

"Do so, the scales have tipped, this war is ours. Send word to heaven also, tell them we shall await our chiefs return at nightfall. Let the war begin."

With that Crater returns to hell leaving Talbot Desdemona to lay waste to the sacred town of Nazareth. Buildings and citizens would really get in the way during an epic battle between supernatural beings, don't you think? Best to just remove them now. The Antichrist grins, oh the satisfaction he gets from doing evil.

"Where do we have to go now?" I ask as Errapel tries to wave us off his property. "Wait," I demand, "What about Dria?"

Errapel causes a moment and considers this last question. Dria is in his house after all, and I don't think she has any intention of exiting anytime soon.

"She may remain until Tom for the war. We should leave together when the time is nigh." He nods as if to say that his own decision was acceptable to him.

"Wait, you're going to fight in the war with us? But you're a healer, not a fighter…"

"Yeah, well, as they say desperate times call for desperate measures. You all are going to need all the help you can get with this one. Especially since the devil has a gun."

"But the gun has no more bullets... He used them all." I try to mentally count all the bullets to make sure I'm remembering correctly.

"Sweetheart I don't mean he can use the gun to shoot any of you. I mean, that blooming gun has done tipped the scales. We're outnumbered and at a major disadvantage. Now you all hurry along. The sun will be down in an hour or two. Dria And I might be a bit late but better late than never. Now shew!" He ushers me along with his hands as if shewing off a stray animal.

I frown and move over next to Michael as we prepare to take off. Dayton steps up next to me and reaches for my hand. I turned my body toward Michael as if I hadn't noticed and asked, "Where will the war be? Where are we going?" Honestly I'm not super interested in the location of the war, but I needed something to ask so it would look like my turning away had more to do with my curiosity, and less to do with the fact that I still feel somewhat betrayed by Dayton.

The shell resting against my neck from my necklace suddenly feels heavier. Of course it weighs no more now than it did when Dayton gave it to me, but somehow the words inside it seem heavier, deeper, and certainly they seek to crush my heart. I swallow hard at the thought of not trusting Dayton. Half of me is screaming *'how can you not trust him? After everything you've been through?'* and the other half is saying *'I should have known it was too good to be true...'*

Michael nods into the distance, as if saying it's that way. Wow, thanks Michael... I give him an annoyed look and wait for an explanation. He doesn't say anything but my dad answers for him.

"North Central Palestine. Specifically Nazareth."

"Oh…" It's all I can think to reply.

Didn't Jesus have something to do with Nazareth? I know he wasn't born there because he was born in Bethlehem. Hmm... Maybe he was raised there? That sounds right... I glance at Dayton, hoping he won't be looking, he is. Our eyes make contact for just a split second before I spin away. The pain that was reflected in his gaze makes my heart ache. I hurt him, but then, he hurt me first. I know he explained himself and apologized and I believed him but I still feel hurt. Like part of my heart has been bruised and now it's sensitive and sore. I can feel him staring at me, begging me to forgive him, and I want to... I do... But I... Well, it's easier to forgive than to forget and it's harder to get everything back on track when you so vividly remember what derailed it in the first place.

Michael announces that it's time to go and everyone unveils their wings. My dad and Michael fly upwards and I do the same, only I'm yanked back down by a firm grip on my ankle. I look around in shock as my feet hit the ground again and no sooner do my eyes land on Dayton behind me than he grabs a hold of me and slams his lips against mine.

I start to shrug him off but he persists and everything in me suddenly longs to melt into his embrace. I stopped struggling and kissing back with as much passion as one could possibly portray in one single kiss. All of my doubts, fierce, and mistrust flow from me in this one instance and I feel empowered. When he finally pulls away we're both left gasping for breath.

"I love you angel. You and only you. For all eternity, I'd swear it on my soul!" He grins mischievously and adds, "Amen." I laugh and choke back tears.

"I know... I love you too."

"So you forgive me then?" He looks nervous as if that kiss hadn't healed a clear answer.

"Yes," a smile before giving him a light, playful shove, "But it better not happen again!"

"Never." He smiles warmly and sweeps me up into his arms like he had on my birthday. Then he shoots into the air, holding me close. I think that was our first big fight... I hope it was the last one, as well, because I can't stand fighting with him.

"What are you thinking?" He whispers in my ear. Wow, he's actually asking me instead of just pushing his way into my head? I smile and give him a quick peck on the cheek.

"Thanks for asking this time. I was thinking about how much I love you." He looks amused by this.

"You're welcome Angel."

Up ahead Michael and my dad have noticed our absence and stopped to wait up on us. But Michael seems antsy and impatient, with good reason
I suppose…

"Are you two lovebirds coming or not? There is a war tonight, in case you have forgotten." If it were possible to tap one's foot in midair Michael would be doing it.

Dayton and I glance resolutely in his direction and Dayton nods hesitantly. I fought in the last war, so no, I'm not too anxious to arrive at this one. I've already cheated death twice, what if it finally catches up to me?

Dayton watches me silently for a moment before saying, "I won't let anything happen to you. I promise."

I'm about to scold him for reading my mind but then I realize, he hadn't, he'd read my eyes... I finally forced myself to nod and we head off towards Nazareth.

~ Aurora ~

It's not a long way from Jerusalem to Nazareth so the flight is incredibly short. We arrive in around 15 minutes and Michael is quick to survey the scene. The town has been practically wiped out and it gives off a very eerie, desolate feeling. The houses have been flattened, destroyed, and left is nothing more than rubble on the ground. Any people that lived here before are gone, and there's no sign of life.

"Where's the Antichrist and the army's and stuff?" I wonder aloud as I take in the sight. My dad is the first to respond.

"We are early. The sun hasn't gone down yet. The armies will arrive nearer to sunset."

" Oh..." I mumble, "So what are we going to do in the meantime?" Not that I don't love standing in creepy wastelands waiting for an army to show up and kill us, but…

"I'm going to send word to Gabriel that we are here," Michael informs as he plucks a feather from his wings, "I'll see if he's heard anything yet." He releases the delicate feather, sending it off to the heavens. Moments later Gabriel appears before us in full on gold and silver battle gear.

"Michael," He addresses the moment he arrives, "Talbot has already sent us confirmation. The war will begin at sunset." Gabriel has an almost frightened look and his eyes flick to the side nervously. This is not normal for Gabriel at all. And I'm not the only one who notices it.

"Gabriel, what is it? What is Talbot up to?" Michael presses the subject forcefully. Gabriel groans but he doesn't evade Michael's question.

"Humans. Talbots using humans in the war. We intercepted the call."

I'm glancing around and it appears my mouth is the only one not open, besides Gabriel's upon hearing this declaration. So what? Did they not expect that?

"But that's... They can't... It's strictly forbidden to include humans in battles of the spiritual realm. That's why they are called spiritual! So they don't include the humans!" Dayton shouts angrily at the idea.

It's weird, hearing them say humans like that... I mean, I used to fall into that category, didn't I? In fact, it's still hard to believe I'm not human. And hearing them say the word human as if they are a whole other species... I mean, I guess they are but I still find it weird to think of it that way. Gabriel shakes his head at Dayton's outburst.

"Yes, it is forbidden under the authority of the Almighty. Unfortunately, the Antichrist has decided that since they have broken every other law created by our Lord that this one shall be no different. Especially since they believe they have nothing left to lose. And I suppose they really don't."

Michael looks appalled by the notion, "How can we fight against those whom we have spent an eternity trying to protect?!"

My dad bows his head sadly, "I fear you shall have no choice. A human's weapons may not can kill you but it can slow you down, wound you. That alone could be the difference between life and death. These humans have taken the mark, they're going to perish either way."

Michael grinds his teeth but not solemnly, not wanting to believe it but knowing that Bokim is correct.

"Fine. Let's prepare. The sun shall be down anytime now and we should be ready. Gabriel, go on ahead and summon the other angels. Something tells me a head start can't hurt in this war."

Gabriel disappears to fetch the army upon Michael's request. Armor forms over Michael, then my dad, and then Dayton. I frown nervously before suiting up myself. A moment later there are a million bright lights to our direct left and I shield my eyes. When the lights dim I can see that every angel in heaven is now standing beside us, Gabriel at the front of the pack.

The sun seems to have disappeared completely and the moon, a deep bloody red, has taken its place. The army suddenly goes dead silent and I follow their gazes towards a swirl of black dust nearly 50 yards out ahead of us. The dust gets larger and larger until finally exploding in a storm of sand that leaves a multitude of demons and humans in its place.

I know we just had the conversation about the fact that the Antichrist had recruited humans for the war but I didn't expect them to magically appear as the demons did. The armor of the demonic army bears is not like I remember from the first war. It's still black and color but now it's more, well, scary. It's decked with bronze spikes and chain mesh all over it and behind their helmets they are not in their semi-human forms. Black, smokey, snarling faces peer out beneath the metal on their heads and they bare razor sharp teeth at us. They remind me somewhat of the villain venom from Spider-Man, only, you know, more realistic. I let out a small whimper at the side of this massive army of monsters before me.

My dad is a demon and Dria basically is… and Dayton used to be, but I've never seen any of them appear this way. Dayton's hand slips into mine and his voice resonates in my mind.

'They can take almost any form. They're trying to throw you off by scaring you.'

I give a sarcastic grunt that resembles a small laugh, *'Oh yeah? Well, it's totally working…'*

'You can't let them get to you. Everything will be fine. Stay strong, and stay close to me. I won't let anything happen to you Angel. I swear it.'

This gives me a slight ease and a comfort as I'm undeniably grateful to have Dayton by my side right now. I look around at the angelic army lined up beside us and spot Dria and Errapel down a ways to our right. They must have just arrived and they are already suited up and ready for battle.

The demon army begins to chant and their cries grow louder and louder. Talbot Desdemona steps to the front and chances well, until the ground begins to shake violently. I grasp Dayton's arm tightly to keep from falling. I'm unsure as to what is happening but I know it can't be good. Every angel around us scowls as the dust in front of the other army swirls in the same fashion it had earlier.

Finally the sand disperses and I see the most horrible thing I could see these days. Satan, still in his dragon form, and Zantouron I'm outstanding before the massive demons, who by this point are celebrating hysterically as though the war is over and they've already won. All seven of Lucifer's heads stretch into the air and breathe out a massive explosion of flames fueled by every ounce of rage he has within.

Despite this display, my intention is focused elsewhere, on Zantouron. He stands defiantly and glares directly at me, his gaze unwavering despite the uproar around him. He blames me for his banishment, also technically Dayton is the one that tied him up and Michael's the one that tossed him in. But it doesn't matter because I started this whole thing, therefore I'm the cause of his imprisonment.

He doesn't give me a creepy smile or blow a kiss or anything like that. I would have probably found these much less frightening than the menacing look I'm getting now. My usual thoughts of him consisted mostly of his being a perverted psycho, but I have the feeling any perverse thoughts he may have had towards me are now replaced by desires to slice through every inch of my skin with the sharpest blade he can find.

I go up and look away but when I turn back I find his eyes still firmly locked on me. Terrifying images feel my mind and I shed her and pull Dayton even closer. I don't want to seem like a coward but I am scared to death, or perhaps I'm scared of it…

~ **Dayton** ~

Aurora's group on his arm tightens continuously and he fears if she doesn't let go soon she may very well cut off his circulation. He scans the field for a reason behind her fearful aggression. His eyes drift over Satan as he rages, no doubt showing off after finally being released. That, however, is not the reason Aurora is freaking out. No, the reason behind that is standing next to the dragon.

Zantouron.

Not only is he back but there's no doubt he's out for blood, and from the direction of his gaze that blood is Aurora's.

'Over my dead body...' Dayton thanks to himself as he scowls in Zantouron's direction. that freak isn't going to lay a finger on Aurora with Dayton around. He casually slides his body in front of Aurora's, sending a clear message to both her and Zantouron. No one is going to get to her unless they go through him first.

The group she holds on his arm loosens just a bit and she recognizes what he's saying. Man, he is so glad she trusts him again. There's no way he's ever going to break that trust again. On the plane before him Zantouron smiles maliciously and the look in his eyes seems to say, 'Gladly'. Dayton growls in disgust.

He would love nothing more than to run Zantouron through but if there's a way to keep him alive until the end of the war he will. Somehow the thought of him burning for all eternity sounds a bit more appealing than just a brief moment of pain. Dayton would love to toss Zantouron into the lake of fire and if given the opportunity he's sure to take it.

But, if it comes down to it Dayton will kill him to protect Aurora. Revenge would be nice but our safety is his top priority. The sky splits open and Christ appears on a glimmering white horse. He rides through the sky, his horse literally walking on air, and lands before the angelic army. Looks like everyone is here now.

This sky thunders and the earth shakes as the two armies screech with fury. Jesus holds up his sword and both armies surge forward, ready to fight to the death. Of course, it certainly makes you wonder, after seeing all of this, how can the humans and Satan's league of troops still be willing to fight alongside him? They just witnessed the son of God right down from heaven on a horse to lead hundreds of thousands of angels to battle against a fire breathing dragon and his legions of demonic forces... If that doesn't send a human packing then they must be beyond deceived. Which must be the case because there they are pushing towards their imminent deaths.

Dayton and Aurora rush into battle, side by side. There's no way he's letting her out of his sight this time. No, not a chance. He slashes through demon after demon, along with the occasional human. Dayton makes sure to keep Aurora in his peripheral vision as much as possible.

'Where is Zantouron?' Dayton tries to look around for the bloodlusting demon but he can't focus for long without another fallen troop attacking him. But there's no doubt in his mind that Zantouron is close by. If he's after Aurora, and she's over here, then Zantouron is undoubtedly nearby. Dayton sees Aurora pull her sword from a demon's chest before quickly spinning around and running it through a marked human behind her.

She makes a face as the human falls to his knees before her and Dayton knows how hard this is for her. He wants to hug her, to tell her it's all going to be okay, but this isn't the best time for sentimental gestures. Another fallen leaps at him and Dayton throws his sword up and defense, striking the demon's blade against his own. screaming pierces through the air all around but one in particular sounds in his ears.

It's a woman's cry and fear clutches Dayton's heart at the notion that it could be Aurora. But no, Aurora is still fighting only a few feet away. Dayton needs the demon in the groin and slices through his stomach with his blade. The body disintegrates and Dayton quickly glances around for the source of the scream.

Dria.

He races over to her. She's lying on the ground, crying and clutching her right side in agony. He lands on his knees next to her and yanks her hand from her side. She has a deep wound and there's a lot of blood.

"It's okay, it's just a flesh wound. You'll heal, hold still and I'll wrap it up and get you out of here." He starts to rip the bottom of his shirt but Drea reaches out and grabs all of his hand.

"No…" She chokes it out through the pain. Her eyes sparkle from the tears if she looks him in the eye and pleads with him, "Kill me…"

She says it so softly, so sadly. Dayton stares at her, shocked, before shaking his head angrily.

"No, I won't do it. Dria You're going to be fine. This will heal, I'll get you out of here. You'll be just fine." He starts to tug at his shirt again but again she grabs him and stops him.

"Dayton please... I'll burn! For all eternity. I. Will. Burn. Please, kill me…" She coughs and a trickle of blood chips from the corner of her mouth. She stares up at him hopelessly and tears form in his eyes. He understands her request but how can he? He has already hurt her and now he has to kill her?

"Please…" She begs, "If there's an ounce of love for me left in you
Dayton then please, don't let me burn... Please…" She says softly and Dayton finally nods. He pulls up his sword, tears streaming from his eyes as he brings it down. He feels the strike hit but his eyes are shut tight. When he finally opens them he can't bring himself to look down. Instead, he pulls his sword up quickly and leaps his feet.

A human jumps toward him but he swings his sword faster than the human can think to stop and slice his right through the man's chest, killing him instantly. Dayton rubs his arm across his eyes before turning back around to once again locate Aurora. She's battling two at once but that concerns him a whole lot less than the fact that Zantouron is making a beeline towards her from the other side.

He has a determined look on his face and he's slicing through angels without so much as a glance on his way. He keeps his eyes and his smile focused on Aurora as he marches through the battle. Dayton wastes no time in bolting towards Aurora, determined to reach her before Zantouron. It's raining again in the Sandy desert They have been fighting on is now a muddy swamp.

It's hard to push through the thick sludge and Dayton resorts to using his wings. He pushes through the air in short spurts of flight, trying to reach Aurora before it's too late. Zantouron seems to have no trouble trudging through the mud and his expression taunts Dayton, as if to say, *'Check mate.'*

~Michael ~

It's an honor, having the opportunity to fight hand in hand with the savior, even if it is under such dire circumstances. Michael stands back to back with his Lord as they fight, protecting one another, as well as the angels around them. Christ handles the demons while Michael takes on the humans, except, of course, when it's unavoidable to fight the other.

However, the humans fighting seem to weigh pretty heavy on his king.

Jesus fights with tears in his eyes, and Michael knows how he feels. Christ died for these humans. He gave so much, went through so much, all to save these creatures who now fight against him in the ultimate battle. It hurts Christ and it angers Michael but it is what it is.

Michael's blade slices through the nearest human's neck, cleanly beheading him. The head rolls across the ground before resting in the mud so that it faces up and the mark on it is there for all to see. That is the hardest part about this; The fact that the human bodies don't leave... Michael and Christ must fight there among the severed bodies bleeding and that makes it all the more difficult to bear.

Michael turns away from the dead human and finds himself face to face with a demon blade prepared to strike. *'Well, this is the end, but it shall be an honor to die in the service of my Lord.'*

This thought passes swiftly through his mind as he stands firm, prepared to die with valor. Suddenly, the demon lunges forward with a very shocked expression on his face. The sword slips from the demon's hand as he crumbles. The following lands face down in the mud, sputtering muck and blood of one to Michael skin.

Confusion settles over Michael as he stares down at the dissipating body below. A hand lands on his shoulder and he jumps before slowly turning. Jesus gives him a soft nod and removes his hand, letting Michael know that he is the one who saved him and he has his back.

"Thank you…" Michael mutters, still somewhat in shock. Jesus suddenly leaps away and raises his sword.

"Heads up!" He warns and Michael spins around, swinging his blade without bothering to look. He misses. The Antichrist stands on the muddy terrain before him laughing. Satan stomps up behind him and the two square off with Christ and Michael.

'So it is time then.' Michael casts a quick glance over at Jesus and receives a nod. *'It is time for the beginning of the end.'*

~Crater ~

That pig Zantouron gets back and thinks he owns the place. As soon as the battle begins the first thing he does is start yelling that the girl is his and nobody else is to lay a finger on her.

'Yeah right, Like that's going to stop anyone.' Crater thinks as he watches Zantouron speed off into the crowd. First of all, Crater's fairly sure only a handful of demons even heard Zantouron, Which means the rest will for sure jump her. Second, Crater plans on getting to her first.

He slinks through the mass of soldiers, fighting off a few angels as he goes. Not to make light of an angel's skills. They are definitely tough opponents; however, crater isn't taking the time to actually have a decent battle with any. If any get in his way he simply swings a few times and then shoves another demon into the battle while he slips away. Some would call it cowardly, but it's not meant that way at all.

Crater would gladly fight any of the celestial breed that dared to cross him. However, Zantouron seems to be slicing through the heavenly host with unfeasible ease. If Crater has any hope of reaching the girl first then he has no choice but to avoid wasting time on any other being. He looks out in the direction Zantouron is hitting and spots the girl, Aurora, holding her own against a demon that Crater doesn't recognize from this distance.

He takes off in her direction from a different angle than Zantouron; He should beat that idiot there. A form suddenly blocks his path and Crater growls angrily.

"Move Dria." He demands but she plants her feet in the dirt firmly. She pulls her sword up before her and glares at Crater with determination. This interests him. She's one of them, more than that she practically led them half the time. Dria was Satan's adopted daughter and although Satan is incapable of love he had a certain respect for Dria. He'd made her the head of many missions since she'd first arrived nearly a century ago.

But now she has changed. Sure, she still got black wings and she'll still burn with them if she survives but she has sided with the enemy and for that Crater shall destroy her.

"All right," He mutters and meets her sword with his, "we'll do this the hard way."

$$\sim\textbf{Aurora}\sim$$

"Two on one? Since when is this fair?" I grumble at my attackers as I try to fight them off. As far as I can tell one is human, the other is not... Although I can't quite tell whether he's a demon or nephilim, but then, I guess it doesn't matter a whole lot. Even being outnumbered I'm not doing too bad, I'm holding my own anyway.

Out of the corner of my eye I see Dayton rushing toward me, panic on his face. The rain has the ground beyond soaked and my feet sink in the swampy muck. I frown as I fight the two soldiers before me.

'Why is Dayton coming over? I'm doing just fine on my own... I mean, his concern is sweet and all but I'm not a child.'

I thrust forward catching the human in the arm, leaving a large cut that gushes blood. I can feel my face flush at the site and my stomach turns. My blade must have struck an artery or something judging by all the blood it's producing. The man falls in the mud screaming and grasping his arm and pain. The demon or nephilim doesn't even miss a beat in leaping at me again, ignoring his fallen partner.

Gathering myself I throw up my blade in defense. Someone suddenly shoots past us and I catch a quick flash of white feathers.

'Dayton?' I don't have time to see where he's hitting because the creature fighting me slices to the air, causing me to dive backwards to escape the sword. Perhaps if my life weren't in danger right now then I would be grossed out by the fact that I'm now lying in a pool of blood soaked mud.

The creature towers above me and brings his sword down towards my drenched body. I roll to the side but the mud slows me down some and the tip of his sword grazes my side. I gasp but I don't stop to examine the wound. Leaping to my feet I jerk my elbow around, popping my attacker in the jaw forcefully. He curses and staggers back, giving me an opportunity to dive at him.

His body falls under my weight and we smack into the ground. We roll around, both getting in some direct hits with our fists before I finally get the upper hand. I sit straddling his stomach as I reach for my sword and bring it down with as much force as possible. I can actually hear the ribs cracking as the sword slices through them. His mouth contorts in a look of horror but he doesn't scream, no, he's dead before he can even process what's happened. The fact that his body doesn't disappear instantly proves he must have been a nephilim.

Beads of sweat trickle down my forehead and mix with my tears. They kill, I kill, sometimes I wonder... How do you define a monster? How am I any different? But then I remember what I'm fighting for. I take this one free moment to lift my shirt and examine the damage. I'm only just beginning to feel the pain, now that the adrenaline is wearing off. Luckily it doesn't look deep, more of a scratch really. Of course, that could just be because it's already begun to heal.

"You'll have to go through me!" Dayton's voice carries through the air and I stand back up and try to spot him, I locate him almost immediately; He's standing close by, between me and Zantouron.

"Oh I'm planning on it." Zantouron smirks and doesn't waste a second before diving at Dayton, catching him off guard.

"Dayton!" I yell and take off towards him. A leg appears before me and I face plant. Great, now every last inch of me that wasn't already covered in mud is now completely soaked in it. Laughter rings out above me and I quickly scramble to my feet. I try to wipe the mud from my eyes. It doesn't do a whole lot of good but it makes it so I can at least see enough to fight.

Crater stands smiling before me, "You missed a spot."

He laughs again but I raise my sword and point it at his face, just between his eyes. His smile fades and his own sword forms in his hand.

"What is it with you female nephilim? You and Dria both, so testy. Of course, it'll kill you, just like it killed her." He shakes his head disapprovingly. My eyes go wide at this declaration of Dria's death.

"You killed her?" I didn't like her but I didn't want her dead. He studies me for a long moment before answering the question.

"No… I merely wounded her. She could have healed." He begins to circle me but I walk with him keeping my sword up and ready.

"Could have?" I ask, seeking clarification.

"Yes, she could have healed easily... If pretty boy hadn't killed her first." He shrugs as if what he's saying has no meaning to him but I can see in his eyes he's taunting me.

"Dayton?" I'm suddenly very confused and I find it hard to believe despite my tingling angel sense claiming that it's true.

"You know," Crater grins maliciously, "I'd heard they had some history. Ha, talk about tough love. He'd probably do the same to you if a new girl came along."

Now I'm seething with anger. I swing at him but he side steps it easily. It's not true! Dayton loves me and if he killed Dria It was for a good reason, I'm sure. Just like it will be with good reason when I kill Crater… With my sword already in my right hand, I form my shield in my left. Crater raises an eyebrow but doesn't form a shield of his own.

"Scared princess?"

I shake my head but I don't bother to say anything. Crater begins to circle me again like a beast would its prey. Again I do the same to him, there's no way I'm giving him any easy chances. He makes the first move this time and rushes at me. I throw up my shield and the battle begins.

Relentless, that's what he is. He lashes out at me like a crazed madman, actually a madman would be a welcome replacement. We dance around each other and I feel rather outmatched. Between Crater and Zantouron it's a wonder I've lasted this long. It's like he can anticipate my every move and match it perfectly. Cat and mouse, he's toying with me. While I'm fighting for my life Crater is playing a game. And he seems to be winning it.

His sword repeatedly rams into my shield, sending vibrations through the metal and up my arms. It's hard to hold on to it against the violent blows it's receiving. With each strike it pushes me back bit by bit. I stumbled backwards, using all my strength to keep the shield between my body and Crater's smoking blade. He's making it hard for me to even stand, nonetheless fight back. But I have to do something, because at this rate I'll be landing in the mud yet again, but I doubt I'll be getting back up this time if I do.

Crater doesn't seem to be tiring at all, in fact, his strength and rage only appeared to grow with each blow. I decided to try something that is most likely very stupid. When Crater goes to strike again I swing my sword around in front of my shield so that crater's blade hits mine this time. I'm not even sure what I'd plan to accomplish by this, all I knew for sure was that if I kept hiding behind the shield I'd be nothing more than a coward.

I've come to realize that in this world you have two options: Don't hide and run the risk of dying, or hide and not ever really live. I'm done hiding... Even if it kills me.

The force at which his sword hits mine pushes my hand into the outside of my shield, hard. Warm liquid oozes down from several of my knuckles but I push aside the pain. I allow my shield to dematerialize and grab the heel of my sword in both hands. Neither of us dare to pull our sword back for the force the other is thrusting with would surely send their blade into our chest.

Crater pushes forward slowly, shoving my sword back towards my face inch by inch. A shape moves behind Crater And I risk a glimpse over his shoulder. Gabriel stands a few feet behind the demon watching us. His eyes are full of concern but he makes no move to rescue me. And I know why…

This is my match. I need to fight this battle no matter how difficult it gets. That being said, just knowing that Gabriel is there and ready should I need him gives me a renewed strength. In a burst of speed and force, that I myself didn't even know I was capable of, I thrust forward knocking Crater back a step. That alone would not be enough to do any good, that is, if it weren't for the shock it caused.

Crater couldn't comprehend the energy burst I had just gained and it left him taken aback. Honestly, I'm surprised myself but I don't focus on it. Instead I swing my sword and manage to knock the demon's blade from his hand. He instinctively follows the blade with his eyes and I take this brief opportunity without the slightest hesitation. My weapon makes contact with his chest, slicing it open from right to left. His eyes flick back towards me as his body begins to crumble. He reaches out to me and grabs a hold of my necklace.

He had no doubt grabbed my necklace and an attempt to stop his fall, however all it did was rip the chain straight off my neck. Crater lands in the mud and pieces of my shell necklace fall from his clenched fist as his body disappears. shattered, the remainder of my beautiful token gets washed away by the rain as I stare down in shock and devastation. Gabriel rushes over and lays a hand on my shoulder but doesn't speak. He doesn't have to.

A yell pierces through the sound of the rain beating down around me and I turn to see one of the most frightening scenes that I've witnessed in a long time. The silver glint travels down deep into Dayton's thigh. He yells again as Zantouron twists the blade deeper into his thigh muscle. Before I even realize I'm moving I'm across the field leaping at the demon that I hate almost worse than Satan himself.

~ Dayton ~

He had one task, protect the girl he loves at all costs, and he failed. At last glance she had been struggling to hold up against Crater's fierce blows, all the while Zantouron I was beating the snot out of Dayton. How it happened he's not quite sure, one second they seemed evenly matched and the next Dayton's being tossed to the ground as Zantouron Bloom's over him gloating.

Dayton's sword is long gone and he tries to reform it only to have the demon kick him in the side. Forming a weapon requires concentration, something that's difficult to do when you're bleeding internally and externally. He grinds his teeth together in pain and tries to get back up. Zantouron laughs and shoves him back into the mud.

"It's no use traitor," Zantouron grins down at him, "my time in the pit gave me plenty of time to think of strategies and build up my rage. I'm afraid you have no chance against me. And I'm going to make you and your little girlfriend suffer."

With that the demon brings his sword down and carves into Dayton's right thigh. The pain is more than he can stand and he cries out in agony. His adversary twists the blade like a screwdriver, embedding it slowly deeper into Dayton's flesh. His body shakes from the pain and he cries out again before sinking into a deep series of moans, drifting in and out of consciousness. Unfortunately, it is not only possible to die of pain but in this case it is a guaranteed result. Dayton can already feel his body beginning to shut down.

'I've failed her…' He thinks as the pain gives way to a numbing sensation. *'I love her and I failed her.'* His eyes begin to flutter open and shut as his mind prepares to shut down. He looks up at his enemy one last time, expecting the demon to be laughing at him on his deathbed. Except he isn't. In fact, Zantouron's expression is one of pure horror.

He releases the sword that is buried in Dayton style and grabs at his stomach with both hands. Dayton is in too much pain to comprehend what is happening. Zantouron pulls his hands away and Dayton can see the blood on them clearly now. All four of them... The fact that he's seeing double now proves the horrible reality of his approaching death.

Someone pulls the sword from his thigh but he's too numb to feel it now. The image is too fuzzy to make out who it is. He's going to die but he needs to say it, he needs someone to tell her…

"Tell… her…" The words come out and barely a whisper and whoever it is hunched over him tries to convince him to hush. But he can't. "Tell… I… love…" He can't do it, he can't finish the sentence because he's so tired. The wave of drowsiness overtakes him and he closes his eyes and prepares to fall asleep.

"No! Don't you... Do you hear... Stay…" someone is yelling at him but they sound a million miles away and he's so tired... so so tired…

~ Gabriel ~

Gabriel had not even had time to react when Aurora took off. Before Gabriel even knew what she was doing Aurora was across the field, running Zantouron through with her sword and shouting obscenities at him. Her language shocks Gabriel and he considers scolding her for it but in her current state it would probably not be advised.

He makes his way over to us quickly. She is hunched over Dayton's body trying to stop the bleeding. His body remains unmoving on the ground, this is good, it means he's not dead yet. Aurora is probably the only thing keeping the angel alive, however, if she stays down like that she will surely be killed.

"Aurora, you must get up!" Gabriel pleads as he approaches them. She looks up at him, panicked and angry.

"I'm not leaving him! I will not let him die!" She screams it to the world and Gabriel knows she means it.

"Fine. I'm not asking you to do either," He leans down and lifts Dayton's
limp body from the ground, "But we need to get you both somewhere safe, off the battlefield."

Aurora nods and trails behind him as he speeds off through the battling soldiers. Gabriel leads the way while Aurora holds off anyone that tries to stop them. She seems to have gone into some sort of attack mode and is doing a great job keeping attackers off of them. They are almost to the edge of the battle lines when Gabriel catches sight of Errapel Fighting a human nearby. It's obvious Errapel is playing with the human. He acts as if he's a feeble old man but when the human goes to strike he's amazed to have missed every time.

"Errapel! Quit fooling around! Kill him and come on. We need your help." Gabriel calls to him and the old man shrugs. Errapel leaps over the human's head and stabs him in the back before flying over to Gabriel's side.

"Can't an old man have any fun?" Errapel asks as they take to the air, leaving the bloodbath behind them.

Gabriel sighs, "In the middle of a war? No."

They land several miles away from the battle but the sound of swords and screams can still be heard, carried by the raging winds. Gabriel lays Dayton down on the ground with care and Aurora, who has not said a word since they had left Nazareth, now begs Errapel to save her love.

"Errapel, please… He is my life... My soul." She whimpers and barely chokes the words out.

Gabriel studies Aurora's face as she speaks. She does not cry this time, she isn't sad, no she's scared. There is no doubt in Gabriel's mind that she would not survive Dayton's death, whether it means she wouldn't survive physically, or mentally, or emotionally… But in some form or fashion she would die along with him.
Errapel seems to recognize this as well but he doesn't wish to give her hope where there is none.

"My dear child, I will not lie and tell you he will surely live. Even if I had all of my herbs and mixtures the chances of his recovery would still be next to none. I shall do all I can but please do not let your hopes get too high... For I fear it will only make for a harder fall."

Errapel turns to Dayton, avoiding Aurora's eyes. Gabriel gives her a sympathetic look and hopes she can take the news she has just received. Aurora is a very strong willed girl and so far it has seemed as though neither heaven nor hell could break that will but this, Gabriel fears, may push her over the edge. Suddenly she speaks, her Amber eyes never straying from her boyfriend's bloody face.

"I have lost a lot of things in my life, especially lately, but I have not lost everything until I lose hope."

Then without another word she flies off in the direction of the war. Gabriel follows her with his eyes until she is out of sight. He can't bring himself to smile at a time like this but he liked what she had said. Although, she left out one thing. Faith. We have not lost everything until we've lost our hope and our faith. Gabriel nods his appreciation to Errapel and then takes to the sky to rejoin his brothers in the battle that is soon to change everything.

<h3 align="center">~ Bokim ~</h3>

Bokim is focused, intent. He is fighting for heaven's side with nothing to gain, but then, also nothing to lose. Every demon on the field believes him a traitor, but then what else could you call his actions as of late? So a traitor he is then, a demon with identity issues. Of course, it's not as if he's the first, no, that would have been Dayton. Bokim tried to hate Dayton, and he certainly had everyone believing he did, but truth be told he respects the boy. perhaps he actually envies him a bit also. But in the end he's glad his daughter has someone like Dayton to be there for her like he never was.

A single beam of radiant light shoots down from the sky and touches Earth somewhere across the field. Bokims eyes go wide and his heart races as he watches the beam. There's only one thing it could be and the idea causes him to break into a run, desperate to reach the light, desperate to see her face again. Heaven is outnumbered. Their only hope is to call back the nephilim from limbo that died before the war. Any who died during the war will not be allowed to return but those dying before can be brought down as a last resort.

This, of course, means heaven is losing the war, and is not to be seen as a good thing. However, the chance to see his darling Shaphir again can only be seen as a blessing in his eyes. The beam slowly begins to rise back into the atmosphere and Bokim arrives within seconds. She's standing at the head of a group of nearly 5,000 nephilim, all with their swords drawn and ready.

"Shaphir!" Bokim yells as he leaps towards her. She turns and spots him instantly and terror floods her face. Bokim stops running and stills. Her gaze is fixed directly behind him and Bokim allows his sword to form in his hand. His wife looks as if she's about to bolt towards him at any second. Someone is behind him, someone Shaphir Sears will kill him and so Bokim does the only thing he can. He turns to face the threat.

Menacing olive green eyes stare back at Bokim from under a stray curl of ash and gray hair. A smile is plastered on Aakar's face as he swings his sword around at his side and watches Bokim.

"Hello son." Aakar laughs as he taunts him with his eyes.

"Very funny Aakar." Bokim raises his sword and the other demon does the same. The sound of footsteps smacking into the mud can be heard behind Bokim but he doesn't remove his eyes from his father in law.

"Oh look," Aakar nods his head as if to point behind Bokim, "My daughter is here to see me."

The urge to turn around is so strong but Bokim resists, even as he feels his wife at a side.

"I hate you." She says softly.

Aakar wags a finger at her, clicking his tongue in amused and fake disapproval. "Now, is that any way to greet your long-lost father?"

Shaphir starts to respond but Bokim grits his teeth and swings his sword. Aakar senses the strap coming and dodges it. Bokim goes to swing again but Aakar grabs Shaphir and puts his blade to her neck.

"Nuh uh uh…" Aakar shakes his head and smiles wide. Taunting. Bokim freezes mid swing and stairs into his wife's eyes.

Do it. She thinks towards him and he moans aloud. She isn't scared, she doesn't care if she dies again, but Bokim can't go through that again. He can't watch the love of his life die a second time. He won't. He drops his sword and hangs his head.

"Good," Aakar says approvingly, "now, Shaphir, You look so much like your mother." Aakar runs his fingers down the side of Shaphir's face and Bokim growls threateningly. Aakar ignores him and traces a line down Shaphir's shoulders. That's when Bokim notices the knife and his wife's hand. It's not a large knife but it's big enough to hurt Aakar enough to distract him. Bokim prepares himself as he waits for her to make a move.

Shaphir's arm suddenly jerks back and sends the knife directly into her father's side. He howls in pain and drops his sword. Bokim doesn't hesitate, the second Aakar releases the hilt of his blade Bokim was already pulling his wife away and diving at him. They both land in the mud, Bokim on top, and begin beating each other. From the corner of his eye Bokim sees his wife pick up his sword and turn back towards them. He holds his arm out to her but she stops and stares at him confused. He looks down and the face below smiles, his face.

Aakar had shifted into a replica of Bokim and Shaphir doesn't know who to give the sword to. Bokim could easily convince her it was him if he had a chance to talk to her… But he doesn't have that kind of time. So instead he resorts to fists again. The two roll around in the mud until Bokim finally lands a hard blow to Aakar's temple. It was such an effective hit that Aakar unintentionally shifts back to himself. Shaphir races over but instead of handing the sword to Bokim she stabs Aakar herself.

Bokim watches as Aakar snarls and his body disappears beneath him. Then he stands and his wife falls into his arms weeping. He's caught completely off guard by this. There had only been two other instances in which he'd seen her cry, the day she had to give Aurora away and the day he'd had to leave her. Pain streaked through his chest as her sorrow seeped into him, but he didn't show it, he simply held her tight. If he could take all the sorrow from her into himself he would, always.

The battle rages on around them but he doesn't care. He holds her as if she were the only thing in existence. Usually she is the one comforting him. So this is definitely a new experience for him. She weeps into his chest and when she eventually pulls away he longs to pull her back. Shaphir Stan's tall and wipes the tears from her eyes before looking at him sadly.

"Are you okay?" He asks her, concerned, as she watches him. She just slowly shakes her head no. Bokim frowns and starts to speak again but she cuts him off.

"Bokim… It's the end…"

His frown deepens in his gay shifts downward. "It'll be alright…" He lies.

She shakes her head again and glares at him. "Don't you dare lie to me. You know good and well what happens when this is over. It's far from all right…"

Bokim says and looks back up at her as tears once again threaten to escape her soft, frightened eyes. He knows what she means and he has the feeling she's on to his plan for dealing with it. So he decides to remain silent and she soon confirms his suspicion.

"You're going to…" She chokes on the words through streams of tears,
"You're going to kill yourself aren't you?"

Bokim grinds his teeth together at the words. It's the coward's way out but what else is there?

"I was…" He avoids her gaze as he admits his Chamberlain tension. She remains silent for a long moment and eventually he glances back up at her face. She stares back at him pleadingly and he feels the need to ask her the question he's been asking himself.

"What else would you have me do? I know it's cowardly, I know it's disgraceful, but what else would you have me do?" He falls to his knees before the one that he loves and she watches him with her in her eyes. Then she draws her sword and nails down next to him.

"When the war ends I will return to limbo for a brief time before disappearing altogether. I may be alive for the moment but I am dead for eternity. If I die again now I shall skip limbo and just be gone. Draw your sword."

Bokims eyes widen at her words and he shakes his head furiously.

"No! I will do no such thing! I know what your plan is and I refuse it. I will not watch you die again." He yells at her but Shaphir doesn't even flinch.

"This body is temporary. I'm already dead. If you wish to die so badly, fine, but you shall not die by your own hand and you shall not die alone. Now redraw your sword." Her hair blows in the wind and she looks so strong and regal.

This time, with rivers of tears flowing down his cheeks, Bokim does as he's told. His sword forms in his hands and he whimpers as his wife guides it to rest over her heart.

Then she places her sword against his chest and whispers, "I love you Bokim…"

He moans in pain and returns her statement. "I love you too... My love for you has no end."

The edges of his wife's lips curve up every so slightly, giving just the hint of a smile. Then she begins to count and Bokim subs harder with each number.

"One... Two... Three."

They both thrust forward as forcefully as they can. Neither cries out or makes any sound at all. their bodies fall to the ground, press tightly together as the life drains out of them. It was only seconds before they vanished into the wind together. Leaving the battle and everything else behind for all eternity.

<h3 align="center">~Aurora ~</h3>

The beam of light in the sky draws my attention immediately. I have no idea what it could be but I intend to find out. As I get closer I see my father battling my grandfather and a hand to hand combat on the ground. Behind them stands a figure that upon recognition causes my heart to stop beating for a moment. Mom. She runs over and stabs Aakar. My father stands back up and she falls into his embrace.

I'm a pretty lengthy distance away but I start to run towards them. A large man suddenly leaps into my path. He's human and pretty easy to beat. It only takes a couple of minutes but it distracts me for longer than I could afford. By the time I manage to kill him and look back to where my parents are I have to hold back a scream. I watch as my mom and dad kill one another and their bodies disappear together.

Agony courses through my body and my knees go weak and crumble beneath me. Strong arms reach around me and hold me up. I don't know who it is but, honestly, it could have been a demon for all I care.

"I have no one left… " I whimper and my body trembles in pain. Gabriel's smooth voice sounds behind me.

"Don't lose faith Aurora. Whatever you do, don't lose faith."

I turn around and bury my face in his sturdy chest as I cry. In my current state I can't bring myself to think about what I just witnessed let alone try to understand why they did it. I don't even know why or how my mom was alive again to begin with. When I saw she was here again I was so... I thought maybe... And then... It hurts, it hurts so bad.

Gabriel suddenly jerks me off of him and whips his blade through a demon that I hadn't even heard coming up behind me. My arm throbs and a bruise begins to form where Gabe had grabbed me. I ignore it, knowing it'll heal nearly as quickly as it has appeared. Gabriel saved my life. I was weak, pathetic, and perhaps I have the right to be. Perhaps when this is over I can break down but this is not the time or the place. I draw my sword, grind my teeth, and race off into battle yet again. I'm determined to keep on fighting, even unto death, if that's what it takes to win this war. Both the physical war raging around me and the emotional war raging within.

~The Antichrist ~

Heaven has called for reinforcements, proving the war is drawing to a close in favor of Satan's side. It appears to Talbot that Satan is not as sure a victory as he is. Talbot can see the way his master carries himself in battle, as if he believes It is his last. nonsense! This war is practically one. Looking around one can see the obvious losses heaven is endured. The battlefield is no longer a crowded mass of bodies that can hardly be moved through.

It's not hard to tell that of the few hundred thousand soldiers left they're practically two demons to every angel. Just before the war Satan had warned the Antichrist saying,

"Do not expect victory, do not even let it cross your mind." What a pep talk huh? Talbot can't begin to understand what Satan had meant by that statement, considering the path to victory is becoming easier traveled by the second. These thoughts had him zoned out for a moment but a yell rings through the air drawing him out of his trance.

The Antichrist looks down below him at the archangel He has pinned to the ground. Michael yells again as Talbot pushes his sword deeper into his shoulder blade.

"Some mighty warrior you are…" the Antichrist grumbles as Michael writhes in agony beneath him. "It's very disappointing actually. I've heard such incredible things about you Angel and was so looking forward to this battle. Shame it's going so pathetically."

Michael's gaze shifts over the Antichrist shoulder but he doesn't turn around. He watches as Michael's eyes widen at whatever he sees behind him. Honestly? Is this what the great archangel Michael has been reduced to? A childish human game of 'made you look?' Well, I will not be falling for it. Michael looks back at Talbot's face and smiles even through the pain.

"The time has come. The war is over." Michael says it confidently and Talbot Desdemona frowns at him.

"Angel, you are going to die by my hand. Then my master and I will win the war and roll together. The outcome is clear, how can you possibly be grinning? Have you gone mad?"

The Antichrist is completely dumbfounded as the archangel laughs at his question. This angel is obviously delusional from pain… suddenly a burning sensation hits talbots back and he whips his head around to see what has attacked him. A bright beam of heavenly fire rains down directly on him, immobilizing him completely. Michael kicks him off and pulls the sword from his shoulder with a sharp wail.

The Antichrist's eyes dart around as he realizes that all of the demons, and even the humans, on the field have been paralyzed by a beam of fire themselves. He's taken aback with waves of confusion.

"I don't understand…" He mumbles as Michael steps over and places him in heavenly shackles.

"They marched across the breath of the Earth and surrounded the camp of God's people, the city he loves. But fire came down from heaven and devoured them. Revelations 20 verse 9. You should not have expected a victory." The archangel shakes his head and Talbot's eyes grow wide.

~Satan ~

In his dragon form Lucifer is a formidable opponent to nearly anyone. But then, he's fighting the son of God, he doesn't have a prayer. Satan smirks at his pun and whips his tail towards Christ, hitting him in the side. It's a direct hit but that means nothing, this whole war means nothing. It's merely one last stand of defiance, one last finger to the sky.

As much as he hates to admit it, he's scared. Satan knows his fate, he knew it would end like this. For the first few hundred years on Earth he tried to deceive himself into believing he could win, but he eventually realized it was impossible to defeat the one that created all things. After that it had been simply a quest for souls. How many of God's precious "children" Could Satan drag down with him?

Lucifer had warned his Antichrist before the war not to expect victory. Even as his servant had nodded in agreement Satan had seen in his eyes that he was going to ignore that warning. Idiot. For the last six millennia Satan has been surrounded by imbeciles. And now he's going to burn with them.

Christ recovers from the blow and his white hair swirls around his head. This battle has been dragging by with neither opponent having caused any real damage to the other. Satan is almost to the point where he's ready to tell Jesus to just end it already. But then, it turns out, he doesn't have to, because Christ gives the signal that does just that. Jesus's eyes light up as if a spark were ignited in them that danced around their brilliant orange hue. He lives his head to the sky and the fire in his eyes summons the fire of heaven.

Satan watches in terror and amazement as the beam shoots down and disables himself and his army alike. The dragon growls as he sees his soldiers' faces painted and fear. Why can't they hide it! show some fortitude, some backbone. His antichrist is yards away being shackled by Michael, and from the look on Talbot's face, it appears he had indeed ignored Lucifer's warning and is utterly shocked by this defeat.

Jesus steps up to Satan and looks him in the eye calmly. "Return to your human form."

Satan growls and blows smoke from his dragon nose but he slowly changes form. "I will not be compared to those lowly creatures who should never have existed to begin with. They are abominations."

Christ vines and shackles him before gesturing to the humans that remained around him. "And yet you shall suffer the same fate. As equals."

The sound that escapes Lucifer's lips is one so dreadful It draws the muddy ground and cracks the Earth into pieces below their feet.

~Michael ~

Michael realizes the Antichrist could have killed him. The sword through the shoulder was excruciating but it was child's play to Talbot. The Antichrist was overconfident and hadn't seen any harm and toying with Michael. Had he forgotten what the outcome would be? Or had he really believed that Satan would ever defeat God? Michael had seen Jesus give the signal and he'd watched as the fire fell from heaven to end the war.

Cloaked with confusion, Talbot murdered about how it makes no sense, how the demons were winning, how he didn't understand how they could have lost. It honestly amazes Michael that the Antichrist had been so confident in the triumph of evil. Sure the angels had their setbacks but God would never allow them to fall at the hands of Satan. Michael fastens talbots hands firmly behind his back with angelic gold shackles before dragging him over and tossing him next to Satan.

Christ has already bound Satan in the same manner and other demons are being hauled over by the $144,000 remaining angels. The angels are covered in blood and dirt and they all look beaten and worn but there's no mistaking the look of relief on their faces. Michael's eyes pan out across the field in search of Aurora and the others and he spots Gabriel making his way towards him. The archangel rushes out to meet his friend and gives him a quick hug.

"Good to see you brother. Where are the others?"

Gabriel gives a sad smile as Michael releases him and steps back to survey his face.

"Aurora is fine, but Dayton... He was injured pretty severely. Errapel is with him now but it doesn't look good. Aurora is heading back to them now. Dria and Bokim... Well..." Gabriel goes silent and Michael knows.

It's for the best.

"We should join Errapel and Aurora. She will need us if…" Michael doesn't finish the statement. He simply waits for Gabriel to not and takes to the sky. They will need to hurry; It won't be long before the humans will all be summoned here and the end ceremony will begin. They have to be back by then if they hope to make it to heaven. Transporting has been blocked since the start of the war and will not resume until the creation of the new Earth. So either they get back before the ceremony or they get destroyed along with the Earth.

~Aurora ~

I have absolutely no idea what's going on. Typical... When I saw streams of fire suddenly cascading down from the sky I actually screamed. I swear the demon I'd been fighting looked at me like I was nuts... The closest pillar of flames roared down directly towards him and while he looked scared, he didn't seem anywhere near as surprised as I obviously was.

The blaze burns into the demon's back and he freezes, rather than trying to run from it. I'm pretty sure if a beam of fire was shooting out of the sky at me I'd run, but all around me demons are standing still and allowing the flames to overtake them. The angels appear relieved and some are even shouting and singing thanks.

So that's it then? That's the end of the war? Should I expect a dragon drawn chariot to appear as well? You know, scratch that, I've had enough dragons to last me a lifetime. But it did feel like that victory was sort of easy... Well... But then when I think of all that we lost, all the lives... No, that victory didn't come quick enough. I watch as the angels begin shackling and dragging the demons across the battlegrounds.

It appears the rain has finally stopped and somehow the ground has magically dried up. I see Gabriel a few yards away and I'm suddenly reminded of Dayton's condition. I race over to Gabriel as quickly as I can.

"Gave! Have you heard from Errapel?" I question intensely.

Gabriel turns around and his eyes quickly look me up and down for injuries before he shakes his head and replies, "No, I haven't spoken with him. He should still be where we left him. I'll take you there if you want."

For the first time since I ran over, I noticed the demon he's holding on to by the chain of a pair of shackles. The demon scowls at me and bares his teeth like a rabid dog. I frown and return my eyes to Gabriel's.

"No, you're busy. I remember where they are. I'll go."

Gabriel nods in acceptance and promises to join us the moment he can, then I head off. When I said I remember where we left them, well, I may have lied just a bit. I remember the general direction but not the exact location. So it takes me several minutes to find it.

When I arrive I see Errapel laying with his back against a pile of rubble. His eyes are closed and he's completely still with no one else around. My breath catches in my throat and my heart starts racing. Where's Dayton? I dive over to Errapel and shake him violently. His chest is moving so I'm pretty sure he's only asleep... I hope he's only asleep.

"Errapel! Wake up! Errapel!" I scream at him and he suddenly bolts up. Various mushrooms and plants roll off of him as he leaps to his feet, eyes darting around in his head like a madman.

"Who, what, when, where?" He twists to and fro as if searching for something, his stance makes him appear ready for a fight.

"Errapel, calm down, It's only me." I try to reassure him and he relaxes a bit, his expression changing to one of anger and accusation.

"Dagnabbit nephilim! You trying to give an old man a heart attack or something? Now look what you did! You made me drop my shrooms!" The old man waddles around picking up his fallen plants and muttering to himself angrily about her interrupting his nap.

"Where's Dayton?"

I'm trying to remain calm, I mean, surely Errapel wouldn't have been taking a nap if something terrible had happened right? But I can't help the anxiety that's bubbling up inside and it seeps out into each word. Errapel stops and looks back at me annoyed.

"Gone. And you woke me from a much-needed nap and I really don't…" he's rambling but I cut him off quickly.

"Gone? What do you mean gone? No… No I don't believe it… Gone where? Errapel! Gone where?!" I'm yelling at him and I can feel my chest constricting and my breathing quicken. He can't be gone. He just can't…

Errapel throws an arm up in surrender, holding his plants in the other.

"How should I know? One second he's here going on and on about there being something he needs to do and then he just disappears."

I stare at him in complete shock. Disappeared? It can't be… He can't mean… A sharp pain streaks through my gut and I moan and wrap my arms around me as I fall to my knees. Errapel watches me in alarm as I curl up on the ground and groan in pain. The look on his face says he thinks I've gone crazy. He sure wanted to judge…

"Dayton…" I guess through ragged breaths. the old hermit raises an eyebrow and shakes his head disbelieving.

"Good gracious girl. talk about your separation anxiety. I'm sure he'll be back before two awful long if he plans to get off this God Forsaken planet before it goes up in flames. Gosh, can't you two go a few hours without each other?"

My eyes shoot open and I bolt upright, staring at him in disbelief.

"What did you say?" I asked, as I try to get my breathing under control again.

"I said, can't you two go a few hours without each other?"

"No, I mean, you said he'll be back? You mean he's not dead?"

"Did, hit no! Whatever gave you that idea?" Errapel shakes his head disapprovingly as if I just committed a crime. I leap to my feet, smiling so wide my jaw hurts, and rush to hug him.

"You are certifiably insane Errapel!" I laugh as I wrap my arms around him. He pushes me away and ends up dropping his shrooms again.

"I am no such thing! They had me tested! Now look what you've done! You made me drop my shrooms again!" He wags a finger in my face.

Thuds sound behind me and I turn to find Michael and Gabriel, both with half curious and half amused expressions on their faces. Michael grins.

"Do I even want to know?" He asks and I speed into his arms. He embraces me and I turn and hug Gabriel as well. Gabe raises an eyebrow as he glances around the area.

"Where is Dayton?" His voice catches slightly in concern. It's as if he was hesitant to even ask.

"Good question" I laugh, "I'm going to find him." I start to fly off but someone grabs my foot, holding me in place. I glance back and find Michael's hand around my ankle, a concerned look on his face, as well as on Gabriel's and even Errapel looks slightly distressed. I land again, a frown creeping across my face.

"What?" I ask and Errapel steps forward.

"It's a big world out there and you ain't got the slightest idea where he went. He'll be back before ya know it but you got no business going on no wild duck hunts…"

"It's goose hunt…" I mutter in correction and Gabriel starts to grin but Michael jumps in to agree with Errapel.

"He is correct. Besides, there is no time for that anyway. We have to get back for the end. Dayton will be back, he knows the time limit."

I glance behind me nervously and frown but nod in acceptance. I want to find Dayton, I want to fall into his arms, but I guess I'll just have to wait a bit longer. We make our way back to the battlefield and arrive just in time. Somehow, millions upon millions of demons and humans are now gathered along the horizon, as far as the eye can see. I glance up at Michael and Gabriel and noticed they are both grinding their teeth, a wave of sadness in their eyes. This must be it... Judgement day.

~Jesus ~

They were waiting on the book of life to arrive when Michael, Gabriel, Errapel, and Aurora land behind Jesus. He turns to greet them and shares a sad look with his esteemed Archangels. Errapel is singing 'Burning Ring of Fire' And Jesus shoots him a stern look to scold his inappropriate song. Errapel doesn't appear to notice and continues right along until

Aurora elbows him and yells,

"Errapel! What on Earth is wrong with you?"

"Golly there nephilim! I'm just trying to lighten the mood." He shrugs.

"Nobody wants the mood lightened! This is serious and sad and not a good time for any song, especially that one!"

Errapel shakes his head but goes silent. The sky lights up and Jesus turns back around and watches as the book of Life descends. When it reaches his arms he sighs sadly and opens it up. All across the horizon the crowds of people and demons bow down for him as the Bible predicted. And Satan's knee is the first to bow.

"Christ travels along the rows, asking names and searching for them in the book. If their name is found it means they had turned to God during the tribulation and they are now transported to heaven. If their names are not found, and sadly this is most often the case, their left standing, awaiting their fate. When Jesus finally makes his way through all of the waiting humans and demons he holds up a hand and the ground splits open into a crevice that goes on as far as the eye can see.

Fire, sulfur, and brimstone rain down from heaven and pour into the crater. Flames climb up the sides and lick at the air. The heat is intense and it swirls through the air enveloping all better here. Jesus holds up a hand and some in Satan to step forth. Satan howls with fury as he steps up and stares Jesus in the face defiantly. Christ's gaze doesn't waver as he watches the fallen king of evil before him.

"For your impudence, rebellion, and all around wickedness, both before and after your fall, you are here by sentence to eternity in the lake of Fire. You will be joined by all those whom you have led astray, both human and angel alike. But first you will say the words that you have denied for thousands of years."

Satan growls but drops to his needs and bowels as he hisses out the words and everyone that followed him does the same.

"Jehovah is God and Jesus Christ is Lord." He almost seems to choke on the words as he spits them out and for the first time in his life Satan appears genuinely afraid. Christ then lifts Satan to his feet and Michael moves to grab him. Jesus releases Lucifer into Michael's grasp and watches with a tear in his eye as Michael tosses the former angel into the flames.

When he had finally come too Errapel had told him what had happened, well, as much as he knew anyways. mostly about Dayton almost dying and Aurora and Gabriel bringing him to him. Errapel said it's a miracle Dayton survived. Then The healer went into a long lecture over the magical powers of mushrooms before Dayton finally interrupted him and informed him that he was leaving.

Errapel asked where he was going but Dayton had simply replied that he had something he needed to do and then took off. He'd known he needed to hurry when he saw the beams of fire shooting down from the sky. Most people wouldn't have risked running off and cutting it so close but this was important, it was worth it. And now he's back.

He made it back just in time too. The angels and nephilim are gathered together preparing to transport to heaven. Dayton rushes over and joins them as he scans the scene for Aurora. It takes him a minute but he finally sees her always ahead standing next to Gabriel and Errapel. She looks tired but otherwise unharmed.

The angels unfurl their wings and wrap them around themselves, and Dayton does the same. The moment he arrives in heaven he fights through the crowd towards Aurora. When he gets close enough he yells her name and the moment she spots him she breaks into a run, diving towards him through the masses. Tears stream down her cheeks and she leaves into his arms.

"Dayton! Oh thank goodness you're okay! I was so worried I'd never see you again. You almost died! Then Errapel made me think you were dead and I thought I was going to die. Then I found out you weren't but I didn't know where you went and…" She finally pauses and Dayton laughs before She continues, "Where did you go anyways? I was so scared that you wouldn't make it back in time…"

A mysterious smile glides across his face and he reaches into his pocket and pulls out a small seashell on a silver chain. Aurora's breath catches and she reaches for it timidly.

"My necklace... But how did you know I'd lost it?" She asks in amazement and she holds the new one in her hand. Dayton's smile drops and he looks down at her neck then up at her again.

"I didn't know you'd lost it…" at his words her smile drops and she looks ashamed so he quickly continues, "But this one is a bit different." He smiles and instructs her to hold it to her ear.

She does if she's told and puts the shell to her ear, awaiting his voice. It's too quiet for him to hear but of course he already knows what it says, he said it after all.

"I love you Angel. Will you marry me?"

Aurora's face lights up and she lets out a shrink of joy before leaning up and kissing him passionately. Her soft lips against his sends butterflies through him as her voice appears in his head.

'Yes! Of course yes! I love you so much! Man I love you so freaking much!'

And with that Dayton is officially the happiest angel in all the history of creation.

While making his way over towards Jesus Michael's attention is suddenly drawn to Errapel, who is dragging a cardboard box full of mushrooms behind him by a rope. That, however, is not the reason Michael's attention was drawn to him.

"Errapel." Michael addresses him.

"Oh, hello Michael. Can you believe this?"

Errapel stops and Michael walks over to him. He knows the old man is referring to the wedding and he shakes his head.

"No, I can't. But Errapel, Why is there an owl on your head?"

The gray owl atop Errapel's head glares at Michael and ruffles its feathers, tipping its head sideways to study him. Errapel looks befuddled by the question.

"I don't have no owl. All I got is this box of mushrooms… Michael, are you alright? Is the stress getting to you?"

Michael again gazes up at the owl who now coos softly as if laughing at him. The front pocket Errapel's shirt moves slightly and Michael glances at it as a small mouse pokes out its nose. Errapel reaches up and pushes the mouse back down, it bites him and he curses it. He doesn't curse at it, he actually tells the mouse that it and its descendants will be cursed for all eternity as he sticks his injured finger in his mouth.

Michael raises an eyebrow, "Errapel, may I ask you a question?"

"I reckon if you must…" The old man pulls his finger from his mouth and glances back down at his shirt angrily, the mouse gives him an almost apologetic look.

"You do not use those mushrooms for anything besides healing do you?"

"Well, whatever else would I use them for?" The healer looks bewildered at the thought and Michael shakes his head and walks off towards Jesus again.

He moves up to Christ's side and Jesus nods to address him. "Michael."

"My Lord…"

"Is there something you wish to say?"

"Are you really going to let them go through with this marriage? We don't know what may come of it…" Michael shakes his head and sighs.

"Michael," Jesus scolds the angel gently. Michael suddenly remembers to whom he speaks and apologizes quickly.

"I am sorry your majesty. Forgive me. It is not my place to question your decisions."

"You are forgiven, do not be upset. I know what will come of this union and I will gladly tell you my faithful friend."

Unsure how to respond Michael simply says thank you and waits for Jesus to continue.

"It will bring about a full blood female angel."

The statement causes Michael to whip his head around in surprise. "But...
There is no such thing as a female angel… Not anymore anyways… There hasn't been since the time of Ezekiel… And even then they were not… Well, regular angels…"

Jesus merely grins and lays a hand on Michael's shoulder comfortably.

"No, there isn't. At least not yet."

With that Christ heads over to where the ceremony is being conducted and marches up to the front of the crowd to begin. Michael takes a seat in the crowd and rises when Aurora appears. She looks absolutely beautiful in her dress, so he wonders where she got it from.She searches the crowd and when she sees Michael she motions him over.

"You look stunning," He informs her as he reaches her side, "is everything all right?"

It's easy to tell she's nervous; partly by the look on her face and partly by how badly she's shaking.

"Umm... Michael... I was wondering, well, you see, I don't really have anyone to walk me down the aisle… so I just wanted to know…. Umm…
Would you give me away?"

The question catches him off guard and his face contorts. She appears to pick up on his discomfort and ducks her head. He tries to find the words and finally gathers his thoughts enough to smile at her warmly.

"Yes. Of course. It would be my honor."

~ **Aurora** ~

Michael walks me down the aisle and I take my place next to Dayton at the altar. He looks gorgeous standing there in his suit, his luscious white wings pulled back neatly behind him. His hair now has blonde highlights sprayed throughout it and his eyes are bright sapphire with merely a ring of emerald left around them.

When he'd first told me of the changes that would occur I had a negative reaction but, well, now I find him even more attractive than ever, which I wouldn't have thought possible. Dayton looks at me with longing and desire so powerful that for a moment I feel heat rise into my cheeks. His gaze is so intent that I try to look away but I can't bring myself to.

We exchange our vows, swearing for better for worse, and then Jesus asks us to exchange rings. Crap! I didn't even think about rings. I didn't pick one out for Dayton and I'm sure he didn't have time to pick one out for me. Suddenly, Gabriel makes his way over to us and presents us a box with two gold and silver bands inside.

They sparkle in the light and I want to ask how and where they came from but Dayton pulls out the smaller of the two and asks for my hand. I grabbed the other ring and we placed them on each other's fingers carefully. Jesus smiles.

"By the power invested in me by my father, I now pronounce you husband and wife. You may kiss your bride."

Dayton leans forward and kisses me like I've never been kissed before. Sensations race down my spine and I lean into him so that our bodies seem almost as one flesh. When he eventually pulls away he whispers in my ear through ragged breaths,

"I love you angel, you and only you."

The End

Bonus Chapter

The Fall of Angels
Dayton's Origin

Heaven is never dark. The glory of the Lord shines so brightly that there's always light. But despite the physical light around, there was a darkness in the air that you couldn't see but you could feel. Something was happening…

Dayton raced through the empty streets towards the throne room. Up ahead he could see him. The most beautiful angel of all. Lucifer. He was the director of music. A high honor and one of the most respected of all the heavenly hosts. Until today. Today he made a fatal mistake. Today Lucifer decided that he should be god. Dayton flew as fast as he could and landed in front of Lucifer and his army, a third of the angels.

"Lucifer stop! You can't do this!" Dayton holds up his arms as if to block Lucifer's way. The Angel of music raises an eyebrow at him and scowls.

"Whose side are you on, warrior?"

Heat rose to Dayton's cheeks and he shook his head. "Nobody's… but this isn't…"

Lucifer shoved into the side causing him to fall backwards and hit the ground hard. Then the angel towered over his body and hissed, "Then get out of my way. This is a war. There is no place for those who don't know their place."

The army continued on towards the throne room and Dayton leapt back up onto his feet. He arrived just behind them and realized there would be no real war. The moment they entered the throne room they were ambushed by the archangels and all the heavenly host that had already gathered to defend the Lord. They were outnumbered and stood no match against the King anyway. The moment He shouted, "Stop" every body in the room froze and fell to their knees.

"What is the meaning of this Lucifer?" The Son stepped down from His place next to the Father. He confronted Lucifer with tears swelling up in His eyes. The angel would not make eye contact with Him, but growled a response.

"I am greater than all of these! I deserve the throne!"

Jesus sighs. "Look at the position you are in Lucifer… pride comes before the fall. Oh how you have fallen Morning Star…"

Then the Lord glances around at each one of those kneeling before Him. His eyes suddenly lock on Dayton and He pushes through the crowd towards him.

"And you, Warrior, choose this day whom you will serve. What side do you choose?" Jesus questions him, a twinge of pain in His voice.

Dayton's eyes fill with tears, "I want no part in any of this… I just want everyone to be together. I… I choose no side."

Jesus sighs. "He who is not with me is against me… Until we meet again, young warrior…"

Then He turns and a wave of wind gushes around Lucifer, his army, and Dayton. The floor of heaven opens up into a whirlpool of clouds and water beneath them.
Then... they fall.

~~~~~

Jesus looks down through the portal as they fall, a tear on the corner of His eyes. The Holy Spirit rests alongside Him.
~~~~~

"That one isn't completely cold yet." The Spirit gestures at Dayton, the last to fall.

The Son nods. "Yes. He will return… after some time and with some help. His story isn't over but he will face much heartache for his lukewarm stance."

"Much heartache…" The Spirit agrees before the portal closes and they both return to the throne.

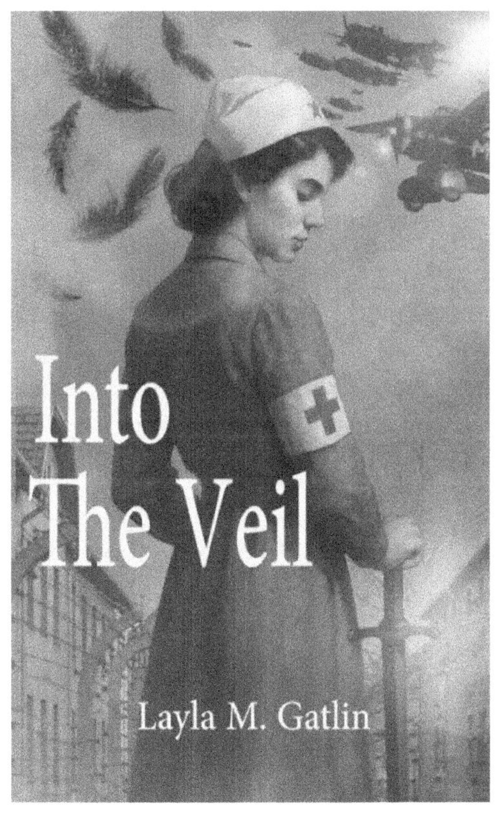
Into
The Veil
Layla M. Gatlin